Wh

M. N. Forgy

Copyright © 2014 M. N. Forgy

CreateSpace Edition

Published by M. N. Forgy

Edited by Belinda Forgy

Cover design by Arijana Karčić, Cover It! Designs

All Rights Reserved. No part of this book may be reproduced or transmitted in any form, including electronic or mechanical, without written permission from the publisher, except in the case of brief quotations embodied in critical articles or reviews.

This is a work of fictions. Names, characters, businesses, places, events, and incidents are either the products of the author's imagination or used in a fictitious manner. Any resemblance to actual persons, living or dead, or actual events is purely coincidental.

This book is licensed for your personal enjoyment only. This book may not be resold or given away to other people. If you would like to share this book with another person, please purchase an additional copy for each person you share it with. If you are reading this book and did not purchase it, or it was not purchased for your use only, then please return to your favorite ebook retailer and purchase your own copy. Thank you for respecting the hard work of this author.

Karen —

Enjoy this dark twisted tale!

M.W. Ford
xx

Dedication

This Book is dedicated to my husband, Derik Forgy, and grandmother, Donna Lonsdale.

Derik, without you, I would have never gotten this far.

Grandma, your skill and memory encouraged me to give it my all.

Table Of Contents

Chapter One

Chapter Two

Chapter Three

Chapter Four

Chapter Five

Chapter Six

Chapter Seven

Chapter Eight

Chapter Nine

Chapter Ten

Chapter Eleven

Chapter Twelve

Chapter Thirteen

Chapter Fourteen

Chapter Fifteen

Chapter Sixteen

Chapter Seventeen

Chapter Eighteen

Chapter Nineteen

Chapter Twenty

Chapter Twenty-One

Chapter Twenty-Two

Chapter Twenty-Three

Epilogue
Acknowledgements
About the Author
Stalk Me

Chapter One
Dani

    I'm startled awake from a commotion coming from the stairs. The room is black and my vision is blurry from lack of sleep. I blink a couple of times and look for the clock on my dresser: 2:15am. You have got to be kidding me.
    I roll back over and angrily close my eyes. I'm sure it's my mother coming home late from work with Stevin. Stevin is my mother's boss or co-worker, I'm not sure. Hell, I don't even know what their jobs are. I don't really care either. She's also dating him, which I find very desperate. Their relationship is weird, and my mother is very private about … whatever they are. He's rich and handsome and he's the sole reason we're living in this savvy apartment in the heart of New York. My mom has mentioned that he has a trust fund from his grandparents, and that his family is wealthy. I'm sure she only told me this as an explanation for moving from the dump we were in. She was a dancer at that time and I questioned how we could afford this new place.
    Without warning, my bedroom door is flung open and slams against the wall, filling the room with a loud thud. The lights flicker on and my mother rushes to my bed, throwing the blankets off me. My eyes feel like they've been slapped, and I wince at the unwelcome brightness.
    "What the hell, Mom!" I yell, still half asleep.
    "Come on, get out of bed. Get dressed and pack a small bag."
    My eyes snap open and widen at my mother's appearance. Her usually sleek, chocolate hair is a tangled mess and there is dried blood from a cut on her cheek. I've never seen my mother so distraught before, and I'm completely taken back by it.

"Stop staring at me and pack a bag. Now. We don't have much time!" My mother snaps at me before I even open my mouth to ask what happened.

Why was she so beat up? Who did this to her? Where's Stevin? And where the hell are we going? I have all these questions and no answers, but I know better than to ask. The look in my mother's eyes and the tone in her voice is not to be reckoned with. My heart jump starts at the notion and I grab my suitcase.

I look down at what I'm wearing; a skimpy tee shirt and panties. I grab a pair of blue jeans; a blue, fitted t-shirt; and my black, knee-high boots. It's not classy, but it will have to do. I run into my bathroom and brush my dark brown, wavy hair. Staring at my reflection, I notice my green eyes look sunk in from lack of sleep, making them seem dull. My eyes are my signature; they are very bright green, almost inhuman. I've been told my eyes are like pools of green ivy, whatever that means. I throw my hair up in a messy bun, and comb through my side-swiped bangs.

I throw some things I've gathered from the bathroom into the suitcase laying open on my bed, along with some extra clothes and shoes. I grab a few other things like my purse, iPod, and sunglasses and head downstairs.

My mother's already waiting for me by the door. I notice the blood is clear from her cheek but her face is still red and a little swollen. She's now wearing a clean white blouse that buttons up the middle. She always dresses to perfection, even in her worst hour, which could possibly be right now. I wish she would tell me what's going on. Am I in danger?

"Come on, Dani, we are going to miss our flight," she says, irritated.

"Mom, what the hell is going –"

She cuts me off by walking out the door of our apartment and into the elevator. I growl in frustration and follow after her.

My mom walks to the curb and yells for a cab. The cool breeze sweeps around plastering my olive skin with goose bumps. I look up at the tall buildings, taking in as much as I can; this might be the last time I see them.

A yellow cab pulls up and my mom bangs on the trunk. It makes a popping noise as it is released. She throws in her bag and yanks mine from my hand and flings it in, too.

"JFK," she tosses at the driver, avoiding eye contact with me. "Quickly, please."

The ride to the airport is silent. I have so many questions but am afraid of the answers I may get in return. I know I should ask, but can't bring myself to speak the words. So I just stare out the window, silently saying goodbye to my life. Well, what life that I have. I have friends but nobody close enough to notice I'm gone. I have a job at the local coffee shop, but they'll just replace me. Actually, being put in such a desperate situation goes to show that I really don't have much to show for my life. It's depressing. Having an overbearing mother does that to you. She doesn't allow much of a social life, so, of course, finding friends in college that like to just stay in and watch movies is hard. Hell, I just celebrated my twenty-first birthday and it was depressingly typical; fancy dinner, wine and parents included.

We arrive at the airport and the cab driver gets our bags out of the car while mom throws some cash in his seat. I grab my suitcase and follow her. I slow my walk as she heads toward a big, burly man with a big gut, who has his arms crossed in front of his chest. He's wearing torn blue jeans and a black t-shirt where tattoos seem to snake out and claim every inch of his hairy arms. My mother walks right up to him, her body language confident, so I double my step to catch up. As I get closer I see his leather vest has patches on it; the left patch reads 'TRIGGER' and the right reads 'Ghost MC.' My breath catches in my throat; 'MC' as in motorcycle club? I have seen enough documentaries and TV shows to know bike clubs are not a force to be messed with.

I look a little lower on his leather cut and see a diamond shaped patch that says '1%'. My throat seizes up tighter as I try to speak, worried what my mom's intentions are. I don't remember exactly what the 1% means, but I know it's bad. "M—mom."

She throws her hand up to shut me up.

What the hell is she doing? This is not some casual pedestrian to ask for directions.

"I'm Lady, do you have something from Bull?" my mother says, assuredly.

Lady? Her name is not Lady, it's Sadie. And who the hell is Bull?

The scary man called Trigger eyes her up. "Yeah, here are your plane tickets. Bull pulled some strings to get you on the next flight. You've got an hour before the flight leaves to L.A." The big, burly man hands my mother an envelope, his voice deep and ominous.

He points at my mother. "You tell Bull this makes us even." He looks at me and then at my mother. "Safe trip, ladies," he says as he walks away.

"Yeah, thanks." She says opening the folder to peek inside.

What the hell? She acted as if she was talking to a damned girl scout. She isn't fazed at all, but I am about to piss myself.

"Mind telling me what the fuck is going on?" I curse at my mother, tired of this whole charade.

Her eyes widen at my language. She is not pleased; go figure. My whole life I've been told how to act and what to say. Always told to stay on the right path; the path my mother and Stevin are paving for me. It pretty much consists of nothing but school. Little does she know, I am still undecided on my college major. She'd have a stroke if she knew I didn't have my whole life planned out. She has never let me do anything wild or reckless. She always catches me right before and then yells at me about how I act just like my father and she didn't go through hell to give me a better life, a better path, for me to mess it up. It seems like that is the only time she is around, to tell me what a failure I am. The last time I tried to gain any independence, I was nineteen and I was tired of being on lock down.

"You look smoking hot, if you don't get laid tonight there's no hope for womankind," Daisy says, eyeing my strapless black dress.

"You look pretty hot yourself," I compliment Daisy, giving a sultry wink. Daisy was the new girl working at the coffee shop, whom I'd taken a liking to. She knew of a club that didn't card, so we were headed out in hopes of hooking up with a hunk.

I eyed myself in the mirror one last time; black dress, red heels, and red purse. Yep. I looked like a vixen.

A half hour later, still giggling, we arrived at the club only to find my mother and Stevin waiting at the entrance.

Fuck! Mother Fuck!

"Danielle Lexington, what are you thinking?" my mother said, grabbing my arm tightly.

"Get off!" I yelled at her, making a scene.

"You look like a prostitute. Get your ass back in that cab and go home now," she yells in my face, spit flying against my skin.

"I'm nineteen years old. I'm an adult. You can't boss me around anymore," I yelled back at her, pulling my arm back with vengeance.

"You want to be an adult, act like one," she hissed back.

I closed my eyes and took a deep breath, rage filled my spine. I wanted to punch the woman who calls herself my mother.

"I'm done with your shit, I have enough money to move out," I said calmly, ready to finally see the blow on her face from me abandoning her. It took me nearly a year to save, but I finally had enough for a decent start; a start without my mother.

She smirked, making my unusual courage flee.

"Oh, honey," she sneered. "I've already cleared that account; you have nothing." Then she grinned like the devil, making me gasp in horror.

"What?" I asked, mortified yet completely enraged.

"Go ahead; leave, move out, go live in the streets. You came from trash, you might as well live like it," she said, pointing out for the millionth time how I'm nothing but my father's spawn. Finally, someone she despises more than me; my father, whoever he is.

"That's what I thought, get back in that cab." She pushed me in the direction of the cab.

"I will try to explain on the plane, Dani. We don't have time right now." My mother's whisper, as she grabs my hand, pulls me from my trip down memory lane.

I found out later that the only reason I got caught that night was because of my damned neighbor that lived on the floor under us. She was my mom's little mouse, always spying on me. She was outside when we got home that night, so pleased I arrived safely and asking my mother if she did her job right. Her job at ratting me out, that is. I was an adult and trapped living with my mom. My mother's and my relationship is a 'go along to get along' kind of thing; even if I'm miserable. Sometimes the streets didn't sound so bad.

It's another hour before we climb aboard the flight. I'm still curious how Trigger got us plane tickets so quickly and who is Bull? My mother sighs loudly, grabbing my attention.

"I suppose I should tell you the whole story," my mother says as she runs her hands over her face, irritated.

"Yeah, that would be nice," I respond, sarcastically.

"I met your father at a party in L.A. about twenty-two years ago. He was quite good looking; you look a lot like him." She looks over at me, her face unreadable. I'm not sure if I'm bringing her painful memories or good ones, but judging by the way she acts toward me, I'm guessing painful.

"We were at a party when some drunk men started harassing me and a friend. My friend sprinted off, but I wasn't as quick. The nasty men advanced on me; I was out numbered. They pushed me to the ground, smacked me around and started to …" She takes a deep breath before continuing. "Well, that's when your father showed up; he beat them to a bloody pulp." She starts to chuckle at the thought, which I find frightening. "He made them get on their knees and apologize to me. One even pissed himself." She shakes her head as if to clear the thought. "I rode to his house on the back of his motorcycle and thought it was the beginning of something special; thought being the key word. I dropped out of school and my parents disowned me after they found out I was dating someone from a motorcycle club." She sighs heavily; so much regret is evident in her voice. I almost feel sorry for her.

"We were together day and night for about five months. Then I told him I loved him and he changed. He didn't call me or talk to me for days, so I went looking for him and found him with some club whore. I jetted out of there on the first plane I could get." She pauses and looks out at the loading passengers. "Anyway, I found out a month later I was pregnant. I didn't want the same path for you, so I didn't tell him. It wouldn't have mattered anyway. He made it pretty clear he didn't want anything to do with me. So I made my way to provide for you, to make sure you took the right path; not like me or your father." She finishes with tears in her eyes and takes a ragged breath. I can tell she doesn't want to tell me any of this.

"Are you with me so far?" she asks as her spine stiffens and she sits up straighter in her seat. Pity mode must be over with.

My head is a complete blur of information. I am following her but feel my nerves fraying around the edges. "Actually I could use a drink," I say, raising my hand to catch the stewardess' attention. All this incoming information has me feeling catastrophic.

"Dani, no! What are you, a drunk?" she asks, eyes wide, shaking her head in disappointment.

"Oh, no, we wouldn't want someone to think that, would we?" I mock. She's always worrying about what others think about her; my behavior giving her the worst of her labels with a child who acts like her deadbeat dad.

She turns her head the opposite direction. "Just like your father," she whispers, annoyed. Only in my mother's eyes would a beer render me as a drunk; even after hearing the crap she just laid on me.

"You going to tell me what happened to your face? And why you're suddenly telling me about my father?" I ask, resenting her by the minute for keeping all this from me. I am never allowed to ask about my father. He is just a sperm donor as far as my mother is concerned. So I'm confused why she is spilling everything I have ever wanted to know now?

Snapping her head in my direction, she loudly says, "I'm getting there," gaining attention from everyone around us, too. Lowering her voice, she continues. "When I left your father I was a waitress at a restaurant in New York for several years, but it just wasn't enough. So, I started dancing in clubs for money. It was sleazy but paid the bills and bought you dolls." She turns her head away again, avoiding eye contact.

"Whoa, you were a stripper?" I ask, shocked. Now my voice is too loud and causes everyone to turn in their seats to look at us.

"Shh, Dani," she says, stabbing me with her eyes and gesturing with her hands for me to lower my volume. "I was an entertainer," she says completely convinced there's a difference in the two.

"Stripper," I mumble under my breath.

I cannot believe what I am hearing; my mother was a stripper. I knew she was a "dancer", but I never would have thought she stripped in a million years. When I was a kid and she told me she was a dancer, I thought she did Broadway shows or something. I can't believe she's been keeping all this from me. All I have ever been told about my father is that he is trash and doesn't want anything to do with us. Well, apparently, just my mom; he doesn't even know I exist. I didn't know he was in a motorcycle club, or that my mother would ever be into a biker.

"Stevin started showing up every night and asking for me by name," she says, grabbing me back from my frantic thoughts. "He told me I didn't need to be in a place like that and I should let him take care of me. I hesitated at first, of course. However, the bills got to be too much to live in New York and my parents weren't talking to me. Then Stevin and I started to connect, so I agreed. He gave me a job and provided things for you and me and I fell in love with him. Until last night, that is." She closes her eyes tightly to avoid looking at me again. Tension suddenly creeps in the air between us, catching me off guard. I focus on her mindfully, trying to figure out why the sudden uneasiness.

"We were in Stevin's office working late and his cell phone started ringing. When he answered it's like his attitude did a 180. He told me to get my things and go home immediately. I guess I wasn't fast enough, though. Two police officers came walking into the office followed by Stevin's two security guards. I was at my desk shutting down my computer when I heard two gun shots. I ran into the office scared they had shot Stevin and his guards." She pauses and scratches her forehead where I notice beads of sweat forming.

"When I saw the cops dead on the floor, I ran. I heard Stevin order his guards to chase me. One caught me and I fought back, only to be slapped by him. I kicked him in the balls and ran to the elevator," she says, frantically. Her words are flying out of her mouth so quickly I can barely keep up.

"Uh," she stumbles. Her eyes are wide with a look of disbelief, "Stevin came out of his office pointing a gun at me, but luckily, the elevator doors closed before he started shooting." Her body is tense, trembling and avoiding. She isn't telling me the whole story; my mother is a crappy liar. Based on her sweating, stumbling words and frantic state, I am sure she is definitely hiding something. This makes me nervous; the danger we appear to be in must be severe. I should know everything, and I don't.

"I called your father. He's going to protect us until we figure out our next move," she says, finally looking in my direction. Her body suddenly seems calm and appeased.

"My--my father?" I stutter, confused why we are running to a guy my mother has wanted to keep away from me, the last person I ever thought my mother would run to for help.

"Anyway, Stevin's a powerful man. I'm not sure how deep his pockets go, so leaving New York is our best option." She looks at me for a reaction, avoiding my question about my father.

"Bull will protect us," she says, nodding her head, so sure of herself.

"This is a lot to take in," I say as I exhale, noticing for the first time I've been holding my breath. My index finger and thumb are worrying my bottom lip as well, which is something I apparently do when I'm nervous according to my shrink, Victoria. When I was younger my mother said I acted so much like my father it worried her, making her feel I needed a shrink. Truth is, I hate Victoria. She always sides with my mother, even when I know she is wrong. The only thing Victoria ever made sense of was the nervous habit I have of playing with my bottom lip. I didn't used to even realize I was doing it, but now I catch myself when I'm lying or nervous, or both.

"Look, I know you can't understand right now," my mother says as she grabs one of my hands in both of hers. This new affection is lost on me; she hasn't shown any maternal instinct since she went to work for Stevin. I drop my fingers from my lips and feel my body stiffen at the contact.

"We need the type of help only an outlaw club like your father belongs to can give us. I won't let them hurt you or drag you into their world of hell. You won't be like them, Dani. You have a future, don't forget that," she says, looking directly into my eyes.

"Uh, okay," I say, shocked at the mother of the year suddenly sitting in front of me.

"They are outlaws, Dani. They will try to drag you into their perverse way of life", she says with a loud sigh "They're ruthless and pigs. Do not let them mislead you." She starts biting her bottom lip reaching up to turn off our overhead lights; as usual she's done talking about this and no amount of arguing will change her mind.

But why will my father help us if he doesn't care about us? Did she tell my father about me on the phone? If this biker club is so morally wrong why are we running to them for help?

Chapter Two
Dani

    I awake as the plane lands and am surprised to realize that I could sleep after all the shit my mother has doled out in the past few hours. I shuffle behind her to the luggage carousel and wait what seems like forever, but is only a few minutes, before we see them on the conveyor belt. I grab mine as it rolls up and head for the nearest exit.

    As I walk out of the airport, the sunlight pummels my sensitive eyes. I stop and reach into my purse for my sunglasses. As my eyes are adjusting, I realize my mother is no longer beside me. I'm not sure who we're looking for, but I notice a large SUV with two black, slick-looking motorcycles parked behind it in the 'NO PARKING ZONE'. There are two men with the bikes and I take a moment to check them out. I'm hoping my sunglasses keep me from looking like I'm staring. One of the guys is leaning against his bike. He is older, maybe in his forties. A black bandanna is wrapped around his head. Long, dirty-blond hair flows from beneath it and rests on his well-built shoulders. A long beard and matching, thick mustache are the same dirty-blond but with white speckles. His mustache is so thick, it covers his mouth to the point I can barely tell he has lips. He's wearing a black leather vest over a white t-shirt and black jeans which reminds me a bit of Trigger from the airport in New York. His legs are crossed out in front of him as he leans on one of the bikes, while his fingers twirl a toothpick in his mouth. His attempt at looking casual isn't fooling me, his whole image screams outlaw.

    The other guy is facing away from me. He has black choppy hair on top of his head and it is shorter on the sides. The back of his leather sleeveless jacket has a skeleton hand crushing a skull on it. It reads 'DEVIL'S

DUST' above the crushed skull and 'California' under it. He's wearing a white shirt with blue jeans and black motorcycle boots. He turns and I stop in my tracks. He's stunning; gorgeous even, and he just oozes bad boy. His skin is tan and I can see his tattoo peeking out from under the short sleeve on his left bicep. I can't make out what it is, though. He looks younger than the other man, maybe in his early thirties. I see his lips turn into a cocky smirk and I realize he's caught me looking at him.

Shit. I smile back. Looking into his eyes, I find that they're a bright blue. Of course, they're blue; the contrast with his dark hair is striking. And these blue eyes have an animalistic presence to them. He stretches his arms out and then crosses them in front of his chest. The fabric of his white t- shirt stretches tight around his arm muscles in the process. My lips suddenly part; I can't breathe at the danger standing in front of me, yet I'm completely intrigued at the same time. Surprisingly, I feel safe for the first time since my mother woke me up in the middle of the night. I have no idea why! He seems anything but safe.

My mother grabs my arm as she catches up and to my dismay, starts in their direction. My mind is still slowly processing the information she shelled out on the plane. I remember we're seeking protection from a motorcycle club and let her pull me along.

The older guy rises from his bike as we approach and the younger one turns toward my mother. "Lady, I presume?" the delicious biker says to her. As we get closer I can see the patch on the front of his vest reads 'SHADOW'. He is even more seductive up close. But behind all that beauty I sense a beast. He has the look of someone who's been damaged, but has a natural allure to hide it. I feel my thighs squeezing to dull the ache between my legs. Fuck! What's wrong with me? He isn't possibly turning me on, is he?

"Hell yeah, that's Lady," the older biker exclaims, his voice raspy with age and cigarettes. "How the hell have ya been?" Up close I notice he has wrinkles around his eyes and mouth, age has not been kind to him.

"My name is Sadie," my mother retorts; her tone cold and unfriendly. This guy obviously knows my mother. The way he's so excited to see her, I feel they must have been friendly at some point. The look on my mother's face, however, is anything but excited to see an old friend.

I feel Shadow's presence and look at him. The depth of his blue eyes stirs something in me and my cheeks flush. I have to look away. I know from past experience that guys like him are usually just womanizers. I haven't been used but I've heard guys talking at college; guys that are gorgeous like that. None of them had ever affected me like this, though. Those guys were mere boys compared to Shadow. Shadow is all man. I hear my mother's words play in my head, "…They are outlaws, Dani. They will try to drag you into their perverse way of life." I close my eyes tightly, trying to shake off the drowning effect this Shadow has me under.

I open my eyes and try to concentrate on my mom and the older biker. I look to find his name patch: 'LOCKS'. Under that was another patch that read 'VICE PRESIDENT' and he has a '1%' patch. 'Locks' is an odd name; maybe he's good at breaking locks or something.

I look back over at Shadow's vest, curious now. 'Sargent-At-Arms' is embroidered on the patch under his name and I notice it has '1%' on it, too. These guys are anything but safe, but I somehow feel they will protect us from the shit my mother has gotten us into. If anything, Stevin will run like a girl when he sees these criminals.

Locks brushes his hand against my mother's cheek and I see her body tense at the touch. "I will kill the fucker that did this to you, Lady. That's a promise!" he says with such fierceness in his tone I know he's not lying.

I look back at Shadow and he's looking at what Locks is referring to; my mother's battered face.

"This is Danielle," my mother says, pointing at me. "Danielle, this is Locks. We go way back." My mother points back at Locks, her introduction takes the spot light off of her.

"Hi. It's so nice to meet you. You can call me Dani," they both stare at me; Shadow's gaze making me uncomfortable. "You... uh... have lovely bikes," I say, nervously. I am trying to be polite, but I just come out as idiotic. Everyone chuckles. Great, I'm sure they're thinking I'm some naive bimbo. I blow air into my cheeks as I sigh in defeat.

"Bull wants us to meet him at the clubhouse to go over everything. He couldn't be here. He had to tie up some loose ends; Club business," Locks explains as he turns back to my mother. "We had the prospects bring the "grocery getter" to lug you and your shit to the club." Locks grabs our bags and heads toward the black SUV.

Wow, it's an Escalade. I'm not sure how an Escalade becomes known as a "grocery getter".

I start climbing into the back seat and am startled by a deep, smooth voice. I jump and turn with a yelp, just missing bumping my head on the door frame.

"Yeah, Locks doesn't know shit about vehicles, unless it's a bike. This Escalade could probably buy his whole fucking house." Shadow smirks, ignoring my startled state. He leans on the side of the SUV, his eyes devouring me; making me feel naked.

Holy shit, he's gorgeous. Up close I notice his ocean blue pupils have a rim of stormy grey around them, painting a picture of an angry ocean fighting a stormy sky. His lips are soft and sensual, his bottom lip plumper than the upper, making me bite my own lip to repress the temptation. I let out a strangled breath I didn't realize I was holding. The affect he has on my breathing makes him a danger to my health. His smirk turns into a cocky grin as he tucks a loose lock of hair behind my ear. He knows the effect he has on me. By the looks of him I'm sure he has panties dropping for him all the time. I get angry as I think about it. What a player. I already want to shove my foot in his ass.

He holds his hand out to help me into the car and I grab it without a second thought. My betraying body instantly heats at his touch like I'm on fire. His grip tightens and he pulls me closer; our bodies only inches apart. I can smell the soapy scent of his body wash blending with low notes of sweat and exhaust fumes; the smell causes wetness to fill my panties. My body leans even closer; I'm almost panting for his attention now.

"Ahem," my mother clears her throat, already in the back seat. "Do we have a problem?" she asks, suggestively, snapping me from the daze Shadow has me in. I clearly didn't have any common sense around him; that alone should make me want to stay away. Who is this guy, and why am I so attracted to him?

I pull my hand from his quickly, shaking my head of anything 'stormy skies and bad boy biker' and climb into the "grocery getter". I take my sunglasses off and turn toward Shadow to thank him, making sure to throw sarcasm in my tone to show I'm not affected; even though it is a big, fat lie. I am anything but not affected by him. When our eyes lock, his smile instantly falls, his jaw clenches, his body goes stiff and his mouth slightly parts, he looks as if he is seeing a ghost. His change in demeanor catches me by surprise. Before I can ask if something is wrong, he slams the door shut.

What the hell? Maybe he is just an ass, getting off at playing games with my mind. If I have any common sense, I will stay away from him. I place my sunglasses back on my face and turn forward. The way my body screams for the guy contradicts the calmness I'm trying to portray. This is going to suck.

Locks and Shadow follow closely behind us as we leave, the motorcycles sending a thunderous roar in their wake. The two 'prospects', as Locks called them, are sitting in front, silent. Their heads are all I can see of them. The one driving has a buzzed Mohawk and the one in the passenger seat is bald with barbed wire tattoos all over his head. My body still feels high from the encounter with Shadow, my skin tingling from every nerve ending. He isn't even in the car with me and he still manages to send butterflies sputtering chaotically in my abdomen. It's taking everything I have not to turn and see the 'sex on wheels' behind us. I wonder if I will get to ride one of those motorcycles before this is all over. I find the motorcycles sexy and dangerous. Ugh, what is wrong with me? I need to snap out of fantasy land. These guys are criminals and I need to be here for my mother. I have to resist Shadow's playboy charm, and stay focused.

It's a short drive before we pull up to a wooded area with a two story building tucked back off the main road. The front has double glass doors with little barred windows here and there. To the right of it is an older tin building with two garages. A parking lot in between the two buildings is littered with motorcycles. As I climb out of the SUV, I hear the rumbling of more bikes. I look over and see Locks and Shadow already getting off their bikes so I know it's not them. Suddenly, a swarm of black motorcycles pulls up and parks next to Shadow and Locks. The group of outlaws makes my hands tremble with fear. How could my mother think this was safe?

"Well, well, well. Look what the cat dragged in. How ya been, Lady?" an unfamiliar voice calls out from the gang that just pulled up. A tall, beefy man, ahead of the others, makes his way toward us. He has dark glasses on his face, and black hair that shags around his eyes and ears. He's wearing a black, ripped shirt with tight blue jeans that tuck into his scuffed boots. His shoulders are broad, and his arms toned and tanned. He reaches down and grabs my mother's hand and lightly pecks the top of it with his lips. She yanks her hand from his mouth with force. I can almost feel the hatred pouring out of her. My eyes dart to the black leather vest he is wearing.

'BULL'. 'PRESIDENT'.

My mind flashes back to Trigger at the airport in New York, he told my mom that this made him and Bull even. This is Bull, this is my father and he is the President of the club. Holy Shit! This is the guy I was always being compared to growing up. The man that paved my road of nothing but disapproving acts; he has made my life hell and doesn't even know it.

"Still just as charming as ever, aren't we, Bull," my mother smarts. "Say hello to my daughter, Dani." She gestures her hand toward me. I notice she didn't say 'our daughter'.

I try to speak, but my lips won't move. I feel my heart skip a beat and realize I'm not breathing. What do I even say to a man I know hardly anything about? Whenever I thought of my father I had always envisioned a rock star or a doctor. The president of a motorcycle club was never on my pretend daddy list.

"Well, hello, Darlin'." He is indeed charming. I put my hand out to shake his and he starts lifting it toward his mouth as he had done with my mother. I slide my glasses off my face and place them on my head to get a better look at the man I am made from. Just before his lips touch the back of my hand, he looks up at me. In an instant his grin fades and his mouth falls open.

"What the fuck is this, Sadie?" he asks, stunned. His eyes snap frantically between my mother and me.

"Obviously she's your daughter, Bull," my mother says sarcastically, with a hint of hatred. "I wouldn't have asked for your help for just myself."

The whole crowd of bikers gathers around me like I'm a freak of nature, like I'm a science project. I have no idea what they are looking at, but the way everyone is gawking at me has me feeling uncomfortable and pissed.

Bull looks back at me and sighs heavily. He grabs his sunglasses and slides them off his tanned face. He has green eyes, like pools of ivy; my eyes. I have my father's eyes. I now know what everyone is looking at. My breathing becomes heavy, I'm trying to control it but losing the battle. There is so much to take in, this is my father. This is his club. It makes sense now why Shadow acted the way he did when I took my glasses off. As soon as he saw my eyes he knew I was the daughter of his president. I look for him out of the crowd and spot him leaning up against the SUV. He pushes off and starts walking toward us. "Yep, no denying that, Prez," he says with a chuckle.

I gasp for air, but come up with nothing. My body goes limp. I try to grab onto something, anything, but there is nothing. The darkness overtakes my vision; my knees buckle and I collapse.

My head is pounding as I open my eyes to a dusty ceiling fan in an unfamiliar room. "Where am I?" I croak out, noticing my lungs are not screaming for air anymore.

"You're in the clubhouse. I brought you to one of the rooms. You fainted," says a familiar voice. "Your mom and Bull are getting shit straight." I look beside the bed to find Shadow kneeling there. "You took a spill right outside the club. How's your head?" he asks, as he brushes my hair behind my ear. His fingers linger by my ear causing a rush of adrenaline to fill my body, making me feel high.

"I-- it's ok," I stutter, that familiar feeling of not being able to breathe creeping its way back into my lungs. The man makes me fluster in a way I have never experienced, I have no control of my body when I'm around him.

"Breathe, Dani. I won't bite unless you want me too." He winks.

Oh my God, don't wink at me. My thighs clinch at the desire surfing up my legs.

I sit up on the bed, Shadow's face inches from mine. My eyes fall on his pouty lips. I wonder what they feel like on a woman's skin. I lick my lips, wanting to taste his; taste him. Breaking my eye contact from his lips, I look up into his stormy eyes and notice he's staring at my lips as well. With a sudden feeling of courage, I push myself forward and brush my lips against his; testing him, hoping for a reaction. He pulls back, studying my face. My sudden feeling of courage rapidly turns back into butterflies. Does he want me as bad as I want him? Does he feel the attraction between us?

He lets out a growl as he roughly grabs me by the legs and swings them over the side of the bed. His fingers dig deep into my skin. Lifting me by my ass, he slams me back against the wall. His lips crash into mine, his tongue demanding entry. I accept the intrusion, he tastes incredible and dangerous. He snakes his hand away from one of my ass cheeks and grabs a handful of my hair, pulling it tightly. He is being rough, as if showing me the kind of guy he is. Little does he know I can't get enough of it. My hands clinch the front of his shirt to pull our bodies closer; my legs wrapping tighter around his waist. I can't believe what I'm doing; my mother warned me to stay away. But, I can't help myself, I know I'm playing with the devil himself and I want more!

Suddenly, he pulls away, nearly dropping me on my ass. "I can't do this, Dani," he whispers hoarsely. "And you would do well to stay clear of me..."

"What?" The fire lit between us is doused with arctic water. I try to compose myself, feeling cheap and easy. His sudden iciness drowns my arousal, drenching me with anger.

"You would just get hurt in the end," he says, running his hands through his choppy hair, his tone arrogant. He looks me up and down, making me feel like I can't handle him. "Trust me."

"I'm a big girl, I can handle myself," I fire back.

He scoffs, pissing me off more. I try to push him out of my way, and he grabs my wrist pulling my body back to within inches of his. I try to pull my wrist free, but he just tightens his grip.

"I am not one of your little boys back in New York trying to play businessman, Dani," he sneers. "If you were mine I would fuck you within an inch of your life every chance I got. I would show you what that body of yours is capable of. He is whispering now, his lips brushing against my skin. "But in reality, you can never be mine." His tone is suddenly cold. He pushes me away from him. My body is confused. Am I turned on or pissed? I hate him, but I still want him.

"You're the president's daughter. I don't look forward to having my nuts on a platter anytime soon," he says with a sudden scowl.

A knock sounds at the door and it immediately opens.

"Shadow, let me have a word with my daughter," Bull demands as he enters the room.

"What's your full name, Dani?" Bull sits down on the bed and pats the spot next to him, inviting me to sit. I oblige.

"Danielle Lexington," I manage to choke out; the severity of the situation still overwhelming.

"I see your mother gave you her last name," he sneers.

"What's your name, I know it's not Bull."

"Leo Goodmen."

"Why do they call you Bull?"

He chuckles, his eyebrows rising, "They say I'm bull-headed."

"Funny, my mother has said that to me countless times," I respond back. I see myself in this man more in the last five seconds than I have my mother my whole life.

He runs his hands through his thick black hair. "If I had known you existed, Dani, I would have been there. I will never forgive your mother. I can only imagine the things she has said about me over the years. When she left, we were not on the best of terms." He looks at me with a sad face.

"Only to say I was acting like my father. If I asked about you, she would just ignore me. She is a very private person, about everything. She works a lot, too. So we haven't really bonded." I respond truthfully. "I just found out about you on the plane ride."

"Well, your mom told me everything that happened. You guys are going to stay here until things blow over, you'll be free from danger here. I would put you guys up in our safe house but we have a charity event coming up and we have other chapters already held up there."

"Charity event?" I was shocked to hear that outlaws were hosting a charity event.

"Yeah, some little boy and his mother were hit by a drunk driver. They can't afford the doctor bills so we rebuilt a bike we're going to auction off for the family. Things will get crazy here during the after party. I know I haven't been your dad more than ten minutes, but I would rather you stay in this room when the party comes back here." He has such sorrow and regret in his voice. I couldn't hate this man if I wanted to. I know as well as anyone my mother is a hard person to love. What happened when they were younger is none of my business, but something tells me he's not as bad as my mother portrays him to be.

My mom opens the door, not even bothering to knock. She avoids eye contact with my father. "Thanks for having us here, Bull, we already feel welcomed," her tone fake as she rolls her eyes.

"Yeah, anything to keep my daughter safe, Lady." He can tell by her tone she is being a bitch.

"Yes, I can see you're such a great father," she retorts, throwing her hands on her hips as her eyebrows furrow.

"If it wasn't for her, I would send your ungrateful ass packing," he yells, pointing at the door. His body, so huge and tense; his voice, ominous and rough, makes me scared. "What you did was unforgivable, not telling me I had a daughter." He's not wrong there. I am still floored she never told him about me; something I'm not sure I will ever forgive her for either.

"Why in the hell would I tell you? You told me you didn't want me. I gave up everything to be with you, and you made it more than clear you didn't care." Her voice is quivering; emotional. I have never seen my mother have any kind of emotion. I never thought she was human enough for it, she practically taught me to hide my feelings.

"That doesn't mean I wouldn't want her, and you know it," he snaps, pointing in my direction. "And, I never said I didn't want you." His vicious tone turns cold, making me shift in my seat. This is so uncomfortable; can I go get a soda or something?

"I didn't want this life for her, she is on a great path, she has a future and it's not biker trash."

Ouch.

He stood silent. This is so awkward, but I am with my father on this one. I glare at my mother, she is pissing all over him when he has been kind enough to help us out with the shit she got us into.

"That's how you see me, huh? Biker trash," he says softly, hurt.

I stand, not sure what to say, but I can't allow my mother to trample on him anymore.

"There's a room at the end of the hall you can stay in, Lady. This is a lot for Dani to take in. I'm sure she could use some alone time."

"Don't tell me what my daughter needs, you know nothing about her," her face scrunches. "She needs her mother and that is what she will have. Don't you have some slut to attend to?"

"Enough!" I yell, throwing my hands up. I can't take this back and forth bickering any longer, damn. I thought Shadow said they were hashing it out earlier.

Bull turns and leaves, slamming the door behind him. My mother falls on the bed and rests her head in her hands.

"I never should have brought you here. I shouldn't have involved you." She lifts her head to look at me. "I know your head is spinning with the disgust of this place, and that man that calls himself your father."

"I agree with him, Mother; I need some space." She looks up at me with disbelief. It's not very often I disagree with her. "I know you are going through something terrible with Stevin right now, but how could you keep all this from me. I deserved to know, and you were selfish not to tell me. Just because Bull didn't want you, didn't mean he didn't want to be my father. Do you know how hard it was growing up without a father, and then to make it worse you refused to tell me anything about him."

She scoffs at my response. "Don't be so dramatic.

"I did what I thought was right, Dani. You are not one of these people; you are better." She shocks me, I have never heard her say I was a good person, or better than anyone for that matter. Who is she trying to fool with this mommy of the year bullshit? "I will give you space," she continues, "but you tell me if you see anything you're uncomfortable with; anything. If one of them comes on to you, you tell me. They're pigs, savages. A beautiful girl like you, they will come flying to your door." She stands, making her way toward the door. "Hopefully they are smart and stay away, you being the president's daughter," she mumbles.

"Yeah, I get it, Mom. They are bad, mean, nasty, biker trash," I mock. I open the door, trying to get her the hell out. I'm confused with all of this, I don't think they are the enemy. In fact, I find it all to be sort of familiar. Maybe I was destined to be biker trash. I can literally feel the walls of school, religion, appearance, anything that wasn't my father; collapsing around me. I am numb now; I don't know what I feel or want anymore. Everything I ever believed is a lie. I don't know who I am anymore.

Chapter Three
Dani

The last several days have been mostly uneventful. My mother keeps her distance for the most part. She just keeps asking if anyone is bothering me; playing her role of concerned mother. Bull and I are getting closer. For the most part, we've only been able to talk about movies and music, because, of course, my mother butts in any chance she gets. She has really been pissing me off.

I also scoped out the rest of the clubhouse and met an 'Ol' Lady' named Babs. She is married to Locks. She has bright red hair and green eyes. Her body is thick and her manner is spitfire; I love her already. She's been teaching me a lot of biker slang, like that 'Ol' Lady' means a woman belongs to a club member and is off limits. I've even met some of the club whores; that's what Babs calls them, anyway; Juliet, a tattooed redhead; Lips, a thick figured brunette with obvious lip injections; and Candy, a busty blond with obvious boob injections.

Juliet is gorgeous. She has sleeves of inked stars and hearts and everything else you could imagine tattooed all over her arms. I'm sure when she's naked there are more. She wears them well. It actually makes me want to get a tattoo. Funny, I used to think girls with tattoos were trashy.

Lips is chunky but not fat. She has light freckles all over her face. She is beautiful and dresses very classy; she doesn't really look like a club whore at all.

Candy doesn't seem to like me; she avoids eye contact and her body language is very cold toward me. She is skinny; like super model skinny, and wears hardly any clothing. Her attitude screams bitch and reminds me a lot of my mother. I'm sure we'll butt heads before this charade is over.

I've seen Shadow pop in and out of the club here and there. He comes in covered in grease and makes my heart do that flip-flop thing. We don't talk to each other; we try to keep our distance. But I catch him staring at me a lot. He stares at me with hungry eyes and the most breathtaking, yet arrogant smile a man can have. He makes my sex clench and dampen with every megawatt smile; he is so infuriating. A few times, when he had to walk past me, he would brush his arm against mine. The spot he briefly made contact with would feel ablaze. It's the worst foreplay ever; pure sexual torture. His pouty lips, beefy arms, chiseled abs, cute butt and amazing dimples make my lips swell with the anticipation of exploring every inch of him.

It's been a few days since I've seen Shadow, so I casually bring up to Babs that I've noticed some of the men missing. "They've gone on a bike run, Hun. Something the boys do to handle club business. They should be back soon." She's wiping the bar clean after feeding me a delicious breakfast. "Other than that, we don't get the privilege of knowing what their runs consist of or how long they'll be out." I am shocked to realize that while her husband is gone doing god knows what or for how long, she just stays at the house and plays Betty Crocker for the rest of the club men. She talks a lot about club rules and the responsibilities of being an Ol' Lady. If this is one of the duties, I'm not sure I'd make a good one.

It's midnight and I'm wide awake listening to my iPod. Music has always been an outlet for my emotions. In my roughest troubles it speaks the words of healing that I can't find for myself. I haven't been able to sleep this entire week; it's all so new to me. My stomach speaks, too, with a growl, so I grab some plaid shorts to throw on. Maybe if I eat I can finally fall asleep. I tuck my iPod in the waist of my shorts and hang the headphones around my neck. I see my bra on the floor and the lacy thing reminds me I am only wearing a thin, black tank top without a bra. It's so late I doubt anyone will be up. I'll just grab a bite and run back here. I open the door and notice most of the lights are off in the hallway. But I can tell there are lights on in the main room that has the bar. I tip toe down the hallway and into the kitchen quietly, not noticing anyone in my quick jaunt.

 I open the big, stainless steel refrigerator and see food stocked on all the shelves; clearly for the upcoming charity event. I grab a dish and open it to find barbecued pulled pork; the smell capturing my senses and making my stomach growl louder. I pull it out and set it on the counter. Plates, pork, buns, and a microwave; perfect! Katy Perry's "Dark Horse" starts blaring through my head phones, reminding me I still have my iPod. I love this song, so I put the headphones back on and start dancing around the kitchen looking for the things to complete my meal. I get sucked into the song and start singing, but try not to get too loud.

 As the song finally finishes, I have everything I need on the counter. I put the pulled pork in the microwave to heat and hear a deep laugh. My heart skips a beat. Yanking the headphones off my head, I spin in the direction of the sound to find Shadow.

 He's leaning against a counter wearing gray sweat pants that hang off his hips in a very delicious way. He's not wearing a shirt, allowing me to see his tight, lick-worthy stomach. He's holding a tub of chocolate ice cream and as his arm moves in to scoop a spoonful, I notice the tattoo on his bicep is a very detailed, black raven sitting on a skull. His hair is wet as if he just got out of the shower. A trickle of water falls carelessly from his hair onto his chest making me pant.

 "Don't mind me, just enjoying dinner and a show. Please, keep going." He winks.

I scowl back at him. How dare he just gawk at me in a private moment and when the hell did he get back, anyway? Then he licks the spoon clean of anything chocolate; his tongue assaulting without mercy. My lips part and a small moan escapes my mouth.

"See something you like?" he asks, flaunting a playboy smile.

I roll my eyes and look back at the microwave, adjusting my plate and BBQ sauce. I try to think of something to say but come up with nothing. The microwave beeps and I grab my plate quickly, ignoring the painful burn the plate brings. I shrug, letting it bang to the counter. "I just notice you're not wearing your vest." I say, not completely lying.

"A vest? You mean my cut?" he asks, almost offended. I shrug again, trying to act disinterested. I know he's still there. I can feel him; his presence. It's beautiful but embodies a hint of beast. I turn my head slightly, catching him in my peripheral. He's still leaning on the counter, watching me.

"Do you have a problem?" I say sharply, turning in his direction. Little fake giggles come from the bar in the next room, catching my attention. Shadow also looks at the door briefly before turning back to me, with a lewd glare. I just put myself in a trap; shit.

"Yeah, I guess you could say I have a problem." He eyes me up and down, his tone sexual, suggesting I could fix his problem.

"Yes, please let me fix your problem," my inside screams within the depths of sexual tension. But I remind myself of his fake charm; how he's so cocky and infuriating; the games he likes to play. He's a womanizer, and I won't be easy; even if it kills me.

I laugh and turn seductively, leaning over the island separating us. I notice his breath catch, confirming that I affect him and making this that much harder. I lick my lips slowly, eyeing him up and down as he had done to me.

"Well, then, I suggest you have one of them..." my eyes dart to the door where the giggles continue, "...fix your little..." my eyes snap to his groin where I'm sure it's anything but little, "...problem." My tone is cold and distant.

I turn to reach for my plate and Shadow leaps over the counter. He tangles his hand in my hair making my scalp burn. Pulling my head back, he thrusts his pelvis into my ass, his length anything but little. The roughness has my veins rushing with erotic pleasure. Warmth floods my wet entrance, shouting for Shadow to have his way with me. My body's reaction causes me to blush.

He leans his face next to my ear, his breath smelling of chocolate making me want him more. I moan, my body defying the warnings in my mind. "You can try and act like you don't want me, that you have control," he breathes into my ear as he thrusts his groin harder against me. He's still pulling my hair, making me arch my back. He slowly pulls his hips away and my ass thrusts itself against his groin trying to regain contact. The action takes me by surprise. Shadow lets out a vicious laugh. "But your body can't lie," he nips my earlobe making me practically come on the spot, the pain shooting to my toes making them curl with pleasure, "you have no power."

He growls and pushes me forward releasing my hair and body. The shocking loss of heat is like a slap in the face. I watch him walk away; his bare back beautifully tattooed with the club name and emblem. Suddenly, I feel cheap and used and I want to slap the cockiness right out of him.

My midnight snack took some of the gnawing from my stomach and after lots of tossing and turning, I finally fell asleep. This morning, though, I just want to stay in my room. I'm still mad at myself for wanting Shadow, and at my traitorous body.

Pacing and arguing with myself isn't solving anything, though, so I finally decide I've somehow been brain washed and clearly do not want Shadow and his scandalous ways in spite of my attraction. Besides, I hear a lot of commotion outside and my naturally nosy self can't resist the temptation to find out what's going on.

Walking outside to the garage, I see some guys pulling out a black bike. I stop to admire the sleek, sexy lines and imagine myself on it for just a second.

"That's the bike the club's donating for the charity," Shadow says from behind me, scaring the shit out of me. "It's a Bobber; not my favorite bike, but it will do. The auction is in an hour." I can only scowl at him, my body still wound up and tight from the games he played last night. But when I see the sincere joy in his face, my anger melts away. Right on cue, my body starts heating up and flashbacks from last night assail my mind. I'm like a dog in heat, sheesh.

I notice I'm playing with my lip and dart my hands to my side, he makes me nervous clearly. "Oh, I thought it was a Harley. Aren't they the best bikes?" I know nothing about motorcycles, only what I've seen in commercials about Harley's and overheard guys at my college say about them being so great.

He clutches his chest with both of his hands and gasps. "A woman after my own heart. Have you ever been on a bike?" His tone seems boyish instead of rugged and dark for a change. He is cute, getting all excited talking about motorcycles.

"Unless you mean a bicycle, no. I live in New York; we take taxis everywhere." I say, smiling.

He grabs my hand and pulls me away from the garage toward the parking lot; toward a different black bike. This one has silver lines all over the gas tank that look like shadows sweeping over a black darkness. I love it.

"This is my bike. It's a Dyna Super Glide." Seeing the confusion on my face, he continues, "This is a Harley. She takes whatever I give her and doesn't bitch. She's the perfect girlfriend." He's smiling from ear to ear. "Let's go for a ride and I'll show you why they are the best bikes. The auction is pretty boring; they won't miss us." He winks, making fireworks go off in my gut.

"Here's a helmet, put it on." He hands me a black helmet. He's not joking; he wants me to ride that thing.

"I don't know, my mom would kill me if she found out," I reply unsure. I know my mother would have a stroke if she saw me climbing on the back of a bike, especially with anyone but Bull. But who am I kidding, Shadow is very alluring and telling him no is not an option; and do I really want to tell him no?

"No she won't. She'll kill me." He tilts his head, cocking his eyebrow, and gives me a megawatt smile. "Besides, you know you want to." He is so cocky, and as self-assured as ever. But he is right; I want to get on that bike with him.

Getting close to Shadow is like playing with fire, but I guess I'm a fire bug because I grab the helmet and put it on my head. The mere thought of going against my mother's wishes is a rush, but the thought of having Shadow between my legs is intoxicating.

He laces the strap under my chin, rubbing one of his calloused fingers across my lips. I forget everything as I stare into those stormy eyes. He shakes his head, as if to clear whatever thought was racing through that gorgeous head of his and effortlessly throws a leg over the bike to start it. It roars to life. The rumble thunders off the ground, up through my boots and in between my legs. Who knew a motorcycle could be such a turn on.

I climb on behind Shadow unsure of where to put my hands. I place them behind me first, then on my thighs. He turns to the side with a smile and reaches back. He pulls my arms around his toned waist forcing my body close to his. I can feel his rock hard back against my breasts. My nipples harden on contact. The mixture of pain and pleasure make my breathing quicken and I just want to rip his shirt off and feel his bare chest.

"You have to touch me to ride: but you're safe with me," he says, snapping me from my X-rated thoughts. "Hold on tight, I like to go fast." My arms and legs tighten around him as he speeds off. He wasn't lying when he said he likes to go fast. He said I am safe with him and I feel safe; with his driving that is. Anything else, I am sure he will trample on, like my heart.

The warm breeze caresses my skin. It makes me feel free; independently free. Shadow's scent fills my lungs; I'm not used to his masculine smell. I lay my head against his back and inhale; not knowing if I will ever be this close to him again. His reactions to me are so unpredictable I don't know what to make of them. He reaches back and rests his hand on the side of my thigh. His touch causes my suspicious thoughts to resurface. Would he just throw me away like a used condom when he is finished with me? Yet even confused, I can't get the thought of having his hands all over my naked body out of my mind. I bet he is dynamite in bed. I'm sure he has been with countless women; just the thought of it makes me uneasy. I don't know why, he isn't mine to lay claim to. Still the thought makes me want to claw my eyes out. I hate how he affects me, I have never doubted myself before, yet here I am punishing myself for not being the ideal girl for Shadow. I'm probably way too inexperienced for a dangerous man like him.

We pull into a parking lot with a sign that says 'Santa Monica Beach'. A breeze flows over us as we park; it smells salty and wet. It smells like a new beginning. Nothing of the past twenty-four hours would have been allowed into my past life. Nothing has prepared me for this emotional roller coaster. I breathe deep and feel my walls of isolation tumbling down. Looking at the physical beauty of Shadow, my spirits soar.

"The beach? Is this where you take all the girls that climb on the back of your bike?" I tease. I shake my head as I remove the helmet allowing my hair to ripple its way down my shoulder and onto my chest. It doesn't sit there long as the breeze sweeps it off my chest and slaps it around my face.

"Actually, I have never had a female on the back of my bike before," he says as he places our helmets on the bike. The expression on his face shows he is both amazed and bewildered by his actions. I look at him in confusion; what did he mean by that, and why was I the first to ride on his bike?

He snaps out of his vulnerable state by running his dexterous fingers through his flawless hair. My fingers twitch at the temptation to grab hold of those gorgeous locks. "Women usually come to me. Besides, if I want a girl I just take her, no questions," he says assuredly, his tone serious. I roll my eyes and am reminded of why I should stay away from him.

We walk onto the beach. I can feel him staring at my back side as I walk in front of him so I sway my curvaceous hips, taunting him. I hear him literally growl in response, making me bite my lips to stifle my laughter. We sit down on the warm sandy beach within inches of each other. He leans back on his elbows, lifting one hand to ruffle the top of his thick black hair. Goddamn he is sex on a stick, and I want to eat, lick, and touch that stick. My hand burns at the thought of tugging his hair, while our bodies are in a sexual embrace. I shift my position, trying to overcome the throbbing in my panties. Embarrassed, my cheeks flush crimson red. I know he can't read my thoughts, but having such a naughty imagination is totally out of my norm.

"So, are you and your mother close?" he asks, snapping me from my kinky daydream.

"Eh, not really. When I was younger we were, but over the past few years we have grown apart. She works a lot, and when she's not working she's with Stevin." He nods his head in understanding, urging me to continue. "I mean, we live together, but we are usually doing our own things separately." I dig my hands into the sand to keep them occupied or I might just start groping the man.

"So you live with your mom? How old are you?" he asks, incredibly.

I don't laugh, or smirk back. The situation with my mother is more than embarrassing. She is the biggest manipulator I know. She keeps me tucked within arm's reach and won't let me leave the nest or do anything on my own. It's like she's keeping me for some reason, but I have not a clue why.

"It's complicated," I reply, looking away.

"Nah, I get it. One look at your mom and I can tell she's a raging bitch on a mission," he comforts. "You in school or anything?" he asks, genially curious.

I sigh heavily. School; another burden my mother forces onto me.

"Well, I'm working on a generic bachelors right now because I'm not sure what I want to do after that. My mom keeps pushing for all these careers like Law Enforcement Officer or Lawyer, but they aren't for me.

"That's crazy; she really is trying to push you in the opposite direction of your father," Shadow replies, shaking his head. "So what is for you then?" he asks, tilting his head, his eyes piercing me.

I half laugh, realizing I'm telling him more than I want to.

"Okay." he says, noticing I'm not answering that question. "Tell me this, is some stuffy businessman wondering where his gal up and left to? What about your friends?" He looks at me with hooded eyes.

How should I respond to that? Even if I say I am seeing someone, it won't stop him if I'm on his radar of future bed notches.

"My mom never liked my taste in men, she always chased them off. She can be fierce when she wants to be." I smile, not answering yes or no. "As for friends, I have a few, but no one close." I doubt they even realize I left.

I feel the hair on my neck rise and my heart beat accelerate. "Why are you staring at me like that?" I ask, before looking at him, uncomfortable under that dark gaze of his.

He smiles, looking down at the sand before lifting his head and catching me with those smoldering eyes. The tenderness I see there makes my heart catch fire.

"You always play with your lip when you're nervous?" he asks. I drop my hands and sigh at myself. I have been around this man for five minutes and he knows my tics; been around my mother my whole life and she has never noticed. "So, what are your plans now?"

Haven't we talked about me enough? I sigh heavily. "I have no idea. After seeing how the other half of me lives, I'm confused on what lies in my future."

"What do you mean?" He throws a sea shell out into the water, making his arm muscles flex. My lips part and heavy breaths escape. I remember him grabbing me off the bed at the clubhouse like I was a toy, weighing nothing. He turns and looks at me again with those heavy blue eyes, then throws me that cocky grin of his. He knows what he is doing, damn him.

"Uh." I pause, trying to remember what the question is. "I mean, I did everything my mother asked without question. She wanted me to stay on some righteous 'path' of hers, never thinking about what I might want. I didn't go against her because she was my mother. I thought this path was for me to have a good future and because she cared. After seeing the bigger picture, though, I think this 'path' is a silent battle my mother has had with my father the whole time." I pause and close my eyes. "I know that sounds like a whiny little princess," I confess, feeling just that way.

He smiles and grabs my hand off the sandy beach, giving it a light squeeze. Even this tender touch makes butterflies swarm in my lower abdomen. This simple gesture says he can relate with being damaged; torn. Shadow is making it so easy to open up to him, which is dangerous. Revealing my vulnerabilities is making me feel close to him, something I know he wants nothing of. I need to reverse the tables on these questions, and fast. He is a player, and he is playing the game very well. I'm not used to someone laying on the charm so thick; I fall under his spell easily.

I lift my eyebrow inquisitively and pull my hand from his. My hand turns cold instantly wanting his touch back. "What's your thing, Shadow? I ask, mocking him from his earlier question.

"Heh, besides the club, you don't wanna know," he says, cynically.

Not sure if he's talking about drugs, or women, or something darker, I turn my head away from him. "Yuck, no I don't," I reply, earning a chuckle form him.

"Club life, baby," he says flippantly. Is it sad I want to be part of his club life? Actually, no I don't, I just want Shadow.

"So what about you, how did you land in a motorcycle club?" I ask, trying to get off the topic of him being a whore.

"'Nother time," he says, standing up. Wait, what?

"What, seriously? I just spilled my whole life story and I don't get anything from you?" I stand up placing my hands on my hips. If he thinks he is not going to tell me something about himself, he's mistaken.

"I just don't open myself up to others, Dani," he replies honestly, with sorrow in his voice. Obviously someone had hurt him in the past and it haunted him.

"I didn't say you had to tell me all your secrets and marry me, but I would like to know something about you. Can't friends talk?" His eyes widen when I say friends. Was wanting to be his friend crossing the line? I want him to open up to me, I want to know everything about him, honestly. He stands there searching my face, I feel like I'm naked when he stares at me with those hungry eyes.

"I was a hang-around at the club for a few years. When your father saw I wasn't going anywhere he made me a prospect. I was a prospect for about a year or so when we were making a run and were ambushed by a rival club. We were outnumbered and they were armed to the teeth. We were shooting back sporadically to conserve ammo, but couldn't get a break. I finally got up from behind my bike and just started shooting at everything. I hit one of their guys and they took off. It was too late for Smokey, our Sargent-At-Arms. The guy I shot later died, too, from what I hear." Shadow closes his eyes and lowers his head. He balls his fists next to his side and shakes his head. He is breathtaking, even in turmoil. "Your dad said I showed loyalty and bravery, that it would be an honor to call me his brother. He patched me in as the new Sargent-At-Arms." He lifts his head and stares at me with those gorgeous blue eyes.

I want to hug him for what happened to them, but I know he is not looking for sympathy. In fact, I'm sure just telling me something that personal is probably hard for him. I really just figured he would tell me his favorite color, or to screw off. Truthfully, he is as broken as I am, we are both damaged. I reach my hand out to grab his, to offer him some kind of peace. He looks down at our hands embraced, his hand much bigger than mine. The fire that was there when our hands touched earlier, starts to ignite again. He pulls his hand away roughly, and shakes his head. What is he shaking his head at? Me, himself, or us?

"Dani, don't read anything into this, there's nothing between us. Being together is a hell we can't afford to explore." He presses his hand on the small of my back to guide me toward his bike. "Come on, let's get you back to the club." His hand on my back shoots waves of ecstasy through my veins. I want him to bend me over his bike and have his way with me; who cares if I'm just a notch on his belt anymore.

I sigh internally. My body, soul, and mind are so confused. I can't deny the way Shadow affects me, but he is right. Anything between us would lead to an even bigger hell than we both already live. My father would kill him, and my mother would kill me, or throw me out on the streets with nothing like she has threatened to my whole life. Our lives as we know them would forever change if we became anything more than friends. I feel alive while I am with Shadow, so high on adrenaline I throw caution to the wind. We are dangerous around each other. Maybe just eye-fucking from across the room would be in our best interest. But being alone in a bedroom, having hell and heaven in the same room, would be monumental.

Chapter Four
Dani

The ride back from the beach is awkward; Shadow is tense the whole time compared to how relaxed he was on the ride there. He keeps his hands on the handle bars and not on my thigh. I can tell he is not happy he told me something personal. I wish I hadn't pushed him to share.

We pull up to the clubhouse and I see my mother outside. To say she has a scowl on her face is an understatement. I climb off the bike and she instantly starts yelling at me regardless of the many people around. Apparently the after party has started.

"Where the hell have you been? Why are you on that bike with the likes of him?" She slurs. I raise an eyebrow. I don't think I have ever seen my mother drunk before.

She grabs my arm as I try to walk past her. "You answer me right now," she yells, gathering more attention from everyone.

I yank my arm away from her and glare in her direction; she stumbles backwards from the force of my tugging. How dare she ask where I was? And why I was on the back of his bike is even less of her business. Screw her and her lies. I am no longer going to follow her every wish and command. It's time to start thinking for myself; living my own life. As I continue past her, she starts screaming at Shadow to stay away from me. I'm sure he won't argue with that.

The clubhouse is crowded with people. I smell cheap perfume mixed with alcohol and cigarette smoke. There's a funny smell that I assume is marijuana. The lights are low so it's hard for me to recognize anyone as I push my way through the main room. Twisted Sister's "We're Not Gonna Take It" is blaring from the stereo system and I think how fitting that song is for what I'm feeling at this exact moment. I'm not gonna take my mother's shit anymore. It'll be hard for her to throw me out now that Bull and I have gotten close. That should piss her off.

    I make my way to my room and lock the door. My dad, eh, Bull, asked me to stay in here so I sit on my bed unsure of what to do next. I don't know if I should call him dad or Bull; everything is still so awkward. I look over and see a laptop on the dresser. Hmm, I wonder if the internet has anything on the club. Maybe then I can see why my mother is so concerned. I reach over and grab the laptop before giving it a second thought.

    When the browser loads, I type in "Devil's Dust Motorcycle Club". The search engine instantly pops up with pages of news articles; yikes. The club has been linked to multiple murders, missing persons, possible gun running, and the list goes on and on. Holy shit, I'm not prepared for this. After opening every news story and article it seems they have never been charged with any of the allegations they were supposedly "linked" to. Witnesses either went missing, were found dead, or changed their story. Hmm? Well you know what they say, "innocent until proven guilty". I slap the laptop closed not wanting to dig any further. Deep down I know better, but this is the story I am sticking to. I feel safe here, maybe it is because I'm the president's daughter. I know nobody will fuck with me, or they will end up in a ditch or with a bullet in their leg. I lay back on the bed. I can hear the music thumping against my wall. I could just go grab a soda and come right back. No harm in that, right? I can even go check on my mother; she was pretty pissed.

    I open my door slowly and peek out; it is still crazy. Cigarette and marijuana smoke fill my lungs, making me cough. It's loud and people are everywhere. I slide out of the door and go to the end of the hall where my mom's room is. When I open the door she is passed out with a bottle of booze next to the bed. Good Lord; how pathetic. I cover her up with a blanket and lock and shut her door as I leave.

When I make my way into the main lobby, I'm shocked. I've never seen so many people with so few clothes on in my life. I see people dancing on each other, giving lap dances, and others just genuinely having a good time. The stereo is now blaring "Figured You Out" by Nickleback, another one of my favorites. Not really noticing anyone, I head for the kitchen. Just before entering, I glance back at the crowd and like the Red Sea parting, there's a clearing of bodies. My vision reaches into the corner where the club whore, Candy, is straddling Shadow's lap. My blood heats to a dangerous level; the scene making me jealous.

Why am I jealous?

She has her bleach blond hair pulled into a sloppy bun with little strands dangling everywhere. Her bright pink tank top is way too tight, and her black shorts don't cover her ass. And those pink high heels... club whore is a fitting name for her. I feel vomit rise in my throat just looking at them. Shadow's eyes lock onto mine; mesmerizing me. I push the vomit down and stare back, not blinking. He raises his left eyebrow; the corner of his mouth curving upward into a smug smile as he pulls Candy closer to him, kissing her neck. His eyes are daring and dark; sending a message, "Look what I got". He is trying to make me jealous. He didn't have to try; I already am and I hate it.

Two can play this game; I walk onto the floor and see a gorgeous man with blond, curly hair and tattoos up and down his arms. It is dark so I can't quite make out what his cut says, but, who cares, he is handsome. I step in front of him and start dancing seductively, hoping my provocative behavior will entice the stranger. He makes claim to my body without hesitation, placing his huge hands on my waist and pushing his groin up against my buttocks. I look down and see "TCB" tattooed on top of his left hand. What the hell does that mean? I sway my hips in time to the music with his. Taking my left arm I bring it up over my head and hook it around the back of his neck. He takes his fingers and slides them down my elbow to my shoulder. Other than a tickle, his touch doesn't shoot sparks or butterflies anywhere in my body.

"Bobby, I didn't know you had a death wish, brother." Startled I look beside us. Shadow's standing there eyeing the man he just called Bobby with a death stare. I look over to where I last saw Shadow and see Candy sitting on the couch with her arms crossed over her chest, tapping her foot, and pouting.

"Don't be a cock block, Shadow. Get lost," Bobby says, pulling me closer. What the hell was Shadow getting at, coming over here acting like that! I smile sweetly at Shadow and let Bobby's large frame cocoon mine.

"She's all yours," Shadow smiles wolfishly; his daring eyes never leaving mine. "I'm sure Bull won't mind if you dry fuck his daughter." He says that last line casually. I glare at Shadow before looking at Bobby. He looks at me closely, then does a double take. He throws his hands in the air like I'm fire; shit. I snap my eyes in Shadow's direction and he's laughing. I whirl back to reassure Bobby, only to find him already dancing with another girl.

"You asshole." I shove Shadow in the shoulder. "Who do you think you are?" I scream, my level of anger at its highest. My violent shove stops his laughter; his face turns serious. I wanted to make him jealous, but did he have to announce to everyone I am Bull's daughter. Between my mother and Bull, I'll never be able to let loose and live.

"If you're going to act like a whore, maybe you should go hang out with them." His tone serious, he points toward a corner full of girls who were half dressed and quite drunk; club whores.

I shove my hand at his chest again. "Fuck You, Shadow!" I scream, hatred lacing each word.

I stomp off to my room, pushing muscle and half naked bodies out of the way; not caring who I knock over in the process. I want to slap Shadow; scream at him for being such an ass. I can't believe how I can be so turned on by just looking at him; yearning for the simple touch of his fingers. And then seeing Candy receive that touch instead... I wanted to round house her ass for just sitting on his lap. I have never been so angry with anyone in my life like I am right now with Shadow.

I make it to my room and stand there; I wrap my arms around my middle trying to settle my manic behavior. My chest heaves and my legs wobble from the anger building within me. He called me a whore, the bastard.

I hear the door open and shut quickly. Glancing over, I see Shadow standing just inside with that toe-curling grin of his. I still want to slap that damn grin right off his face; he loves that he's driving me crazy. The anger inside amplifies at the thought. I walk up to him, pull my hand back and slap him. His head whips to the side. He clenches his jaw and stares at me with hooded eyes. My hand stings from the harsh contact, but I refuse to acknowledge the pain and raise my hand to slap him again; not having felt any relief from the first one. He catches my hand by the wrist, mid-air. I raise my other hand in an attempt to slap him and he catches that wrist, too. He whips me around and slams me against the door; both of my hands are now pinned above my head. I look into his eyes, they're dilated with anger.

He lets go of my hands and punches the door behind me. His growl makes me jump with fear. His face is red with rage, his fists balled at his sides. He's pissed!

"Get out!" I yell, pointing at the door. He turns and looks at me, his eyes now savage. Making me his prey, he stalks toward me and pins my arms above my head again;

only this time I don't fight him. Why? "Yell at him, tell him to fuck off. You want nothing to do with him. He called you a whore," I scream internally.

He pulls my chin up to face him, and lowers his lips just above mine. His breathing is harsh and deranged; his lips barely a hair's breadth away, "I'm sick of these games, Dani!" he snarls.

"You? How do you think I feel"? I say roughly. I turn my head, his lips brushing against my skin in the process. "Leave me alone. I want nothing to do with you." I whisper, venom pouring over each word.

"You want me to leave you alone, huh? Is that what you really want?" He shakes me against the door like a disobedient child. I stare into his sinister blue eyes, now a darker hue. I don't know what I want anymore. I know messing with Shadow is a signed death certificate but I can't shake the magnetism I have for him. Telling him I do want him would mean he wins; a game of control he clearly needs. Can I give control like that to someone I barely know?

Taking advantage of my hesitation, he leans in close. "I call bullshit," he whispers, his lips brushing my own. This fight is pure sexual tension. I cannot deny it any longer, and by the look in his eyes neither can he. So what if I'm just a one night stand? So what if I'm just another notch on his belt? Maybe having sex will finally get him out of my system. The way my body craves his touch makes me take the risk.

"I want you," I whisper, my admission catching me by surprise. Did I really just say that?

"Say it again, Dani," he demands. Our rage and anger melt into sexual energy. His alpha male attitude makes me delirious with arousal.

"I. Want. You." I form the words with each sultry breath.

He releases my arms and swiftly lifts me up. My legs instinctively wrap around his waist. I grab his head and tangle my fingers in his messy black hair. Pulling his face close, I smash my lips into his. His lips part mine as my tongue demands entry; he tastes of alcohol and weed. Our anger replaced with raw passion; we bite, lick, and suck each other's mouths; savoring the taste of one another. A moan escapes me as I draw my head back, allowing Shadow to dive into the crook of my neck, kissing and nipping, causing me to moan louder.

Shadow pulls back. "I win," he hisses. His tongue licking up my jaw line causes me to breathe heavily. His eyes show me the beast that lives within, circling in its cage waiting to be released.

He's right. I just verbally confirmed that I want him. Who knows what twisted demented things he will do with my confession.

"Goddamn, you smell like heaven," his lips whisper against my skin. "It's not that I didn't want you, you know. I've wanted you since I first saw your stuck up ass walk out of the airport," he confesses. He pulls back again and looks into my eyes. "But this could get me killed." His voice is solemn, taking me out of the moment.

He licks the sweat beads forming on my neck and my legs naturally tighten around his waist. His lips spread across my neck and jaw bone like wild fire; igniting a spark I desperately need for him to put out. I reach for the bottom of my shirt and his hands support my back while I pull it off over of my head. He pushes my body higher against the door and lays wet kisses in between my breasts. He walks us to the bed and gently lays me down as he slowly lowers his own toned physique over my tiny frame. He rests his weight on one elbow and using his other hand unclasps my lacy bra. My nipples instantly harden from the cool air when they are released from their cups, causing me to gasp.

"You are fucking perfect." His calloused hands greedily grab my breasts, kneading and teasing them, causing my back to arch into his touch, pleading for more.

"Dani," he pauses to catch his breath and lifts himself up some. My body immediately aches for his touch. "If you're having any second thoughts, we need to quit right now because I won't be able to stop once you are all mine."

His gesture is kind, but my need is crude. At this point I don't care, I just want more of him; now. "Don't stop, Shadow," I whisper, my breathing sporadic. I clench my hands in his shirt, pulling him back to me.

He removes his leather cut and tosses it on a stained chair in the corner of the room. He pulls his shirt over his head, revealing perfectly toned pecs and a slim, tight abdomen. A happy trail leads down into a V that disappears into his low cut jeans. Oh, holy mother of God, give me strength; I want it all!

My tongue darts out to lick my bottom lip; I want to eat him up. I kiss his chest, licking around his nipple before giving it a light tug. He moans as my teeth pinch the soft skin. He unbuttons his jeans and tugs them off his hips. Once they're down to his ankles he uses his feet to push them off each leg. My eyes widen at the impressive length pressing against the fabric of his white boxer briefs, demanding to be released. My cheeks suddenly flush, my body temperature rising. He arrogantly smiles, before he climbs back on top of me, spreading my legs open with his. His hand rubs the inner crotch of my jeans, causing my panties to dampen. He knows every button to push, there is no question there, and he is about to find out just how inexperienced I am. He may not like it if I surprise him with something like that. He starts sucking on my earlobe as his hands fiddle with the button on my jeans. Shit, shit, shit!

"Uh, Shadow," I say, nervously.

"Yeah?" He answers, pulling my fingers away from my lips. Shit, I didn't even notice I was doing that again.

"I, uh, I'm a virgin." I sputter, awkwardly.

He lifts off me instantly. Shit, I should have just let him figure it out.

"Fuck," he pauses. "I mean, I thought you might be."

I turn my head and look at the wall, biting my lower lip in embarrassment.

"Hey," he whispers, pushing a strand of hair behind my ear. He is so sweet when he wants to be. "We can go as slow as you like, Dani. I'll be gentle" I swear he is cooing.

Holy shit, who was this man, and where did my bad ass biker go?

I nod my head, afraid I may chicken out if I give myself the opportunity to speak.

He unbuttons my jeans and pulls them off of me. Then he tucks a finger under each side of my white, lacy panties and slowly slides them down my legs, his fingers blazing a trail of fire all the way to my toes. He leans back on his heels and looks at my naked body displayed before him. Leaning in, he takes one of my nipples between his teeth and gently bites down, blending pleasure with pain and making me feel buzzed. I can feel his engorged manhood against my already wet heat. I slide my feet up his legs to the waistband of his underwear. Tucking my toes under the elastic, I push them over his cute firm ass and down his legs. His cock springs free against my abdomen.

"Anxious, baby?" He asks arrogantly. I roll my eyes at his self-assured tone.

He grabs me by the hair and pulls my head back. "Don't fucking roll your eyes at me," he hisses, kissing my jawline. His demanding ways make me whimper, but in a good way. His tone is serious, and anything but playful, but I can't help but be aroused at his roughness.

His fingers spread my sensitive folds to allow entry. He suddenly dips his fingers in my wet heat, spreading the moisture up and down my clit. I dive my hands into my hair and arch my back, rocking my hips into his touch.

"Holy shit, you're wet," he whispers, breathlessly.

He lifts his fingers and slowly slips them into his hungry mouth; he sucks hard, savoring my juices.

"Keep your eyes on mine," he says, ducking his head in between my thighs. I raise up on my elbows watching him lay light kisses on my clit before going further down and plunging his warm tongue deep inside. I collapse off my elbows and fall back, moaning loudly. Thank God the music is so loud that nobody can hear me. It feels so warm and wet, my sex clenches wanting release. He takes his other hand and presses lightly on my stomach lowering my arched body down onto the bed. He flicks his tongue between my folds, teasing me, and then sucks my clit into his hot mouth roughly. My body pushes back into the bed and my hands fly into his messy hair.

"Don't you cum," Shadow orders, as he lifts his head up from between my thighs. My wetness drenches his stubble and lips. He puts his hands on my knees and positions his pulsing erection against my wet opening. I close my eyes tight, waiting for him to plow into me.

"Open your eyes, beautiful," he says sweetly. I comply and open my eyes, slowly.

"Shit, hang on." He climbs off of me, exposing my body to the coolness of the air. I hear a foil wrapper rip and watch him roll the rubber onto his shaft.

"Okay," he says, climbing in between my legs again.

I look deeply into his beautiful, stormy eyes as he pushes the tip of himself into my wet opening. I wince, and dig my nails into the sheets as he slides in deeper; his eyes never leaving mine. It's the most erotic thing I have ever witnessed.

"You okay?" he asks, concerned.

"Yeah, just don't stop," I reply back, my breathing now chaotic.

I can feel myself stretch and pull to accommodate his impressive size. It stings yet feels amazing. Once he is in as far as my body will allow, he stills, letting my body acclimate to his length.

"The hard part is over." He leans down and kisses me hungrily, biting my bottom lip as he rocks his hips back and forth.

"Here comes the fun part." He smiles, from ear to ear, causing me to smile too.

My legs wrap around his body as he thrusts his way in and out of me. He lifts his hand and grabs my right leg pulling it even tighter around his waist. The sound of our sweaty bodies smacking against each other fills the room. There is nothing, just me and him. The music is muffled by our heavy breaths and light moans. Time is standing still as I lose my innocence to the devil himself.

He grabs my ass cheeks lifting me slightly off the bed. He thrusts harder making me whimper. "You are so fucking tight; I don't think I will last long." His confession heightens my arousal that much more.

I detach my nails from the sheets and explore his immaculate chest. His head falls back and he lets out a raw growl with my touch; his hips pick up speed. One of his hands finds one of my over-sensitive nipples and pinches it as the other hands trails down my stomach, over my pubic hair, to my clit. He starts to move his finger in circular motions over my clit; it's my undoing.

Warmth floods my feet, making my toes curl, shooting the flame up my legs and in between my thighs. My body convulses with explosive tingles, my sex clenching his cock like a vice. My nails grab at his back as I arch my body into his. I scream out in pleasure, as he thrusts harder. I thrash my head to the side and bite at the loose sheet as his body stiffens. I feel his thick warm seed fill the latex, before he falls on top of me.

    We lay there panting, trying to catch our breath. Shadow slowly withdraws his rock hard erection from my wet sleeve, making me wince from the void his absence has left. He rolls the condom off his length with his fingers and tosses it into the corner of the room. Is there even a trash can over there?

    "Sleep," he whispers in my ear. He pulls my back to his chest; his body cocooning mine. This feels so right, but so wrong. After coming down from my sexual high, my rationalizing comes in. I can't stomach being another notch on his bed post, but I knew that was a possibility before I handed him my virginity on a silver platter. I know deep in my gut Shadow is anything but out of my system, he's an addictive drug and I want more to satisfy my craving. I close my eyes, trying to summon sleep. Listening to the loud crowd in the club and the thud of the music slowly takes me under.

Chapter Five
Shadow

    I feel smooth legs wrapped around mine, and silky hair on my chest. The smell of Dani's intoxicating perfume fills my lungs. Peaches and sandalwood; the smell of her alone could make my dick hard. I'm hard now, shit. The events of last night play in my head simultaneously; what the fuck was I thinking? I have had her in my damn head since the day I saw her high maintenance ass walk out of that terminal. I tried to stay away. Hell, I tried to push her away. But when I saw her dancing with Bobby last night, the thought of someone else having their hands on her or possibly in their bed... I went caveman. I wanted to drag her to a room and fuck her within an inch of her life.
    I open my eyes to find Dani's head lying on my chest and her body clung to mine, our legs and arms tangled. I'm speechless at the angelic beauty sprawled out before me, and completely appalled. I have never had sex like last night. When I'm with one of the flavors; that's what we call the whores who hang around the club, I usually bend them over something or have them on their knees. Then I send them packing; no skin contact, no cuddling, and sure as hell no staying over.
    And I sure as hell never messed around with a virgin before. I should have bailed as soon as she pulled the 'V' card out. Fuck. Fuck. Fuck. I had hoped after getting my dick wet by Dani, I wouldn't want her anymore. I just wanted to prove to her that she couldn't resist me; and

prove to myself I just wanted her because I couldn't have her. But looking at her this morning I could definitely take her again; I still want her. But I don't deserve her and I can't afford the distraction.

I can't help but slide my hand up and down her bare back. Her olive skin is so silky. My dick twitches at the skin contact, making me frustrated. All these feelings I'm having are fucking mystifying. I need to get out of here and clear my head. I slowly move her head over and try to untangle my body from hers, trying not to wake her.

"You're still here. I thought you would be gone," she mumbles with sleep in her voice.

Shit, I woke her.

"Yeah, uh, I gotta go now," I say, slipping off the bed. I grab my underwear and jeans and put them on quickly.

She sits up in the bed grabbing the white sheet with both hands to cover her perky tits. I need to hurry up and get the fuck out of here before the urge to fuck her consumes me. I'm sure her bitch of a mother will be barging in here soon.

I grab my cut off the chair and risk a look at her. Her face is down and she looks ashamed. Shit. This is why I don't mess with chicks outside of the club. Club girls know what to expect out of a brother; nothing. Civilian bitches, girls who know nothing about club life, expect more and look deep into things; leaving shit like this to happen. I actually feel guilty for wanting to leave Dani.

"Church," I respond, trying to ease the leaving situation. Why I give a shit; I'm clueless.

"It's not Sunday?" she questions, with a cocked eyebrow. Her question actually pisses me off. Doesn't she know who the fuck she's talking to? But her innocence makes me want her more, I swear. She is nothing but purity, a breath of fresh air. Something I have never been around. Girls like Dani don't hang around the club.

"No, not that kind of church. I have to go to discuss club business. It's at noon, and it's noon now. I gotta get before they come looking for me." I pull on my shirt and leather cut. It's the same shit I had on yesterday, but I don't have time to change.

I open the door a sliver and peek out. I don't see anybody so I slip out and shut the door quietly, not giving Dani another look. I feel guilty as shit as it is, I can't stand to see her in pain any longer. The main room of the clubhouse is a fucking mess, and there's naked chicks scattered everywhere. The prospects have black trash bags picking up trash, and some of the Ol' Ladies are throwing clothes at the naked girls trying to get them decent and out of the club. I walk into the kitchen and grab a cup; I need some coffee to help process what the fuck is going on in my head. I just slept with the devil's daughter. I'm a dead man walking.

"Where the hell did you disappear to last night?" Bobby spits at me from behind, making me spill coffee.

"Nowhere, why?" I ask, irritated.

"Oh, I dunno. I saw you chase the president's daughter down the hall and haven't seen you come out until just now." His tone is accusing.

I glare at him. What is he getting at? Bobby and I go way back, even before the club. I know we are close, but the club is a brotherhood. I'm not sure he wouldn't tell Bull I fucked his daughter. Hell, I felt like shit keeping this from Bull, but I'm not sure he wouldn't put a lug in my head if he knew I banged his daughter.

"What the fuck is that, brother? Please tell me you had a bloody nose or some shit." Bobby points at my hand. Looking down at what he's pointing at, I tense. Shit, I have blood on my fingers; how did I miss that. It must have gotten there when I took the condom off last night. Trying to hide that I fucked Bull's daughter was not going to be easy with the loss of Dani's innocence all over my fucking hands. I walk over to the sink and start washing my hands, ignoring Bobby.

"That's not what I think it is, is it?" Bobby asks, pulling me from my thoughts.

"Fuck off, Bobby, it's nothing!" I bark, his persistence is really starting to piss me the fuck off.

"You get in a pissing match with me for dancing with that bitch last night; then you disappear into her room for the night... just looking at her... I'm pretty sure that is exactly what I think it is," he says, gesturing toward my hands again.

"What the fuck did you just say to me?" Pushed to my limit, I shove Bobby and get in his face. Him questioning me has hit its toll.

Not one to back down, Bobby gets right back in my face. "I think you're the one with a death wish, brother. What the fuck were you thinking?" He pushes me in the shoulders, his voice snapping and authoritative. He's right, though; what the fuck was I thinking? I knew better than to fuck with Dani.

I back off and throw my hands in my hair, unsettled by my own actions. "I wasn't thinking. The bitch had me twisted, acting like she didn't want me. I just..." I pause trying to figure out what the fuck I was thinking last night. "I wasn't fucking thinking," I whisper.

"This can't be good, brother. You know this shit won't go down well," Bobby whispers back and walks out of the kitchen.

He is right. I feel different around Dani, I know that. But I also know she would be better off without a piece of shit like me. I'm fucked up in the head; not right. If Bull didn't kill me first, my way of living would devour Dani, thus causing Bull to kill me. The way I see it, Dani's a loaded gun either way.

Sitting at the table waiting for the other brothers to show, Bobby eyes me from across the wooden top. He grabs a piece of paper from the center and starts drawing on it; snickering as he scribbles. What the hell is he doing? He slides the piece of paper across the table at me, and looks over his shoulder as if he's in middle school passing a note.

What. The. Fuck? It has a stick figure with a disproportionate cock fucking another stick figure with big boobs and a gun to the male figure's head. I crumple the paper in my hand as he laughs; pleased with himself.

"First order of business," Bull says as he lowers himself slowly into his chair. He looks like shit. I'm sure he partied hard last night. Bull is always one for lots of bitches and booze and he is paying for it this morning. "Bobby what do ya have to report, son?"

Bobby was sent on a run to Nevada to investigate a deal the El Locos, another motorcycle club, want us in on. They want us to run guns with them and buy their stock weapons. Not knowing much about them, Bull sent Bobby to check out their credibility and their stock and report back to us for a vote.

"Eh, they seem sketchy, a fly-by-night operation, if you ask me, Prez. " Bobby leans back in his chair, his childish behavior vanished. "The containers they have the guns in were beat to hell, and the AK-47s have seen better days. I didn't even want to test 'em out, they were that banged up; seems like they went through hell. Their club seems too eager to sell them, too."

"Think they're hot?" Bull asks, wondering if the other club stole them from the competition. If they were, buying them would mean more trouble for us, something we don't need right now. Our club has been attracting heat since a rogue prospect shot a cop a while back. Now the competition and the cops were dying to get a shot at us. Needless to say, that prospect will never be found, I took care of it personally. I knew that fucker was worthless when I first met him.

"The shape those guns were in, possibly a robbery gone wrong," Bobby says, scratching his chest.

Bull rubs the stubble on his cheeks as he processes what Bobby is saying. "Alright, I don't think this is something we want to get involved in, who agrees?" Bull asks. Ayes are spoken around the table in agreement; we don't need to make waves.

"Tie up that loose end, Bobby," Bull says, pointing at him. "Next order of business. Locks, any word about the girls and this Stevin fellow?" Bull lights a cigarette.

"Not a damn thing, Prez. I called out to the Ghost's in New York and asked them to find the fucker and follow him; see what his next move was. Nobody in the area has seen him or heard from him. Fucker is MIA." Locks replies, lighting a cigarette as well.

"Shit, not sure if that's a good thing or a bad thing." Bull says.

"Yeah, he could have gotten spooked and split town, is lying low, or he is out looking for the girls," Locks chimes in.

"Don't make sense to me," I think loudly, not realizing I said the words.

"How so?" Bull asks, taking a drag from his cigarette. His eyes narrow and I'm not sure it's just the smoke.

"I just don't get how a powerful man like Stevin isn't heard of around there," I justify.

Bull nods his head in agreement.

"Considering how sloppy he was in killing those pigs in his office, I'm shocked to find out he hasn't left a trail, either," I admit.

"Yeah, something is fishy," Bobby says, agreeing.

"Hmm... Find out who this fucker is, Locks, and get back to me. I want everything, from his real estate to who he has in his pocket," Bull announces. Usually powerful, wealthy men like Stevin have lots of people on their payroll; greedy fuckers only wanting money. Maybe if we can find one of them we can buy some information and get a lead on Stevin.

"Let's get the safe house cleaned and stocked up; get the girls out there. I want three men on them at all times. Shadow, I want you on Dani, she seems to like you."

Bobby snorts, at that comment; fucker. I kick him under the table to shut him the fuck up.

"Bobby, follow Lady around. Good luck, she's a bitch," Bull laughs, "and get a prospect, too. If you two need to be elsewhere you get someone to cover your spot," he commands as he stands.

"You got it," Bobby replies.

Bull slams the gavel down and everyone gets up to leave. I look over at Bobby who is red in the face from trying to keep his laughter in.

"What's so fucking funny?"

"You are so fucked, man," he laughs.

I throw the crumpled up piece of paper I held in my hand at him. Fucker, so glad he thinks this shit is funny.

Chapter Six
Dani

A vibrating noise on the night stand next to the bed catches my attention. It is Shadow's cell phone. In his rush to avoid me this morning, he forgot it. I pick it up. It reads '1 missed call'. I wonder who called him. I can't stop the suspicion in my gut, so I open the cell phone. The missed call is from someone he's dubbed 'BITCH'. I'm sure he has lots of bitches. He should probably number them, bitch 1, bitch 2, I could be bitch 3. I growl at myself, thinking I, too, am just some bitch to get his rocks off. I bet tonight he will be in bed with a different bitch. Well, I'll just make sure he thinks of me while doing it.

I open the contacts to put my cell number in. For a contact name, I start typing 'Dani'. Unexpectedly, his voice echoes in my mind from last night; "Goddamn, you smell like heaven". I smile at the memory. I delete what I typed and put in the name, 'Heaven'. I angle the camera at myself, sex up my bed-head with my fingers and pinch my cheeks. I pull the sheet up over my breast, bite my lip and take the picture. Not too bad. I look like I was just fucked seven shades from Sunday; exactly what I was going for. It will make a great contact photo. If he doesn't delete the picture, he will always remember me and him last night.

How pathetic am I? Even with the thought that he used me, I still want him.

I get up to put some clothes on. Stepping over my white panties reminds me of the loss of my purity. My clit tingles just thinking about how Shadow took me with his deceitful ways. My body betrays me as easily as he did. Grr... I need to push him out of my mind; forget him. But having given Shadow something as special as my virginity makes me feel connected to him in a way I know he doesn't share. I feel stupid, and to be honest, a little hurt.

I grab my suitcase to see if I have any clean clothes left. I should probably see if there's a washer and dryer in the clubhouse. How convenient; a black bra and panties set; that should match my promiscuous ways. When I start to slide on my panties I see blood between my thighs. Shit, I need a shower.

I let the hot shower wash off everything from last night. It is bitter sweet. I want proof of what happened off of me, but don't. I grab some soap and lather it up between my hands, it smells like Shadow. I smile at the recognition. I rub the dried blood off with the soap, the smell of Shadow soaking into my skin.

I slip my sinfully colored panties and bra on and open the closet to see if there's any kind of shirt I can throw on. Luckily, there are a few with the Devil's Dust logo of a skeleton hand crushing a skull. I grab the black one and put it on. It engulfs my slim figure, so I tie the bottom corner hem into a knot. Reaching back into my bag, I find some blue jean shorts to put on.

A smooth voice startles me. "Damn, you were born to wear that shirt." It's Shadow, studying me from top to bottom with beastly eyes. The sound of his voice brings hurt to my soul and desperation to my loins.

"You're back," I respond, trying not to sound excited. "I didn't think I would see you again today."

"Yeah, I forgot my phone," he says, grabbing it off the night stand.

Awkward silence fills the room; neither of us knowing what to say about last night.

Great, here it comes: "I didn't mean for last night to happen," or, "it's not you, it's me". I don't think I can handle the rejection. Even though I knew this was a probability, actually hearing I was just a one-night stand coming out of his beautiful mouth might kill me.

"You don't need to explain, Shadow. I get it." My eyes start to sting. Holding back my emotions may be harder than I thought. I stare out the window trying to avoid eye contact.

Shadow scoffs, "I'm glad you understand what's going on, because I ain't gotta fucking clue." His confession throws me for a loop. Is he just as confused about our chemistry as I am? Is there chemistry? Maybe I'm not just a one-night thing. I shake my head; I'm getting ahead of myself. These games are exhausting.

"So, why don't you clue me in, seeing as how you've got it all figured out," he says, his tone unreadable.

When I face him, his expression is sincere. He looks lost even.

"Dani, last night-" Shadow is cut off from a knock at the door. Panicked, I start looking around the room; looking for somewhere to stuff him. I start pushing Shadow toward the closet in a desperate attempt to conceal him.

"Are you fucking serious?" he whispers, when he realizes I am shoving him into the closet.

"Yes, I'm serious," I whisper back. "What if it's my mom or dad? Go, and be quiet."

I shut the closet door and notice the condom on the floor next to the trash can. Shit. I grab it and throw it in the bathroom trash; I grab some toilet paper and throw it on top to hide it. I run back and open the door my mother is pounding at, trying not to seem panicked.

"Are we over our temper tantrum"? My mother asks, walking in. She looks like shit. She's pale and still wearing the same clothes from last night.

"Mom, I –" she cuts me off, pointing at my shirt.

"What. The. Fuck. Are. You. Wearing?" she snaps, her eyes as wide as saucers.

I look down at the shirt I'm wearing. "I found it in the closet. It looked comfy," I profess.

She walks over to me and tugs at the top, trying to take it off me. "No. No daughter of mine will wear this shit," she says, frantically.

"Stop it," I yell at her, but she keeps grabbing at me. "Get off me!" I can feel my face turning red; my body temperature rising; my vision blurring with rage. Finally having enough of her scratching my arms and neck to get at the black shirt, I snap.

"Back off, damn it!" I push her violently, her body flying to the floor like dirty laundry. I jump back; startled by my lack of self-control and anger. Where did it come from? I have pushed my mother before, yelled even, but never have I practically tossed her like a rag doll.

She is trembling as she stands. "What's gotten into you, Dani? First you are riding around with... with that biker trash; then, wearing that God awful shirt like you're a club member; and now you're violent to your own mother." She is hysterical now. "This is wrong. I raised you better than this. I gave you a better life than this; hell, I gave you life." Other than trembling, she isn't moving a muscle.

"It's a fucking t-shirt," I shout at her as she eyes it with a deadly stare.

"No, No, it's more than a fucking t-shirt. You are becoming one of them; biker trash. You're becoming your… your father." She went from being loud and hysterical to whispering those last few words. I may have barely heard the words, but even her whisper was dripping with hatred.

"Yeah, well, I never asked for your lies and betrayal," I snap back at her in self-defense.

"You know, I had a premonition when I realized you shared your father's green eyes. I loved those eyes until he tossed me aside. I knew I had to hide him from you; keep you on the right path, or you would turn out just like him."

She's avoiding eye contact which always raises my suspicion.

"What's so wrong with being like him?" I ask.

"Really?" she says, snidely. "You have been here but a minute. You have no idea what he is capable of, any of them. They lie, cheat, murder, rob. They are unstoppable. You stand in their way, they will kill you."

She points at me. "That boy you are hanging around... keep your distance. He just wants in your pants; you being the president's daughter won't stop him. I got an earful of the kind of man he is. He is a womanizer and he's messed up in the head," she bluntly spits at me.

Now I can't look her in the eyes. I'm afraid she might see I'm not as pure as I was when we arrived here.

"Everyone has a few skeletons in their closet," I justify. Looking at my closet right now, I can relate.

"If I hear of that boy trying to push himself on you, I will get your father involved. Messing with the president's daughter does not go without repercussions."

Gee, I wonder if she said those same lines to all the boyfriends I had growing up, that would explain them suddenly dumping me.

"Why did we come here if you hate my father so much; if you hate everything about this place," I calmly point out.

She sighs wearily. "I had no choice. It's what had to be done," she whispers, her head hung low.

She steps close to me. "Before you go thinking you belong, know your place here. There are club laws; some you will never be able to identify with." She straightens her clothes and leaves.

I sigh tiredly as the door closes. Wow. Who knew just wearing a t-shirt would make my mother go bat-shit crazy. Maybe she needed my shrink more than I did. Seems she has a lot of issues with the Club, so being here is still a mystery to me. And what did she mean by she got an earful of how Shadow was messed up? I turn to the closet, waiting for Shadow to come out.

"Shadow?"

He opens the door and walks out, his presence actually bringing calm to my battered psyche.

"You okay?" he asks.

"As okay as I can be. Sorry you had to hear all that." He shakes his head as if he's not bothered by it.

"What did she mean about you being messed up?" I ask. I got the part about him being a womanizer. That was no shocker. It still stung to hear it after just sleeping with him, though.

"Everyone has a past, Dani. I'm not perfect; I told you that before you climbed in bed with me," he barks back.

Another knock at the door snaps us from our conversation.

"Damn, you're popular," he says irritated. I raise my eyebrows and dart my eyes toward the closet. "Again, really?" He asks flippantly while climbing back into the closet.

With Shadow hiding, I yell, "come in!"

In comes Candy; this ought to be good. She has on a tiny black dress with black hooker-heels. Her blond hair is in beautiful curls hanging loosely around her shoulders. She is beautiful, yet slutty at the same time. I hate her.

"Is Shadow in here?" she asks sweetly.

"No, I'm staying in here," I inform her.

"Right. I'm pretty sure I saw him come in here," she replies with a high amount of bitch in her voice.

"Right. Well as you can see, no Shadow in here." I return with as much bitch as I can muster.

"You're cute." Her sweet tone is as fake as her boobs.

"I can see why Shadow likes you," she laughs like she has a secret I am oblivious to.

"Is that right?" I ask, curious at what she is getting at, but trying not to sound it.

"He's going to eat that innocence and spit you out, honey. That is, if he hasn't already." She puts her hands on her hips, proud of herself.

"I don't know what you're talking about." I lie, still feeling defensive.

"I have been with Shadow for years. I have seen girls come and go. You don't think just because you're sweet and innocent that he cares about you; that you can tame him, do you? As soon as he's done with you, he'll come running back to me. He always does. In the meantime, next time you kiss those lips remember they were on me not so long before you. His cock? In me as well. Shadow can't get enough of Candy." She sticks her nose in the air as she verbally slaps me.

My palms are sweaty and my breath is getting shallow. Here is yet another confirmation that I am just a notch on Shadow's bedpost. How many times do I have to hear it? She gets to have Shadow as much as she wants and she's rubbing it in. I am jealous of the whore; what an all-time low.

She turns to walk out but stops; her body half out of the doorway.

"Oh, and shame on you. If Bull finds out you are fucking with Shadow, only God knows what he'll do." She turns back around and rests her hip on the door frame. This isn't the first time I've heard that my dad will kill Shadow for messing around with me. It's hard to wrap my mind around.

Seeing the turmoil on my face, she laughs. "It's law. No one can mess around with the President's daughter behind his back and not be punished. "Despite the smile still on her lips, her tone is serious. "And I'm sure your mother won't like it either. Seems you and she are whores in the same, huh, sleeping with men you have no business messing around with." She spins on her shiny black stiletto and walks out.

I let out the breath I had been holding. I am more of a mess than I want to be over Shadow. I thought I would be okay being a one-night stand or maybe even a causal fling. But after hearing it from the two most spiteful women I've met in my life, the pain seems unbearable. The thought that I was nothing but sloppy seconds after Candy hit all the wrong notes.

Shadow opens the closet door slowly. My body is wound as tight as a viper. He approaches with caution. "Dani?" he says with concern.

"Just get the hell out." I say quietly, avoiding eye contact.

"Dani, calm down and let me explain," he demands.

There is nothing to explain. I am just a challenge for Shadow; a score for him. Not only did he get to bang the president's daughter, he also got to take her innocence. I'm just one big joke to him. I feel regret wash over me. I want to go back to feeling numb. Feeling numb wins over feeling used.

"No, I don't want you to explain, just get the fuck out of my room now." I look directly into those damaged eyes. "I don't want you near me, ever," I say calmly, hoping to get my point across. He just stands there, looking dumbfounded.

I push him at the door, trying to hold back my tears. "Get out, biker trash" I yell, noticing in my time of distress I sound exactly like my mother, and damaging my ego that much more. "I will not be your shiny new toy whenever you're bored." I slam the door in his face.

I lock the door and slump to the floor. How could I be so naive? Did I really think that just because I gave Shadow my virginity that we would somehow be a couple now; that he would suddenly care for me? Man, I'm clueless. I was just new ass to him; a game. His words from our first kiss instantly play in my head, "But in reality, you could never be mine." I am so angry at myself, how could I see Shadow as anything less than a playboy. Why would he want someone like me, when he had biker babes dropping their panties for him?

"Whats going on out here?" I could hear Bull through the door.

"Eh, she's not happy I have to follow her around everywhere," Shadow says. What? This is news to me. Why does the asshole have to follow me around everywhere? As if I wasn't humiliated enough, now I have to endure being around him 24/7.

"Yeah, I didn't think she would be happy about it," Bull proclaims. "Her mother will be even more pissed."

"Dani, open up." Bull demands.

I sit here against the door, ignoring his request. I need time to process everything, alone.

"Darlin, I just need to make sure you're safe. Not only from your mother's shithead boyfriend; we have enemies too. It's just safer this way. Shadow won't mess with you. If he does he will answer to me." His voice is sincere; he's just trying to make sure I stay safe. I still can't bring myself to respond, all I want is to scream.

Now is when I wish I had a best friend; someone I could spill out everything to. They could tell me what to do. I'm sure my shrink, Victoria, would have a field day with all this information. I have to get myself together; I can't let Shadow or that whore, Candy, see how distraught I am. I knew when I let him take me, it might end badly. In all honesty, I would rather live with this regret, than to never have had the experience. I've felt so alive being with Shadow. It is going to be hard going back to the numbness that succumbed me before.

Chapter Seven
Dani

Apparently the safe house has been cleaned and readied for our arrival. I use the time cramming my dirty clothes back into my suitcase to steady my breathing and calm down. I don't know how long I'm going to have to endure Shadow as my bodyguard, but I know I need to keep my wits about me. I go to my mom's room to check on her but she's still trying to gather up all her belongings, so I head out to the parking lot alone.

As I approach the vehicle taking us to the safe house, a blond, curly haired guy with tattoos all up his arms reaches out for my bag. A tattoo on his left hand catches my attention: TCB. My eyes widen; my body goes stiff. This is the guy I used to make Shadow jealous last night; Bobby, if I remember right.

"Well, hello there." He's charming, like all of the bikers I've met so far.

"Uh, hello," I respond, unsure if he recognizes me and feeling like a complete idiot. He has light blue eyes and little freckles here and there across his cheeks. He's pretty. Yes, a pretty boy. Bobby looks like he belongs on the cover of a magazine despite the tattoos and biker aura. Looking at the knock out grin, I'm sure he is just as much of a panty dropper as Shadow.

"I got her bag, Bobby. Thanks." Shadow comes up behind me, taking the suitcase from Bobby's hands. The man is relentless. What did he not understand about stay away from me? What is his angle, to try and keep me as his shiny new toy, or did he feel sorry for me? Either way, I wasn't giving him the satisfaction!

"I can handle it myself, thank you very much." I grab the suitcase from Shadow, who won't let go.

"Give me the damn suitcase, Dani," he barks, with cold finality in his voice.

Bobby's mouth raises into a Cheshire cat grin. "Trouble in paradise?" he asks amusingly, staring at both of us. I'm sure we look a mess, playing tug of war with a pink suitcase.

"Fine, take it," I say, letting go. Growling within his muscled chest, Shadow throws my bag in the back of the SUV.

"Can one of you make yourselves useful and grab my bag, it's heavy," my mother interrupts, stumbling out of the clubhouse doors.

Shadow and Bobby eyeball each other before Bobby gives in and grabs her bag.

My mother and I settle into the back seat as Shadow and Bobby straddle their bikes behind us. The prospect with the Mohawk who brought us from the airport is behind the wheel of the SUV again.

"What's your name," I ask, tapping him on the shoulder. "You have driven us around twice now and I still don't know your name?" I'm surprised at my sudden boldness.

"Charlie." I waited for him to say more. Nope, short and to the point.

Seeing he isn't much for talking, I sit back and remain silent for the rest of the ride. My mother is busy messing with her phone; she is always on that damn thing. Her face isn't swollen anymore. She looks like her normal self.

We drive north out of L.A. and I watch the urban streets fade away before we pull into a suburban neighborhood. We stop in the driveway of a two story house. It is cute and simple from the outside; not something I would peg a motorcycle club to have. When we climb out of the SUV, Bobby and Shadow pull in behind us. The raw masculinity coming from the bikes makes my body vibrate with arousal.

Shadow climbs off his bike and pulls his phone from his pocket. "What!" he barks into the line. He takes his other hand and runs it over his head back and forth, fluffing up that sexy black hair of his.

"You don't know what you're talking about. I don't have anything... Don't make threats at me, or I'll fucking put you in the ground!" He stabs his finger at the end button in fury and jams the phone back in his pocket. Bobby raises his eyebrows in concern, but Shadow throws his hand up like "not now". Odd.

I don't even attempt to grab my suitcase and risk having another episode in front of my mother. I walk up to the door and wait for everyone.

"It's a three bedroom," Bobby says as he unlocks the giant white door. "The master is downstairs; I figured you would want it, Lady. Upstairs are two bedrooms and a small bath. Shadow and I can bunk in one room and you can have the other, Dani."

We step in to a small entry area with stairs leading to the second floor immediately to the right. The living room is to the left and is done in soothing tan with touches of red and black. It looks very inviting and cozy.

As I start up the stairs, my mom catches my elbow. "Are you going to be alright up there by yourself?" she questions, as she eyes Bobby and Shadow. Ah, she's off her phone and back in "concerned mom mode".

"Yeah, I'll be fine, I'll lock the door. No worries," I respond, pulling my elbow from her grip.

I stop at the top of the stairs; unsure of where to go. Across from me is one of the bedrooms and there's a hall that shoots off to the left, where I assume the bathroom and other bedroom are.

"Bobby and I will take this room; it has two beds in it. You can take the one down the hall," Shadow says from behind me. I can hear Bobby's muted voice explaining where everything is to my mom. I'm sure she is ignoring him, though.

I grab my suitcase from Shadow's hand, our fingers briefly making contact, causing electricity to fly through me. I hold my breath and turn down the hall where the other bedroom is in an attempt to show the touch went unnoticed. As I am walking away he grabs the belt loop to my shorts.

"I still want to explain things," he says softly. As much as I want him to explain, it's best if he doesn't and just stays away.

"I think it's a little late for that, don't you"? I say raising my eyebrows in irritation. I start walking down the hall and he grabs me by the arm, halting me once again. His touch sends a blazing fire of warmth rippling up my sensitive skin.

"No, it's not too late if you will stop being a stuck up bitch for a second and hear me out," he protests.

Infuriated with his tone and his accusations I pull my arm from his grip and continue down the hall. I really want to slap him in his face again.

"I'm not Candy, Shadow. You were right, I shouldn't have gotten involved with you. I expect a little more than to be someone's sloppy seconds. I take responsibility for being inexperienced and expecting more," I say, with animosity lacing every word. I open the door to the room I am staying in and turn to slam and lock it in Shadow's face.

"You can't avoid me forever, Dani," his muffled voice vibrates through the door. He is relentless and I hate him for it. If he keeps this up I don't know how much longer I can resist him. I want him, but I don't want to have him unless I know he is all mine.

"I see you already managed to fuck that up," Bobby's voice is mumbled so I gently place my ear against the door to hear better.

"So when Bull kills you, can I have your bike?" Bobby asks, his tone completely serious.

"Why, tired of that Bobber? Ready for a real man's bike," Shadow jokes.

"Yeah that's it."

"She's being a bitch. I knew I shouldn't have fucked around with a civilian, especially her." Shadow says, his tone serious now. What does he mean by civilian? Is the club that out of civilization that I'm considered a civilian?

"Might be for the best, man. That's one pussy you don't want to fuck with. Cut your losses." Bobby says, his voice clipped and cold.

Instantly, I'm pissed. As much as Shadow and I should stay apart, that's not what I want: no matter how much I tell myself it is.

"I can't even fucking think straight," Shadow admits. I smile knowing I affect him, I wonder if any of the other girls he's been with affect him to the point he can't think straight?

"Whippah!" Bobby hollers. Not sure if I made out what he was saying through the door, I press my ear harder against it.

"I am not pussy whipped, fucker." Shadow protests.

"Whippah!" The sound comes again; Bobby is making fun of Shadow. I clasp my hand over my mouth trying to restrain the giggle rising in my throat.

"Man, fuck you!"

Well, it seems Bobby knows about last night. He and Shadow must be pretty close because I can't see Shadow going out and telling everyone he slept with me; unless he honestly has a death wish or he's really, really proud of himself.

My room here is a lot nicer than the one at the clubhouse. The walls are light purple and the sand-colored carpet is stain free. A queen sized bed takes up most of the bedroom with purple, black, and white covers and pillows filling it. The blankets look and smell brand new. There is a honey oak dresser with a mirror attached, and a floor-to-ceiling mirror on the back of the closet door. Some of the Ol' Ladies must have helped decorate this place; it was far from the club decor.

I start opening my suitcase when a light knock comes at the door. I swear if it's Shadow I'm going to kick him in the balls.

"Dani, It's me. Open up," Bull says. Funny I hadn't heard the sound of his motorcycle pull up. Then again, I was busy trying to resist Shadow, and eavesdropping.

I unlock and open the door. There stands my father in loose, faded jeans; a distressed Rolling Stones t shirt; and his black leather cut. His dark hair is all messy, and his vibrant green eyes are striking in contrast. Even as an older man, my dad is stunning.

"You getting settled in okay?" he asks, eyeing the room behind me as I step to the side to let him in.

"Yeah. It's much nicer than the clubhouse. Thank you," I respond sincerely, inspecting the room with him. Even so, I suddenly realize that the club had felt more familiar to me; strange.

"Yeah, the Ol' Ladies got together several months ago and decorated the place. Cost a fucking fortune, too." He shakes his head as if trying to forget how much it must have set the club back. "I had them buy new blankets this morning, though. God only knows what was on those sheets after last night," he adds, pointing to the bed.

"I thought they looked new; thanks."

"I was going to have one of the boys pick up pizza and movies later for you guys. You like sappy chick flicks like your momma?" He sits on the corner of the bed.

My mom liked sappy chick flicks? I never knew that. In fact I couldn't remember the last time my mother sat down and watched a movie with me.

I shake my head from my pity party, "uh, anything's fine. I watch anything really," I respond, sitting beside him. He knew so much about my mother and I felt like I knew nothing. What I did know about her seemed completely different from the person he was talking about.

"What happened between you and my mom? I mean, she told me her side of the story, but what's yours." His eyes shoot to mine. They go from vibrant and playful to downright sad in a flash. Maybe this topic was truly his living hell, but I need to know. Growing up in the shadow he unknowingly cast for me hadn't exactly been a picnic.

He rubs the stubble on his cheeks, making it sound like sandpaper, lost in thought.

"Your momma and I were inseparable; wherever I was, she was. I remember it like it was yesterday. She was here on spring break when we met. She never went back to New York and dropped out of school to be here with me. Her parents disowned her. They were a couple of Bible-thumpers; so when they found out she was sinning away with me, they cut her out of their will," he pauses and looks into my eyes. "She was different than any girl I had ever met; classy. She always acted like a lady, but when you crossed her, she was fierce. She told me she loved me one day and I freaked out. She didn't understand the club... hated I spent so much time there. Hell, I wasn't even president then, my pops was. I didn't think I was capable of falling in love and I thought she deserved better. I just needed to get my head straight, ya know... figure out where we were going; where I was going." He cracks his knuckles and takes a deep breath.

"We had a chick named Roxy, who I slept with a lot before I met your momma. She came to the club one day and started stripping in my room. I told her that shit between her and me was over, but she just kept running her mouth and climbed up on my lap. That's when your mom walked in. I'm sure it looked terrible. I should have pushed Roxy off my lap, but I didn't, and the fact that I was high on enough blow to kill a horse didn't help. Lady ran out before I could catch her and explain." He exhaled deeply like he was finally releasing the breath he had taken minutes ago.

Did my mother know it wasn't what it looked like between my father and this Roxy girl? Knowing her she wouldn't have cared; my mom has too much pride. Still, I hate the image she casts on my father when that image is blurred. If what he is telling me is true, then he is not a bad person. Well, not in the romance department anyway.

"Word around the club was that Roxy had been telling Lady she didn't belong and that I would tire of Lady and come running back to her. She was in Lady's head deep, from what I'm told. I was blind to the whole fucking thing; your mother never said a word to me about it. After I heard Roxy had been tormenting her, I took care of it."

This sounds eerily familiar.

"Roxy doesn't come around much after the ass beating she got from the Ol' Ladies, but now her daughter's a hang-around. Guess being a club whore runs in the genes of that family." He says exactly what I'm thinking.

"When your mother called me the other day I actually thought I might get her back; that I could fix what I fucked up. But when I saw her, I knew she had made her mind up about me a long time ago, there was no going back." He is slumped down, his elbows on his knees staring at the wall. I rub his back in respect, not sure what to say.

He cocks his head to the side and looks up at me. "It's for the best; club life isn't for the weak. It's rough on a woman, especially a lady." His words are laced with regret and blame. I feel for both of my parents at this point. I have seen the women around the club; it is tougher on girls.

"Who is Roxy's daughter?" My nosy side wants to know which of the current whores carries her genes.

He looks at me curiously; wondering why I would care, I'm sure. "Candy."

Her name hits me like a bus; my breath catches in my chest. The comments she made earlier make more sense now. "Seems you and she are whores in the same, huh, sleeping with men you have no business messing with."

I don't want my father to see the effect that wench has on me. I can handle my own battles. So I swallow the lump in my throat and try to sound as casual as I can.

"Oh yeah, I think I've seen her around the club; the skinny blond?" ...that looks like a coke whore and I want to plow my fist into her face... Man, I've got a lot of aggression built up inside.

He nods his head in acknowledgement. He seems unconcerned; mission accomplished. Me disliking Candy, though, just went to an all-time high. She can thank her mother for that.

"Well, I've got club business to get to. If you need anything let one of the boys know. I'm usually at the club, but, if not, they know how to get in touch with me. We will get this Stevin fucker eventually. He's MIA right now, but you're in good hands, sweetheart; got one of my best guys following you." He leans down and kisses my forehead, his lips soft on my skin. I've never felt fatherly love before. It's nice.

He leaves me alone with my thoughts. I wonder why he hasn't told my mother she pegged him wrong. Even if she couldn't believe him then, she might now. Then again, maybe he has already and he was right; she didn't care. Who knows. Their relationship is as complicated as ever; it makes my head hurt just thinking about it.

Maybe Shadow doesn't think I'm club-worthy. It would explain a lot. Seeing how Roxy was a shit starter, maybe I should take what Candy says with a grain of salt.

Or maybe I should just beat the last twenty-one years of my life out of Candy since it was her mother who really paved my road of hell. I sigh. Where are all these ferocious thoughts coming from? I have never been violent, not even in my thoughts. Maybe my true colors are starting to come through being around my father; my true blood.

Chapter Eight
Dani

It's dark, all I can see is glimpses of Shadow's sweaty face from the moon light casting a glow through the window. Our bodies are slick with exertion, and our breathing harsh and needy. My body vibrates with greed and intimacy. Shadow's body clings to mine as he thrusts deep inside of me, grunting like a beast.

"I'll die before I let you go, Dani," he whispers against my cheek, his stubble scraping my skin, reminding me of the masculine man that claims me. My body arches for more as I plead for him to take me. I don't care if my mother finds us, and he doesn't care if my father kills him. We cannot deny the attraction that consumes us, brands us.

"Yes, Shadow, I'm yours," I pant. "Take me."

I feel a feathery light touch caressing my cheek, waking me from my dreams. My eyes flutter open and I see Shadow standing above my bed. His calloused fingers cup my chin. I sit up and rub the sleep from my eyes with the back of my hand; his touch sensual. He's wearing those low-slung sweats and nothing else again. My hands ache as I try to keep them from reaching out to touch that silky smooth chest.

"You've been asleep for a few hours. We got movies and pizza if you want some; you gotta be hungry." His voice is deep and raspy and caring. The butterflies form in my stomach and my body flushes with the arousal I'm trying to conceal.

"Uh, yeah. I'll be down in a few minutes," I respond, trying to look at anything in my room but his god-like perfection. The raven on his bicep, however, lures me into its trap like the ominous predator it is. I'm hypnotized at the way the bird dances on his arm.

"Okay." He stands there as if he wants to say more but eventually turns on his heel and walks out. The spell broken, I just catch his feet before the door closes. Shadow barefoot is somehow very appealing and lovable.

I stop in the bathroom on my way to join the others to splash my face with cold water, my dream left me a sweaty mess.

I walk into the living room to find the guys huddled around a couple of open pizza boxes and some movies. They're cussing over which one they are going to watch. I bet none of them asked my mom if she wanted any pizza, but who can blame them. She hasn't been the most approachable human. I walk over to my mom's room and hear her talking. The door is slightly open so I stop right outside of her line of vision and listen. Being snoopy is the only way I can find out anything around here. I should have started this a long time ago.

"It's not like I had much of a choice in coming here!" I hear her snap at whoever is on the other end. "Are you serious? You want me over there?... Fine... She will be fine here. I can come back and if she has seen anything... Yes, I'll go now," she says angrily.

Where is she going? What does she mean if I see anything? This is what eavesdropping gets me; more questions and no answers.

I don't hear her voice anymore, so I knock on the door.

"What!" she yells. I open the door and see her phone in one hand and her chewing her nails on the other. I wonder who she was talking to. Maybe it was my father, but I would be crazy to ask.

"They bought pizza and movies; want to join us?" I ask lightly, not wanting to piss her off any more than she seems to be.

"What? No, I'm fine. I'm going to the club. Will you be okay here by yourself?" she asks, putting her shoes on.

"Yeah, I'll be fine. I have my cell phone if anything goes wrong," I remark, trying to ease her mind from leaving me behind. But why was she going to the club?

"Great. If you see anything you're uncomfortable with, give me a call, okay?" She walks past me into the living room.

"Can one of you take me to the club?" She worded it like a question, but her voice made it sound like a demand.

"Shit," Bobby says, taking a slice of pizza. "Yeah, I can if you let me eat first. I'm starving."

"That's alright, I got it, boys," Charlie says, finishing a slice of pizza.

"Great! Let's go," she says, walking out the door.

My mother hates my father, I wish I could say I was optimistic and my parents will get back together, but I know hell would have to freeze over for that to happen.

I grab a slice of pizza and flop onto the couch opposite of Shadow and Bobby. I dig my phone out of my pocket to stalk the social networks; anything to keep from having to look at Shadow and his gorgeous body. I can feel him looking at me; eye-fucking me. I need to keep him at arm's length. I have been burned enough.

"Ping". My phone lights up alerting me to a text message from an unknown.

"Seems someone has been playing on my phone. – S"

Shit, that picture I put in there this morning, before everything really went to shit. What was I thinking?

"Just delete it, it was a mistake, don't read into it. - D"

"So, you moaning my name in your sleep, was that a mistake? - S"

My nostrils flare, and my face turns red with embarrassment. Before I can reply my phone pings with another text.

"Oh, and I'm not deleting it! I want to remember you like that, thoroughly fucked by me. - S"

Reminded that I am nothing but a sex toy to him, my body vibrates with rage. At one point, a point when I was over stimulated and high on Shadow, I didn't care what the terms were I just wanted him. After realization slammed into me this morning, I cannot allow myself to be that weak again. I have to maintain my self-control. I turn my phone off and shove it in my pocket. I focus my eyes on the movie; it appears to be a comedy of some sort. I can feel Shadow staring at me, making me uneasy. I glare back and he gives that wolfish grin that makes my panties wet.

"Well, that movie sucked," Bobby proclaims, after the ending credits come up. He reaches forward and grabs his beer off the coffee table, his TCB tattoo again catches my attention.

"What does TCB stand for, anyway?" I ask, genuinely curious.

Bobby eyes his hand. "Taking Care of Business. You like it?" He flexes his fingers making the tattoo move slightly on top of his hand.

"Like the song, 'Taking Care of Business"? They both start laughing; full-blown belly laughs. What's so funny? My ears and cheeks go warm, the blood rushing to them in embarrassment.

"No, it's just something we say a lot around the club. Taking care of business," Bobby informs me, after he gets his laughing under control. I look over at Shadow, his eyes hooded with desire. It seems like every time I make a fool of myself he gets turned on.

"Oh, do you have any other tattoos?" I ask Bobby, knowing he'll show me. He rises from the couch and pulls his worn black shirt over his head of blond curls. His body is as toned and tanned as Shadow's but covered in tattoos. I stand up and with my finger trace a skull tattoo he has along one pectoral muscle. Without breaking contact, I glide my fingertip across his golden chest to follow the outline of 'Live To Ride, Ride To Live' inked just above his other nipple. I can feel his body stiffen under the caressing trail my fingers leave behind. He is definitely ravishing, but I don't feel anything when I touch him; not like the flames I feel with Shadow. I look over and see Shadow's jaw clenched, he is staring straight ahead and taking a swig from his beer intently.

"They're nice," I say cheerfully. "I would like to get a tattoo myself." Seeing all the ink around me these last few days has me seeing tattoos in a different light.

"You do?" Shadow and Bobby say at the same time, clearly shocked that someone of my upbringing would want to ink herself.

I trail my fingers over Bobby's shoulder blade and make my way to the kitchen to grab a beer for myself. I can't resist looking over my shoulder to see how my actions play out.

"I think she wants me," Bobby teases Shadow as he grabs his beer off the coffee table and takes a sip. Shadow punches Bobby in the arm, reverberating the room with a 'smack'.

"Ow, fucker!" Bobby yells, rubbing his arm where Shadow just plowed his fist.

"So what are we watching next?" I ask, plopping down on the couch opposite of them. I take a sip of my beer, watching Shadow as he stands up to put in the next movie.

"I got one for you," Shadow says, his gorgeous mouth curved into a malicious grin. As soon as the movie starts I hear eerie music playing. He sits down right next to me.

I know what he is doing. He put a scary movie in hoping I would edge closer to him at the scary parts. Bastard. I scoot as far away as I can on the couch. Maybe not being able to eye-fuck each other will allow me to actually watch this movie. But sitting near him brings his scent to my nostrils and my body becomes aroused instinctively. His presence right next to mine might make this harder than eye-fucking from a distance.

Just like Shadow planned, every time something unexpected happens in the movie I jump and edge myself a little closer to him. Near the end of the movie I am so close, I can feel his hot breath on the back of my tender neck. He lays his hand on my knee, teasing me as he slides it slowly up my thigh. My heart is racing; thumping so loud I'm sure he can hear it. I look up through my thick dark lashes and see his stormy blue eyes staring back at me intently. I'm drawn to Shadow like a moth to a flame. I stand no chance of defying his magnetism. Whether he wants me only for sex or something more, at least he can't seem to leave me alone either.

"Oh shit!" Bobby exclaims, making us jump apart and snapping me back to reality.

I need to distance myself from Shadow. Being this close to him is a sure way to wind up in bed with him again; only waking up regretting my actions.

"Uh, I'm going to bed," I say, jumping up from my seat.

"Night, Darlin'," Bobby says, waving his hand in the air, not taking his eyes off the screen.

Shadow stands up as I start walking up the steps. "Please don't follow me. Please don't follow me," I say to myself. He doesn't and now I'm kind of disappointed. My body and mind are making me feel bipolar.

I slip off my shoes, socks and shorts and untie the knot in the Devil's Dust shirt. I remove my bra like a ninja but leave the shirt on to sleep in. I'm not even tired; I guess I can listen to some music. I dig through my purse for my iPod when all of a sudden I hear something similar to firecrackers.

Pop! Pop! Pop! Pop!

The walls vibrate with every pop. I fall to the ground and put my hands over my head in panic. I hear someone yelling my name from a distance. Suddenly, my door flies open and Shadow throws himself over my body.

"Stay down, Dani," he shouts above the chaos. I can feel his heart beating as his chest covers my back, protecting me from the hostile world around us.

As fast as it started everything goes silent and still.

"Wh- what was that?" I ask, frantically.

"Bullets. You okay?" he asks, lifting his body off mine.

Bullets? Someone was shooting at us? I can feel my hammering heart trying to catch up with my frenzied breathing, causing me to feel light-headed.

Shadow takes my face in both of his hands. "Look at me. Breathe, baby," he says calmly, his tenderness not going unnoticed.

I grab his wrists and stare into his stormy eyes as I inhale a deep breath.

"Baby?" I repeat, confused that he would call me that. Baby is a term you use for someone you care about. I'm not that, am I?

Shadow's eyes widen. He didn't even realize he called me that in the heat of the moment. He drops his hands from my face, breaking contact instantly.

I look down at my body and feel around; making sure my limbs are still intact. Still looking down at myself, I spot blood dripping on the floor. Where is that coming from? I'm sure I wasn't hit. I retrace the thick bloody drip to find it coming from Shadow's arm.

"Shadow, you're bleeding. You've been shot!" I yell, pointing at his arm.

He looks down at where I'm pointing, "Oh, shit. I have been shot," he says surprised.

"I'll be fine. Are you okay?" He looks at his arm again then back at me. Seriously, that's his reaction to being shot? I nod my head that I'm fine, physically. Mentally, I'm not sure yet.

"She okay?" Bobby asks, running into the room.

"Yeah, she's fine. I caught one though." He lifts his arm to show the damage.

"Did you get a look at who it was?"

"Nah, man. Motorcycles, but I couldn't tell who," Bobby says, taking a look at Shadow's arm, then at me. Suddenly I'm aware that I'm only in a t-shirt and underwear. I grab the bottom of the shirt and try to pull it further down to cover myself, but I'm not accomplishing much. Shadow grabs my shorts from the floor and hands them to me.

"Put these on, you're killing me in that damn shirt." His confession makes me smile, I love knowing I affect him.

"I'm gonna call Bull," Shadow says, pulling his phone out of his pocket. His arm is still dripping dark red blood onto the tan carpet. The Ol' Ladies are going to be pissed. I run into the bathroom and return with a soaked towel. I wrap it around his arm and pull tight to knot it. He winces at the harsh contact the towel makes when it squeezes his wound shut.

"Yeah, she's okay," he says, surveying my quick work. "Just me... Nah it's not bad, but I'll need the Doc... I don't think it was her, unless she joined a club lately... Yeah, we'll head that way now." Shadow pushes his phone back in his pocket.

"What's the word?" Bobby asks.

"He wanted to know if I thought my mother was behind this. She left a voice mail demanding drugs or money or she would take Dani. You said they were on bikes, so unless she's joined a club lately, it's not her. I'll tell you more later. Let's get." He's speaking to Bobby as if I'm not even in the room.

Bobby nods his head in understanding. I'm flabbergasted. Who is Shadow's mom? What kind of a mom demands drugs? How did she know about me? Why would she use me as a bargaining chip? I open my mouth to voice the questions but Shadow cuts me off.

"He wants us at the club; it's not safe here anymore. Pack your shit, Dani." He pauses and points at my handiwork. "Where did you learn to do this?"

"T.V., of course," I say, smiling proudly, getting a lopsided grin from him in return.

Chapter Nine
Shadow

Dani's petite arms are wrapped around my waist as we head back to the clubhouse on my bike. Having her arms around me helps with the pain clawing in my right arm. It's helping with another pain, too, but I'm not sure I'm willing to admit that yet. When I heard the first shot, I ran across the living room up the stairs as fast I could; my only mission was to get to her. I even caught a fucking bullet in the process. I didn't even realize I had been hit, my adrenaline was pumped so high. Having a feeling other than wanting to stick my dick in Dani, has me nervous.

When I'm around her, though, I think about someone other than myself. And she makes me feel respected; like when she dressed my bullet wound, no one has ever shown such care for me. I'm loyal to my brothers and would put my life on the line for them, and they for me. But there's no company like a woman's, and Dani's company is much to be desired.

I love Bobby like blood, but when Dani had her hands on him, I wanted to put my gun to his dick right there. And him seeing her in just that Devil's Dust shirt and underwear made me see red. I'm not the jealous type; this bitch has me twisted something deep. I've been trying to deny that there might be something deeper than sex with Dani, but that was before bullets went flying at the safe house. I have never been so frightened for someone else's safety in my life, except for Bobby. That fucker has had some close calls.

Women are a scary breed. I have seen first-hand how women can be pernicious and venomous, like my mother. My walls are built thick with vile scars, but having it thrown at Dani like that is the first time I've felt regret.

Getting through those walls might be more than I'm willing to give; and more than Dani is willing to handle.

It's quiet when we pull up to the clubhouse. Most of the boys are at home with their Ol' Ladies.

When we walk in, Bull is at the bar with Hawk, our treasurer. Hawk is older than dirt and has been around here longer than any of us. Always chimes in with how the world is shit today, and back then he had to walk through snow both ways, kind of bull shit. We have to sit there and listen to the old bastard in respect, but man, is he an asshole.

Bull gets up and heads straight toward Dani, inspecting her for any scratches or wounds. No doubt if the club princess had even a scratch on her pretty head, it would be my ass.

"You alright, Darlin'?"

"Yeah, I'm fine. It was a little scary, but I'm fine." You can tell in her voice she's trying to be tough, but deep down she is scared as shit.

"I couldn't fit her or her mom's shit in my saddle bags; might send Charlie over to get it in the truck."

"I'll send someone over in the morning. I don't want whoever that was to come back around and have one of my men in there packing. Let's go figure this bullshit out; we can catch the rest of the boys up in the morning." He runs his hand over his scruffy face. He always does this when he's trying to figure shit out.

"Where's my mom?" Dani asks, looking around the room. We haven't seen her mother for hours; I'm curious where the bitch is as well.

"She was shootin' the shit with some of the girls; drank a little more than she could handle. She's in the room she was staying in at the end of the hall. Old girl can't handle the booze like she used to, that's for sure," Bull chuckles to himself.

Dani's emerald eyes go hollow with a lost look, a look she often gets when Bull speaks of Lady. The woman he talks about and the woman we see are completely different. I think it fucks with Dani; she doesn't really know who her mother is. At least I know my mother is a piece of shit.

It is killing me not to touch Dani; to comfort her in some way. What the hell am I thinking? Fuck! The pull she has on me scares the shit out of me. Bull always says, this life is not meant for women. Pick your women carefully and tread lightly around them when it comes to club business. Poor Dani hasn't been treated lightly; she's been thrown deep down in club shit. I want to protect her; from the club and from myself. Bull has a saying, passed down from his pops, he tells all of us often. "Lust like a saint, trust like a sinner." I remember how confused Bobby and I were when he told us that the first time. He made us ponder on it for awhile, but it still made no fucking sense. Bull eventually told us, 'Lust like a saint', means nobody is as good as they seem, even saints. And 'trust like a sinner', means trust nobody because nobody will trust the sinner you are. Something I need to remember often around Dani.

"This..." Bull pauses, trying to choose his words carefully, "what happened tonight... she's going to go through the roof," he finishes, exasperated. No doubt Dani's mom will freak out; who knows what she'll do. I don't trust the bitch, I know that.

"She doesn't need to know," Dani says, with such force that it shocks me. "We can make up a reason we need to be here, instead of the safe house." Maybe she has a little more fire under her ass than we take her for.

Bull laughs; hell, we all laugh. "My daughter. I think there is some Devil's Dust in there after all. Lying to your momma, making me proud and shit." Bull has the biggest, goofy-assed grin I have ever seen on his ugly face. I swear if that shit smile widened anymore his face would crack.

Truth is, as angelic as Dani looks, I can see the darkness that runs through her veins swimming around like meat-eating sharks, waiting to be released. If I can see it, I'm sure her mother can too. Explains a lot about why her mother sheltered her from the rogue life for so long, but even I know you can only trap a darkness, a beast for so long. Of course, the darkness that swims in Dani's DNA pool seems like a minnow compared to the rest of us, to me.

"Go get some sleep. You're safe here, Darlin'. We will figure out who those assholes are." Bull treads lightly, giving Dani a kiss on her forehead. I want to put my lips on that angelic face, too. I can think of a couple of places where I want to put my lips on that knock-out body of hers. I sigh heavily in defeat; the attraction I have for Dani is exhausting.

"What then? I mean after you find out who is responsible?" she asks, snapping me from my daze. Bull stands there with his back to us, rubbing his face again.

"Then we kill the fuckers." Bull just throws it to her straight. Dani nods her head in knowing and takes off to her room; my room. I wonder what is going on in that mind of hers; wonder if she thinks we really are the beasts her mother has been crying to her about. We are; I am.

"Shadow, Doc is on the way; 'til then, fill me in." We sit around the wooden table where we handle club business. My arm is on fire, making it hard to focus.

"We were sitting around watching T. V.; Dani went up for the night; next thing..." Bobby throws his hands up in the air, "bullets came fucking flying into the side of the house. I grabbed my pistol and went toward the shit storm-" Bobby stops short.

Bull points at me. "Where were you?"

"After I realized we were under attack, I went to make sure Dani hadn't been hit. Must have caught the bullet when Bobby threw the door open." I eyed Bobby. Fucker never feared death; always went running toward the bullets instead of away from them. Bull nods and looks back at Bobby to continue.

"They were shooting with pistols; I think five gunmen on bikes. That's all I could make of 'em." Bobby shakes his head, ashamed he can't ID who it was. He hated when he couldn't deliver 100% to the club. He'll be drowning himself in cheap booze and worn out pussy for the next twenty-four hours.

"Pistols," Bull repeats, astounded. "For a drive-by?" Usually, a drive-by is handled with fully-automatics; more damage and half the time. To use pistols seems amateur.

"Tell me more about the call you got from your mom." Bull points at me again. I hate when he calls her my mom; bitch is not my mother, just a fucking junkie who carried me for nine months.

"Called me this morning saying she wants a kilo in coke or twenty thousand... if I didn't deliver she was, uh..." I pause. She said she was going to take my new little girlfriend, but I'm not about to fucking tell Bull that. I'm not even sure how the junkie knows about Dani. She must have followed me around to insinuate that Dani is mine to even take; and that will raise questions about Dani and me. Her threatening me pisses me off to a whole other level; makes me see black .Throwing Dani into the threat, though, makes me feel something I can't even put a name on. All I know is Dani's safety has become my number one priority.

"She was going to take something else, like the girl," I finish, avoiding eye contact with Bull. I hate fucking lying to his face, but if he thinks I am after Dani in any way, he'll kill me. Bobby eyes me suspiciously, he knows I'm lying. I hate that he knows me so well, no doubt I will be hearing it from him later. He's worse than a bitch sometimes, always nagging me.

"Said she needed the money badly. Haven't heard from the bitch in years; not since she put me down as an emergency contact after her junkie boyfriend and drug dealer," I scoff. I remember getting the call; the nurse said my mother was incoherent from a drug overdose and they needed to know if they could treat her. She was too fucked up to sign herself in, or some bull shit. I don't know, as soon as the nurse said her name I told her to take me off the damn emergency contact list. I could care less if the bitch died in a fucking ditch; putting me on the list seemed asinine.

"What about Lady's ex-boyfriend?" Bobby asks, to no one in particular.

"Could be. Might have found out she ran back here. Maybe thought he would put a club in his pocket, have them take out his witnesses." Bull rubs his scruffy jaw again; that shit irritates me. "Hawk, we good on shipments and dues?"

Hawk gruffs under his breath before answering; bastard's mean as a snake.

"Have I told you we were off? We are still on for the drop in two days, supposed to call us tomorrow with the drop location," he huffs under his breath again. Bull raises his eyebrows waiting for Hawk to answer his question. "Yes, Princess, we are good on dues. See, that's the problem with this club today, you get these pretty boys in here to do your-"

"Thanks, Hawk!" Bull cuts him off. Hawk gruffs, but continues his bitching under his breath. Only Bull could get away with that shit. If we did something like that... if Bull didn't pistol whip you first, Hawk would break your fucking arm. Bobby knows.

A knock came at the door.

"What!" Bull yelled at the door, his body rising slightly with the force of his voice.

"Doc's here," Charlie says, poking his head in between the double doors. He isn't allowed in the meeting since he hasn't earned his patch yet. He's a good prospect, though; I'm sure he'll get it before too long; always gets the bitch jobs and never complains.

"Alright," says Bull. "I will have Locks check into some local clubs, make sure we don't have any problems..." Hawk raises up out of his chair and eyeballs him, pissed that Bull isn't trusting his word.

"Just to make sure, Hawk. If you want to double check and get back to me, you can do it. See if they've heard anything, or if other clubs have been hit." Bull throws his hands in the air in surrender. Even he is afraid of the old fucker.

Bull comes around and pats my shoulder. "I want you, Bobby and Locks on the drop. Dani and Lady will be safe here." I nod; I don't want to leave Dani, but I can't stray from club business.

"You think you can ride with that arm?" Bull asks, pointing to the blood-stained rag tied around my bicep.

"Yeah, just another day," I respond.

"Get that lug out and get some sleep; both of you," he says to me and Bobby before walking out.

Dr. Jessica comes in with her black bag. She's hot, I'll give her that, but she doesn't put up with any of the guys' shit. They've all tried to get in her pants. Only guy she's slept with has been Bobby; so he says. She helps the club out under the table, repaying us for some shit she was in a couple years ago. Her husband beat the shit out of her on a daily basis, then started to hit on their little girl too. She tried to leave him and he nearly killed her. He was powerful and rich as fuck. She was in a shit spot. She showed up at our doorstep one day all battered to hell, offering to help us if we would help her with her problem.

It's not normally our style, to take in strays like that, but Bull had a soft spot for her. He can smell a pig a mile away, so if he said she was okay, then we were okay with her. So we killed the husband and disposed of the body; didn't have to worry about his sorry ass anymore. She was a tough bitch and great at her job so it was worth it in the end. I've killed for less, that's for sure.

"If I had known you were coming, I would have shot myself!" Bobby jokes at her as she walks in. Her long blond hair is hanging down her back and she's wearing blue scrubs; she is cute as hell in those damn things. We have two docs; her and some old fart. We're always thrilled when she shows up; sexy girl playing doctor is always a win over an old fart.

"If I knew you were here, I would have brought my gun and shot you myself, Bobby," she says with a wolfish grin. One thing's for sure, she can handle herself.

"How ya feeling, Shadow?" She pulls up a chair and angles herself around my arm. "Nice job; putting pressure on the wound. Saved yourself some blood with that little number," she says as she starts to unwrap Dani's handiwork; I'll have to tell her the Doc approved.

"I've been better, Doc." I wince when the pressure is released, watching blood trickle down my arm.

"He didn't do that doohickey on his arm; his ball and chain did," Bobby says, with a shit eating grin on his face, pissing me off.

I pull my gun out from behind my waistband and set it on the table. "You might stay around, Doc, cause I'm about to fucking shoot him myself."

"It wouldn't be the first time, dick." Bobby spits at me, his goofy grin gone, causing me to grin. When we were younger and we got our first guns, we were out shooting cans for practice. Bobby was great at shooting and didn't feel any remorse in letting me know how much better he was at it. Let's just say I accidentally shot him in the foot.

"Please don't shoot him, Shadow, it's late; and stop calling me Doc, damn it. All the damn cartoons my kid has me watching; you remind me of a damn rabbit." She pulls out a syringe with a long-ass needle. I hate this part. I should be used to that needle as many time as I've been shot, but it still makes my lungs seize up.

"You're going to feel a sting." She pushes the long needle in; instantly I feel numbness licking up my arm.

"How is your little girl?" I ask, trying not to watch her as she pokes and prods for the stray bullet lodged in my bicep. My head suddenly feels a little light so I rest my head on the back of the chair and breathe deeply.

"She's alright, got a spelling bee next week." Her blue eyes stare intently at the wound. She has such focus. She obviously loves her job, even if doing it includes working on us outlaws.

"She'll do great. Smart as hell, like her momma," Bobby says, trying to charm her. And he calls me pussy whipped. Jessica doesn't even look over at Bobby. I wonder what their story is. She seems to be the only bitch he's ever chased. She acts uninterested, but maybe that's just a front.

"Alright, you're all done. Take it easy for the next twenty-four hours. I would tell you to stay off your bike, but I know you won't listen." She sets the bullet she pulled out on the table, it's a little bloody, and then starts to wrap up my arm with white gauze and tape. I didn't even notice her stitch it up; she works quick.

"Take these pills every few hours, don't mix with alcohol; but I know your stubborn ass won't listen to that either. I'm not even going to bother with a sling because you won't keep it on." I laugh, because she is right. I will be back on my bike tomorrow and drinking before the night is over. That sling wouldn't be on more than five minutes before I would be sick of it. She sets the orange bottle of pills on the table before turning to leave.

"Bobby, take care of him." She winks at him as she leaves the room. Maybe she does want him. He jumps out of his chair and runs after her. Pussy.

I better go check on Dani, see how she is coping with all this shit.

I look up and down the hall before entering the room. Dani is sitting on the edge of the bed, staring at the stained floor, deep in thought. She's still wearing that black shirt that brought me to my fucking knees; God give me strength.

"Got the bullet out. I'm going to live." I say, trying to break the silence. I rub the blood off on my shirt and toss the bullet at her. It falls right in front of her, catching her attention.

"This was in your arm?" she asks, shocked as she picks it up off the floor. I nod at her question. "That's fucking cool!" She eyes the bullet and then my arm.

"You doing alright?" I ask, concerned. There have been hang-arounds and Ol' Ladies around the club for years who have seen less shit than Dani has in her short week with us.

"Club life, baby. Right?" She quotes me, reminding me of the time we were on the beach. Her smart-ass mouth makes me want to spank her. She turns me on in the way she defies me. No other girl has ever had the balls to get remotely fresh with me. The pain barking from my arm snaps me from the image of me spanking Dani's ass; seems the numbing shit is wearing off quickly. I need those pills and some Jack.

"I gotta do a run tomorrow, someone else will be here to watch over you." I lean against the door, trying to read her body language.

"Oh goody, another babysitter," she says coldly, sarcasm in her voice.

"It's not like that, you should know as well as anyone. It's so you don't get hurt."

"Hmm, really?" She bites the corner of her bottom lip and looks down at her hands.

"Are you going to hurt me, Shadow?" She fiddles with her fingers, before looking up through those long, black lashes. Her emerald eyes pierce my fucked-up soul, as she looks at me. We aren't talking about her physical safety anymore, that's apparent. She is talking about this magnetic force that keeps pulling us together, even when we try our hardest to defy it. Her and I together will never happen like she wants it to. If not because of who I am, because club life won't allow it. There is no white picket fence in our future, and her dad would kill me before I could prove that to her, anyway.

It doesn't stop me from wanting her, though. I can't tell her that I won't hurt her. Truth is, I don't know that she won't hurt me, as pussy sounding as that is. Every time I'm around her, I can feel more of my wall of distrust crumble. It scares the shit out of me that I can let her in where nobody has been before. If she sees the beast I am, will she take flight? It's what any normal person would do. But watching Dani in the last twenty-four hours, I'm starting to wonder just how normal she is.

I break eye contact, ignoring her question.

"Night, Dani." I lock her door and go to a different room for the night; these pills are calling my name and I have a long ride tomorrow.

Chapter Ten
Dani

The sun is screaming through the small, bare window. It takes me a second to realize I'm at the Club again. Shadow's manly scent lingers on the bed sheets; I roll over and inhale the pillow as hard and long as I can. On the ride back from the safe house last night I had become angry. I didn't even know I was in danger from Shadow's mother, and then on top of that, I was still coming to terms with the fact that I don't even know the woman I call a mother. I'm tired of not knowing anything; of everyone keeping secrets from me. I was less than thankful to Shadow when he came in before bed. I even threw him an off-the-wall question, which he ignored. He didn't need to answer, we both know that us coming out on the other end of this whole is unlikely. Even so, after seeing the look of pure fear on his face when we were being shot at, I refuse to believe that he would intentionally hurt me.

I lie in bed thinking about everything that has happened between Shadow and me. I'm so confused on what I want from him. Trying to stay away from him, like I swear I'm going to do, is breaking my heart as much as I know being with him will. When we're apart, all I can think about is how in sync our bodies are together, how he makes me feel, how attracted I am to him. He has to feel something, too, because he keeps coming back to me.

I roll over and see my pink suitcase by the door. Shadow must have brought it in here while I was asleep. I look down at my position on the bed and see that I'm half naked and the sheet is tangled at my feet. I'm sure the pervert got an eyeful before he left. I get up and unzip the case, grabbing some distressed jeans and a green tank top.

I sniff for cleanliness; they don't smell dirty. I head to the shower.

Everything is wet and warm when I climb into the stall. Shadow must have showered while I was asleep. Man, I must have been out of it. I wash my hair with his shampoo; the smell of him so strong I close my eyes and take it in. I imagine my fingers in his hair instead of mine, loving the way his hair curls and grooves around my fingers, it's so silky. My own long, curly wet locks are not doing the trick for me; they're not Shadow's black messy hair. I call defeat and shut the shower off. I grab the damp towel off the rack and start drying myself. My body tingles at the thought; everywhere the towel touches it has touched Shadow just moments before.

I spot the counter and see toothpaste spit all over the sink, men are so gross. Seriously, he couldn't wash the spit down? His red toothbrush is sitting right next to the sink. I grab it. I rub my finger across the grooves of the wet bristles, smelling of mint. My lips turn into an upward smirk as an outlandish thought forms. I squirt toothpaste onto his brush and start brushing my teeth with it, feeling naughty at the thought of secretly using someone else's toothbrush; his toothbrush. I rinse the spit out of the sink, and put my clothes on. I finger brush my long dark hair, letting it fall at the peaks of my round breasts. I put my shoes on, put my phone in my pocket, and head out of the room.

Walking down the hall, I can hear Bobby's voice becoming clearer and louder as I get closer.

"All I'm saying is you're not yourself, when we get back you're getting laid." I walk around the corner and see Babs behind the bar and Bobby, Locks, and Shadow sitting in front of it, eating breakfast.

"Hey there, babe, you hungry?" Babs spots me from around the corner. She has her red hair all poofed out in curls like in the 80's. She's wearing a leopard print shirt that is really tight around her bust and tucked into a pair of black jeans that come halfway up her stomach. She wears it well, with her bright red hair and pale skin.

My eyes lock with Shadow's intense, blue eyes and my body instantly becomes alive. My skin pricks with goose bumps as I feel him ogle me. He has on some clean blue jeans and a white t-shirt under his cut. His hair is all tousled on top, screaming for my fingers to tug on it. He is so rugged looking; he makes my mind scream.

An old man with slicked-back, peppered hair and matching beard and mustache comes walking through the clubhouse door. His beard starts all the way up his cheeks and hangs well below his chin. I haven't seen him before. He stops and looks at Bobby, eyeing him with disdain.

"Your eggs are the best. Locks is a lucky man to have you cook for him," Bobby charms Babs.

The old man that walked in starts to grumble as he makes his way to the kitchen.

"What was that?" Bobby yells at the old man. The man stops and turns his head.

"I said, fuckin' fruit cake!" the man bellows at him before he enters the kitchen.

"Don't man, you're gonna get your fuckin' arm broke again and we have a run to make. I'll be damned if I have to make the run with that bastard." Shadow eyes Bobby.

Bobby drops his fork on his plate, making a loud clatter. "No. No." Bobby says, shaking his head. "He didn't break my arm, Shadow, he sprained it; there is a difference. And I told you, I had a sore throat for like a week before that happened. I clearly was not in my prime!" I can't help the giggle that escapes my mouth at the thought of Bobby getting his ass handed to him by an old guy.

"You wanna go again? I'll break that fucking arm this time, pretty boy," the old man yells as he slams through the double doors of the kitchen.

Bobby shakes his head and keeps eating his eggs, not even looking at the old man who is fast approaching him.

"You couldn't take it, old man."

The old man is behind Bobby now. He grabs his arm and twists it behind his back in a flash. For an old bird he sure is quick and strong. Bobby falls to the floor, knocking his stool over in the process. I look at Shadow, who is shaking his head and finishing up his eggs. I look at Babs and she's just rolling her eyes. I guess this is normal?

"Say uncle or I'll break it!" the old man gruffs under his mustache.

"Break it off!" Bobby screams at him.

Bull walks through the doors of the club with mail in his hands. He peeks up at the commotion only to roll his eyes, too. "Hawk, you break his arm you're taking his place on the run today." He steps over Bobby's body which is lying on the floor after the old man, Hawk, had let go.

"You spoil these city boys. Back in the day we rode with a broken arm if that's what we had coming to us." Hawk points at Bobby on the floor, "damn fruit cake."

Bobby jumps up and starts swatting the dust off his pants. "Mean ol' bastard. He clearly came up behind me taking me by surprise. You saw that right, Dani!" Bobby asks me. I just smile, not sure what to say. "If I hit the ol' fucker I would kill him." Bobby eyes everyone.

"Well shit, boys, we better get," Locks says as he kisses Babs on the cheek. "We should be back tomorrow night sometime, babe."

"How are you feeling today?" I ask Shadow, worried about his arm. He looks up from his plate after shoveling in the last bite of scrambled eggs.

"Better, it will be fine. You sleep okay?" Shadow asks, his eyes staring intently into mine.

"Let's ride, Boys." Locks exclaims as he busts out of the kitchen, placing dark sunglasses on his face.

All the boys walk out of the club leaving their plates for Babs to clean up. Shadow turns and winks at me as he goes out the door making my face split with a smile out of this world and my cheeks turn as red as fire. I'm tired of fighting the feelings I have for him. If it wasn't for my mother and dad, I would throw him down on the club floor and have my way with him. My heart and head are so muddled, I don't know which one to follow.

I pull my phone out of my pocket and find the number he texted me with yesterday, wanting something to say to him before he leaves.

"I used your toothbrush. – D"

As soon as I hit send I slap myself in the forehead, baffled that that was the best I could come up with. I was hoping he would hear his phone go off before climbing onto his bike. I sit staring at the phone, waiting. I'm not sure what I expect him to say, I just want him to say something after the question I tossed at him last night, I don't want to scare him away before I even have a chance to have him.

"I don't mind. – S"

My heart instantly does a back-flip. My cheeks feel like they are going to split at the goofy grin I have on my face. He didn't tell me he loved me; he didn't tell me he wasn't going to hurt me; but his simple text justifies that he thinks of me as more. I bet he doesn't let Candy use his toothbrush.

"I know that smile; that's love. Your man miss you back in New York, Babe?" I hadn't noticed Babs sitting on the other side of the counter, I was so intent at staring at my phone. How long had she been sitting there? She slides a plate of eggs over at me, and lights a cigarette.

"Uh no, no, man. Just messing around on the net," I lie. Shadow is the reason behind my giddy state, but nobody can know that.

She throws her pack of cigarettes on the counter, and shakes her head.

"I don't much care for the internet, not my thing. I just have my cell phone to call Locks on, that's about as high tech as I get." She seems to really love Locks. I imagine you would have to really love someone that is in a club though.

"Why do they call him Locks? Is he good at picking locks?" I ask, picking at my food.

She laughs and takes a big drag off her cigarette. "Nah, that was a good one though. Fuckers call him Locks because of his long blond hair. You know, Goldilocks." I spew O.J. all over the counter, imagining Locks as Goldilocks is not something that would normally come to mind.

"They call me Babs because they say I talk a lot; assholes. Trust me, it's not a name I would pick. I was thinking more of Red, 'cause of my red hair and I love the color. But you don't get to pick your name around here," she says, picking her bright red fingernails. They are so long I bet she could mess someone up if they crossed her.

"Does everybody have a nickname?" I ask, trying to gain my composure from the O.J. I spewed everywhere.

"Mostly. Some prospects don't, but they will in time. Only person that doesn't is Bobby, and that's because 'Overgrown Child' is too long to put on his cut. I'm sure you will get one, you stay around here long enough." She pauses, staring at me intently.

"Are, ah, are you staying?" she asks hesitantly. I sit there thinking about her question, I'm not trying to be rude, but I honestly don't know how to answer. Truth is, I don't want to go back to New York, to the life I lived sitting in a house, studying and watching TV, because my mother thought if I was given the chance I would stray off the right path. Sadly, she is right. After seeing how the other half of me lives, it seems mundane to go back to

New York. I want the Motorcycle Club world, at least what I have seen of it. Living on the edge is way more appealing to me than anything my mother could ever offer. Maybe that's why I didn't feel like I fit in, in New York. My blood knew I was born with more tenacity than what I was giving myself credit for, and to finally be around what I was bred to do seems fitting rather than immoral. I hadn't even been shocked last night when Bull said they were going to kill the fuckers who had shot at us.

"Well, I know we all would love it if you stayed. I'm sure we could get you a little apartment or something; get you all set up. You think on that, doll." She grabs my plate of half-eaten eggs and strides into the kitchen, leaving me with thoughts of actually having a life here in L.A. and getting away from my mother. Maybe I can start my life over doing what I really want to do and not worry about what my mother would do to disown me.

I look around the club, noticing only a couple of guys are left. Prospects from what their cuts say. Where are all the Ol' Ladys? Every time I'm here all I see is Babs.

Babs walks out of the kitchen holding a cup and eyeing me as I look around the club. "You looking for someone?" she asks over the rim.

"I just noticed I never see any Ol' Ladies here but you. Are all the guys single, or something?" I ask, seeing how most of these guys are brutes, that wouldn't be an unfair assumption.

"Nah," Babs says chewing on ice. "There are a couple Ol' Ladies, but they're not allowed here unless a family gathering is going on. Club Law." She raises her eyebrows as she says club law.

"I'm here because Bull favors me. I clean up all the shit around here and do what needs to be done. Could have one of the skanks do it, but they don't do it near as well," she says, putting glasses under the bar.

"Oh," is all I can muster.

"and… I can make sure Locks keeps his dick in his pants," she says slamming the cabinet door, "Win, win for everyone." She walks back in the kitchen, leaving me a little shocked. Locks cheated? Why would she stay with him? Do all the guys cheat behind their Ol' Ladies backs? The more I hear about being an Ol' Lady, the more I don't want it.

I need to go check on my mother and make up a lie about leaving the safe house. Last night I could tell my dad did not want my mother to know about the drive-by, and neither did I. She would just make everyone's life hell, and she would be on top of me more than ever.

I knock on the door of the room my mother is staying in; I can hear her grumbling as she stomps over to the door.

"What!" she snaps, as she flings the door open. She looks like shit and that is putting it nicely.

"What are you doing here?" she asks, shocked to see me.

"There was a huge leak at the safe house; flooded the whole damn place," I lie. It was the only thing I could think up. I stare down at my feet avoiding eye contact, my mother has always caught me when I've lied before, but I'm hoping her hangover wins over her asking me questions.

"So we're staying here?" She unsteadily walks back to her bed and climbs under the blankets.

"Yeah, for now, anyway."

"Good, I want to be here." My eyebrows shoot to my hairline in surprise. Why in the hell would she want to be here instead of the safe house? One thing is for sure; my mother is high maintenance and the club is anything but fancy and classy. That may be why I love it, I am pleased by simple rather than extravagant, but my mother is a different story. And after the phone call last night and my mother's random behavior, I can't help but wonder what she's up to. I'm going to be beyond pissed if she's trying to patch things up with Stevin behind my back, especially after he tried to kill her... or so she says, anyway. Before I can ask she is falling back asleep.

Walking back to my room I see Candy coming down the hall to one of the guest bathrooms. She has on a white dress that is way too tight and very short, and her nipples are poking through the top. She is clearly not wearing a bra. I try to get over to my side of the hall as far as I can, if herpes can jump, they'll be throwing themselves off of her.

"Well, well, look what the dog dragged in," she spits at me as she walks by. Her neck nearly snaps as she watches me. If I stop to argue with her, I will drop her ass to the ground. I can't stand her, and after learning who her mother is, I want to beat her ass that much more.

My days are passing slowly and boredom is knocking loudly while Shadow is gone. I spent a lot of the first day talking to Babs. I can see why they call her that. She talks about everything from her dog to her arthritis, but she is, at least, someone to talk to. And Candy doesn't even look my way when I am around Babs; in fact, she avoids us like the plague. Babs gives Candy the most malicious glares when she walks by. There is definitely some tension between the two. I can't help but wonder if Candy slept with Locks.

My mother did come out of her room to get some food after the guys left, but she ended up throwing it up. Babs took care of her more than I did that day because I have no sympathy for her. Call it revenge for the last twenty-one years if you must, but being around my mother is like nails on a chalk board anymore. She's spent the last two days sitting at the club talking to Babs and Hawk about the club. They tried to change the subject several times, but she's not having it.

I tried to just sit and listen for a while or to help Babs with food preparations to waste some time, but I prefer being alone. I feel the numbness that was my life before, devouring my emotions. I need Shadow. He is all I can think about. He is my drug, my obsession, my addiction. Just as I did in New York during my lowest points, I grab my iPod and headphones. Listening to music helps. When I worked at the coffee shop, most of my money went to buying songs so I have a ton of tunes on the damn thing.

I lay in bed listening to Avicii's "Hey Brother", thinking of Shadow. He was supposed to be back today and I can't help but worry. The hour is late and he still isn't here. I could text him, but I don't want to seem clingy. I think about the words Candy spat at me; how she has slept with Shadow and how I don't belong here. Maybe I don't belong here, but I have my father's blood in me; surely I have some outlaw in me somewhere. It would explain more than enough as to why my mother sat on me like a damn mother bird my whole life, afraid if she turned her head I would burn the whole town down.

My father's blood running through my veins; maybe that's why I get so mad and jealous. Who am I to judge Shadow's past, maybe he is even trying to change. All I know is I would do anything to have him hold me like he did the other night. I wouldn't care if he were mine afterwards. I would be happy with him being mine briefly if that's all I had.

I wake up with my iPod screeching a Bruno Mars song. I pull the headphones off and see it's 3am. Laughter outside my room catches my attention. I can hear Shadow's voice. The butterflies that left my abdomen when he left on his run come roaring back with urgency, making me feel giddy. I get up and turn the lights on to inspect my appearance. I want to look appealing when he sees me. I want to make things right between us. My hair is tousled down sitting on my breasts as usual. I grab the black Devil's Dust shirt that drives him crazy and some jean shorts that are ripped a little too high up on my thigh, making me feel sexy. I take a deep breath and open the door.

I stop to inspect where the laughing is coming from; it must be by the bar. I walk barefooted toward the sound of laughing and voices. When I turn the corner, I'm dumbfounded by the scene before me. Bobby and Shadow are on the black, leather sofa with a bare-breasted Candy sitting between them. Bobby is snorting a white, powdery substance off Candy's nipple; cocaine.

"You want any?" Bobby asks Shadow, who is eyeing her bare chest. Bobby then slides his hand in between Candy's thighs and up her skirt. He leans over her, whispering something into her ear that causes her to throw her head back with fake giggles.

Shadow leans over the same bare boob and flicks his tongue over the powdery residue left behind. Then he sucks the perky nipple into his mouth. Candy moans in response as he pulls away, making a smacking sound.

An uncontrolled yelp escapes my throat in disbelief. I cover my mouth with my hands to stifle any other noises that might escape, but it's too late. All three of them look up at where the sound came from, spotting me.

"Oh shit," Bobby whispers, before looking over at Shadow whose face seems more than alarmed at my presence.

I turn to run back to my room, traumatized by all the emotions flooding my mind and heart; jealously, rage, regret. I hear steps coming my way and I try to walk forward but my feet won't move.

"Let 'er go, Shadow, princess doesn't belong here anyway and she doesn't deserve you." Candy's words hit me like a ton of bricks.

I instantly sober; my pain replaced with pure rage. I turn back on my heel and stride toward Candy, barging past Shadow on the way. Bobby jumps off the couch, seeing I am not to be messed with. I am a venomous snake, ready to strike.

"Oh shit, cat fight." Bobby exclaims, beside me now.

"Dani, wait!" Shadow says calmly. I throw my hand up to shut him up. This is between me and Candy-pants here. I will deal with him later.

Candy stands up, our faces less than a foot apart. Her faked-tan bust is barely inches away from me. My breathing is harsh and hostile, my body wound up and ready to strike. The tension in the air thickens significantly. If she thinks she can run me out of here like her mom did to my mom, she's wrong. This is where the cycle ends, bitch.

"Sweetheart, go sit down before you break a nail." She puts her hands on her hips, waiting for my come back.

I can feel my nostrils flaring from the amount of air I'm pushing through them. My rage is poisoning my wholesome blood. I ball my hand, pull back my arm and slam my fist into her cheek as hard as I can. She tumbles over the arm of the couch and flat onto her ass, her legs spread wide. She's not even wearing any panties. Of course, she isn't.

"Damn!" Bobby yells.

I walk up and stand over Candy's prone body; she looks up at me, her cheek split where I hit her. Suddenly, she kicks her legs up and hits me square on my ass, sending me flying forward and landing on my hands. I'm shocked; from the blow she took to her cheek I was sure she would stay down. Catching me off guard, she flips me over on my back and straddles me, her massive, fake boobs bouncing with her quick movements. Before I can manage to get her off of me, she rears her hand back and bitch-slaps me, her nails leave little stings from skidding across my silky cheek.

Seriously? I punch you and you slap me back?

I rear my hips up, bucking her over me, her erect, pink nipples skidding across my face in the process and leaving behind a cheap smelling perfume. I stand up and she grabs my shirt to pull herself up, ripping my shirt right across my chest with her nails in the process. My black, lacy bra plays peek-a-boo with the small slits she's made.

Damn it, I like this shirt.

"You don't deserve to wear that shirt, you bitch," she yells at me, out of breath and pointing at the Devil's Dust shirt I'm wearing. She starts trying to rip the shirt off of me again, pulling on my bra, making one of my tits pop through the slits in my ripped shirt. I push her back so I can hit her again. I pull my sore fist back and I throttle her right in the nose. She squeals as she falls back onto the couch. Her nose is bleeding all over her hands and down her tanned chest.

"I'm just getting started, whore!" I throw my arms out and give a 'come and get it' gesture with my hands.

"Oh no, you don't, you're done!" Shadow yells in my direction, grabbing me by the waist and pulling back.

I kick and slap at Shadow. "Fucking let me go!" I scream.

"Ah, man, you take all the fun away," Bobby complains, clearly enjoying all the boob action.

Shadow eyes Bobby aggressively. "Call the fucking Doc, man." Shadow places his hand on the small of my back and pushes me toward the room. Looking back at Candy's bloody state, I think she has learned her lesson on trying to run me out of here.

Chapter Eleven
Shadow

I follow Dani back into the room, she stands staring out the window worrying her lip with one hand while the other arm holds her body. Man I fucked up. I shouldn't have listened to fucking Bobby. Asshole has been in my head since we left the other day. The run went relatively smooth and we could have been back that night if it weren't for Bobby and Locks. Every damn time we make a trip to Las Vegas they think they have to hit up casinos and strip clubs. I'm usually all for it, but I just wasn't in the mood this time. Today we went to the strip club; Bobby kept saying I needed to let loose. I didn't argue, because I did need to unwind. When Locks was in the back with one of the strippers, Bobby started chirping in my ear like a fucking female.

"That's the third bitch I've seen you turn down for a private dance since we've been here, bro, what the fuck? It's Dani, isn't it?" his eyebrows lifted in question.

"Let me tell you something, Shadow, I have dated chicks like Dani. They only mess with men like us to get back at their parents or they think they can change us into what they want, or what they think they want, anyway. Her world and our world don't mix; look at how her parents turned out. Get her out of your head, man, and have some fun with one of these sexy creatures walking around here."

Bobby slid his hands up a girl's torso as she walked by. "Besides, if Dani doesn't stomp all over you, Bull's boot will." I grunted at his assumptions. "I'm only telling you this because I can see you opening yourself up to this broad, and I'm telling you it won't work out."

I heard what he was saying and he was right. Dani did have issues with her parents, so she fit the bill and every time I went near her she would become reserved. I hate how I have her in my fucking mind all the time. If she is the kind of girl Bobby thinks she is, then she's going to chew me up, spit on me, and rub it in with her stiletto. Just the thought makes my chest ache; feel hollow. I feel like such a pussy.

When we got back to the club, Bobby ended up calling Candy; wouldn't be the first time we screwed Candy together. Bitch took whatever we would give her; most girls did, in hopes of being patched in as a brother's property. We usually called a couple of girls when we got back from a run to relieve stress. But I didn't want to see Candy this time and that pissed me off. I knew exactly why I didn't want to see Candy. I fuck anyone I want with no remorse, yet just the thought of anyone besides Dani had me second guessing myself. As Candy was sprawled out on that damn couch half naked, my mind kept going back and forth if I should go see what Dani was doing, or if she was awake, and did she want to see me? The smell of her, the feel of her warm body against mine, her long beautiful hair, and those fucking eyes. Bobby offered me coke, and I wanted to relax my mind. It wasn't anything more to me than coke on a slutty tit.

Dani's reaction was a surprise, and that's putting it fucking lightly. She didn't fall to the ground and cry, or let Candy walk all over her. Her reaction proved she is where she was born to be, and if I was just something to prove to mommy and daddy, she wouldn't have gotten so upset with me fooling around with Candy. Bobby was wrong about her, she was not that high maintenance, stuck up bitch he pegged her to be; that I pegged her to be. Seeing her beat Candy's ass like the club brat she is was also the most becoming thing I have ever seen, and it left my dick rock hard. I'm tired of playing these games with her. It's time to find out where the fuck this is going; whatever the fuck this is.

I shut and lock the door. Dani turns, impaling me with those emerald green eyes of hers. She is wearing the Devil's Dust shirt again, well, what's left of it. She's a fucking vixen in that shirt. A couple of scratches feather across her left cheek, no doubt from Candy's fake nails. I can hear music playing from her headphones on the bed. She walks over to it and stops the music. I notice her knuckles are bruised and bloody; I'm not sure if it's her blood or Candy's. I would inspect further, but I'm not looking for an ass kicking myself. I'm sure I'm the last person in the world she wants to touch her. Candy made me out to be in it for nothing but sex when it came to women, and it usually is, but with Dani it's different. I can't get her off my mind, and I feel for her on a different level than I have for any female.

"Dani, look, the other night… tonight, I just..." I can't spit the fucking words out, I have never had to explain my actions before, especially to a woman. It really isn't easy with Dani just standing there with a vicious glare.

"You don't have to explain yourself, Shadow. It was just sex, no labels, right?" She's trying to sound stern and sure of herself, but I can see through her; she wants more from us than sex.

"I think we were both okay that night with just sex," I run my hands through my hair; this always seems to catch her attention, "but, I can't get you out of my fucking head." I point to my head in explanation. "I don't know what this is; if this is even anything to put a label on, but I would be willing to put my life on the line to find out where it goes."

I shock myself in my admission, but it's the truth. I have never been this twisted over a female before, and I would be a fucking fool to turn away from it. Most girls that come through here are looking for a free ride; wanting to become an Ol' Lady; wanting protection or drugs. They'd be in your bed one minute, then with another brother's dick in a second if they thought it would get them up the ladder quicker. Dani was different, she came to me pure and innocent. She makes me work for her intimacy, and will push me away in anger. The only thing I can see she wants from me, is me. My only fear of that, is if she can handle all of me. So In the end, I'm glad I said it.

She turns her back on me and scoffs. I widen my eyes in disbelief. I just opened myself like a damn book and she turns her back on me?

"Right. Do you usually fuck around on people you want to be with?" She is so sexy when she defies me, but she is also pissing me off. What the hell does she mean "do I usually fuck around on people I want to be with"? I have never wanted to be with anyone before.

"Dani, I have never had a relationship with anyone; never wanted more than just a one night stand with anyone. You're the first," I say, letting out a breath. Maybe I should have never said anything. Maybe this was all just a big mistake.

She turns, her eyes are watery like she's going to cry, staring at me like I just said words of gold. Shit, I hate it when chicks cry. I need to set her straight on what I am, what we are, before she thinks I'm some Romeo.

"What did you expect, Dani? When Candy told you a fraction of the man I am, you went running for the fucking hills. I'm the fucking Sargent-At-Arms of the Devil's Dust Motorcycle Club. I'm a murderer, an outlaw, a fucking beast. There are no white picket fences and Sunday brunches on this side." I stare her in the eyes as deeply as I can. I want her to know I'm no fucking Prince Charming, not even close. This is the man I am; if she wants me, this is who she gets. There is no changing me to some Mr. Perfect.

Her eyes darken. "Ah, I get it. You think the same thing as that bitch out there; that I don't belong here," she says, snidely.

I can tell her exactly what she wants to hear, that I never thought that, but I would be fucking lying.

"At first I didn't believe you belonged here, no. I thought that you were some stuck-up bitch; one that I wanted to fuck into her place." Her eyes widen with shock. "But then I got to know you a little better; and now, after that little charade in there..." I point through the wall to where she just beat Candy's ass moments before, "... I know you have Devil's Dust Blood in you, and I think you know it, too.

"I saw the ferocious woman in you finally escape tonight; the woman your mother has been scared shit-less to let out. You are your father's daughter, no doubt," I chuckle. Watching Dani let loose on Candy was like letting a caged tiger out into the wild. Its primal instincts kick in, and it is where it belongs.

She wipes a tear from her face, letting her hands fall to her side. She's no longer trying to shield herself, maybe I haven't fucked this up.

I walk up to her and grab her hands in both of mine, I don't know, isn't that suppose be romantic or some shit?

"I have never done this before, so be warned. I'm going to be a shitty romantic, and you're going to be pissed off at me more than you actually like me. If we do decide to go forward, you are mine! I own you, do you understand?" I tuck my finger under her chin making her look at me. "I won't let you go, and I sure as hell won't let you go back to New York." I lean in and kiss the scratches on her face. I have never hit a woman before but after seeing the scratches on Dani's beautiful face, I want to bitch-slap Candy, I want to fucking beat the shit out of her mother for her neglect. I want to protect Dani from everything bad.

Dani's green eyes pierce mine, as she nods her head. "Say it, Dani. Say you're mine and you understand."

"I'm yours and I understand." Her voice is so quiet it makes me nervous. Then again, this whole thing makes me nervous.

I dive in and bite her bottom lip, sucking it into my mouth before demanding entry with my tongue. My cock, that was already hard from all the tits and ass being thrown around the club, throbs against my jeans, screaming to be released. The back and forth between Dani and I, has given me horrendous blue balls on more than one occasion.

She pulls away, placing both her hands on my chest and looks down. I can tell she is over-thinking something. "What is it, Dani?" I pull her chin up, her skin is so silky and soft against my rough fingers. I bet telling her I own her has her rethinking everything.

"You're mine too, right? No more Candy, or other girls?" She's so damn cute. I guess she has point. I can't ask her to only be mine and fuck around on her. I know brothers do this; mattress hopping isn't uncommon in the club, but I just can't see myself doing it to Dani, she's different.

"I'm all yours." I smile wolfishly as I turn the lights off. She wants me all to herself. Nobody has ever asked such a thing of me before. I'm sure before this is over she is going to be throwing me at someone else.

I claim her sugar lips; licking, nipping, sucking every drop I can get from her delicate mouth. I can hear her breath become heavy. Her hands fly to my shoulders; climbing me, clinging to me like she can't get enough; like I am her next breath. I grab the back of her thighs and place her legs around my waist; she weighs nearly nothing, making it easy to move her around. I take one hand and place it on the back of her head before letting us both fall on the bed, protecting her head from the forceful fall. She moves her head to the side, giving me entry to the crook of her neck. I skid my lips across her peach smelling skin, teasing her porcelain skin with my hot breath. She whimpers and starts to pull my cut down my arms and my shirt over my head. I sit up on my knees and help her remove my shirt; her fingers fly to the zipper on my jeans. The need in her eyes is almost too much to handle. I tug the button off my jeans and shimmy out of them, leaving me in my white, boxer briefs. Her breath catches at the sight of my length fighting against the thin fabric. Her fingers grab the waist band and start pulling them down. She places tender kisses across my chest making a beastly growl escape my mouth. I grab what's left of her shirt and pull it over her head. Her dark hair falls across her nipples. Her breasts are not as big as Candy's but they are natural and suit her beautifully. I grab her shorts and panties and yank them down as one, urgent to be inside of her. I place tender kisses over the scratches on her cheek; fucking Candy. She throws her legs around my waist, knocking her iPod off the bed.

"Oh, shit." She jumps in panic, our heads almost hitting in the process. "I didn't break it, did I?"

I lean over and grab it off the carpet, making it come to life. The screen lights up the dark room.

"No, it doesn't seem to be broken." I instantly see Whitesnake, press play and set it down beside her head. "Is This Love" filters through the headphones filling the room. Well, that's not what I had in mind exactly. Fuck it.

I gently pull her legs apart and kneel in between them. I rub my dick against her wet opening. When I push the tip of my cock in, she throws her head back into the pillow and moans. I love the sound of her moaning; it's so erotic. I push in deeper causing my own head to fall back. It feels so amazing. She's so tight and warm, it's like heaven. She moans louder when I'm in as deep as her sweet sex will allow. I lay my body on top of her small frame, putting most of my weight on my knees so I don't crush her. I can feel her nipples gliding against my torso as I lower my elbows beside her head. I start to thrust and her sweet mouth forms into an "O" and her breath comes in short spurts. She's so fucking sexy, just the look of her as she takes me is killing me. I nip and suck her neck, the smell of her is fucking intoxicating. I grit my teeth; the amount of pleasure she gives me is borderline narcotic, a high I only get with her. I nip her earlobe and skid my teeth along her jawline gently, before taking in her sweet lips; tasting anything and everything she is willing to give me.

"Shadow," she whispers into the dark. My name slipping through those angelic lips nearly has me busting my load.

I take her bottom lip into my teeth and give it a light tug before leaning up and catching those eyes staring back at me breaking walls I never knew were there. I have never loved before, but I would think it would take longer than the time I have known Dani.

Her nails skid across my back as I feel her vaginal walls squeeze my cock; she's getting close. Her tits bounce while I thrust into her, screaming for attention. I reach down with both hands and grab onto her perky tits as I plow into her softly. Her hands come up and tangle into her own hair; her body arches and she spreads her legs wider inviting me in deeper. I can feel the fluttering sensation race deep within me, licking up my dick. I start to piston my hips faster. She moans louder and untangles her fingers from her own hair to fly at my back, her nails digging into my skin, claiming me. Her legs tighten now around my waist while she climaxes. The sight of her is it for me; I throw my head back and explode inside her.

I fall next to her trembling body; mine feeling like Jell-o; a first for me. She rolls over and places kisses on my chest, knocking the iPod off on the floor again and stopping the music. She doesn't panic that she might have broken it this time. I don't even know if Whitesnake is still playing, I am so caught up in us. Then it hits me; we just made love. Last time we did it was a bit more animalistic. This time was sensual, deep and tender. What the fuck is happening to me?

I tuck her head under my chin and give it a kiss. Her hair smells like my shampoo, making me grin. Laying there we try to catch our breaths while I try to reel in what the hell I'm doing. Have I fucking lost my mind? I can feel Dani's breathing slow, as her body starts to go limp.

"Sleep, Baby," I whisper into her hair.

"Shadow," she croaks out, sleep heavy in her voice.

"Hmmm?"

"We didn't use a condom," she whispers against my chest.

My eyes snap open. Shit, how could I be so careless? I didn't even think about a condom. This is yet another example of how I cannot think clearly around Dani. I have always made sure to wear a condom; never thought for a second to go without one. Even when I was a kid fucking around, I always used a condom.

"I'm clean. You're the only girl I have had sex with unprotected."

"Yeah... but I'm not on the pill."

Fuck. Of course, she's not on the damn pill; she was a virgin until a few days ago, why would she be on it.

She pulls her head from under my chin and looks up at me. "Maybe Bobby can talk to Doc for me or something. We will figure it out. We will be more careful, though." She kisses my lips tenderly, causing me to sigh into her.

"Good night, Shadow." She whispers against my lips.

Fuck.

Chapter Twelve
Dani

I feel fingertips sliding up and down my bare back, waking me from my slumber. I open my eyes to a tanned chest and remember my night with Shadow. A grin instantly plasters itself across my face. I look up at him and his gorgeous, blue eyes are looking back.

"Good Morning."

"Mmmm..." I respond. I grab the sheet and pull it over us, tucking us both into the bed. I don't want this to end; whatever is outside that door can wait. I don't even mind his morning breath, not that mine is any better. He grabs the hand I hit Candy with, lifts it to his mouth and kisses each knuckle. How can he say he is a shitty romantic when he does things like this? When he acts like this, I have no problem being his.

"I want to take you out this evening," he says. I look up at him, shocked. His face looks shocked, too, that he even said it.

"Really?" I respond, stunned. I didn't take him as a date kind of guy.

He nods his head yes.

I feel giddy, like a teenager being asked to prom.

"What are your plans today?" I ask him, trying to find a distraction from the awesome feeling bubbling inside of me.

"I got church; gotta let the Prez know how the run went; see if anyone heard anything back on the shooting or that Stevin guy; then probably work on my car some." He starts rubbing his rough fingertips up and down my back again. The feeling is so sensual; I love it. Wait, he has a car? I haven't seen it.

"What about you?" he asks.

I sigh heavily. "Oh, probably helping Babs or laying around in here. It's pretty boring here." I am glad I have someone to talk to like Babs, but sitting around here doing nothing is driving me crazy.

I run my hands across his chest; his body is so toned and perfect. I feel his length pressing against my stomach as I caress his chest. It makes me feel needed. I throw the sheets over my head and lower my body down the bed. I find Shadow's impressive length instantly.

"What are you doin'- aaahh!" I lick up Shadow's shaft before he can finish his sentence. I flick my tongue at his head and cup his balls with my hand. I sheath my teeth with my lips and plunge my hot, moist mouth around his erection. His body comes off the bed as I suck on him like a Popsicle. My hand grabs the bottom of his shaft to keep it still while I assault him with my mouth. He groans as I flick my tongue on the underside and continue to suck him without mercy. I feel his length pulse and tighten as I bob my head. I hollow out my cheeks and suck harder, making his body tremble. He places his hand on my head as I continue to suck him like a vice. His shaft tightens and pulses inside my mouth again as he groans.

"I'm going to cum, Dani," he whimpers in warning as his back inclines off the bed. I don't slow down. I grab at his balls and continue to suck him halfway down my throat. Suddenly, salty warm fluid spills into my mouth. He tastes amazing; I milk him of every drop. I feel him fall back down on the bed, huffing and puffing.

He pulls the sheet off me. "Do you have a fucking gag reflex? Holy shit!" I smile at him, not sure what to say. I have never done anything like that. I've just seen it in smutty films when I was home alone. Looks like I can please my man better than a whore, judging by his reaction.

I hear a ring coming from the floor and Shadow gets up off the bed to grab it. His body is so sexy; I don't think I will ever get used to his god-like perfection.

"Yeah," he answers. "What time is it? Oh shit... Yeah, I coming now." He stuffs the phone back into his jeans pocket, grabs his briefs off the floor, and starts to shimmy his legs into them.

"It's near noon. I gotta get to church, babe." He pulls his pants on and looks around the room for his shirt and cut. His bed-head hair suits him so well and my fingers itch to play in it.

He leans over and kisses me on the lips before he hops to the door, battling to put on a boot. I can't help but giggle.

I hate that we have to hide. I'm sure my mom will blow up, probably even threaten to burn this place down. I say go for it, I have finally found a place I belong and I'm not about to turn my back on it.

Shadow's words from last night come to mind: 'I won't let you go, and I sure as hell won't let you go back to New York.'

Honestly, I don't think Shadow would let my mother take me, and I'm glad because I don't want to go back. This is my home now, and I think she knows deep down that this has always been my home.

I guess I should get a shower, though I hate to wash the smell of Shadow off of me. I get a shower and brush my teeth with Shadow's brush again, I put on my pink lace bra with matching underwear, some khaki colored shorts and a yellow tank top. I walk out and spot Babs behind the counter.

"There you are. I'll make you whatever you want this morning; you name it." Her tone is a little more enthusiastic than I was expecting.

"The Club Princess has arrived. Babs, you better make her what she wants or you may end up with a black eye." Locks winks at me. Shit, the whole club knows about what happened between Candy and I. I look over at the meeting room to find open doors. Looks like church was quick this morning.

I try and paste on a smile, but my fear is that if the whole club knows, then my mother has probably heard as well. Shit. I don't think I can lie myself out of this one.

Shadow comes in the door covered in grease and sits down next to Bobby. The grease on him makes him look so rugged; I'm drooling for another round in the bedroom with him.

"Well, if it isn't the Club Princess," he smirks at me; smart ass. But, man he is a sexy smart ass.

"You should have seen it, Babs, it was like fire flying across the room." Bobby looks at me with a sudden awe in his face. "Like a firefly."

"Oh, I like that; Princess Firefly," Babs nods in agreement.

"I could see her as a firefly," Shadow agrees.

"Wait, what?" The whole conversation confuses me.

"Your 'road name', nickname, what have you," Babs clarifies.

My dad walks in through the club door. "Dani, follow me." His tone is flat and his face is impassive. I'm sure he knows about Candy; shit.

I follow him into the chapel and sit down at a huge wooden table. He sits at the head of the table, leans back in his chair, and lights a cigarette. He sits there playing with his red lighter, not even looking at me. The awkward silence gets the best of me so I look around the room. Ten chairs are scattered around the table and I wonder which one Shadow's fine ass graces during "church". There's a fan in the window behind me and the wall I'm facing has frames with worn cuts in them.

"Fallen members," my father answers, watching me look at each of the frames.

"You want to explain what happened to Candy?" His voice is calm and eerie, snapping me from the frames. I can't tell him that I am jealous of Candy; that I want to be a part of Shadow's world. I start picking at the worn table, not sure what to say.

"She has a broken nose and stitches in her cheek. Judging by the scratches on your cheek and knuckles, I know you did it. What I don't know is why?" He takes a long drag from his cigarette, blows a puff of smoke into the air, then looks right at me. I've not seen this side of my father before; he is usually so tender and caring. Right now, his voice is strong and wicked. It's scary as shit.

"You guys fighting over one of my boys, Dani? They know better than to come near you. If I find out this is over one of the guys, it won't be pretty. You're club property and- "

"She said I didn't belong here, and that I didn't deserve to wear the Devil's Dust shirt I was wearing. I just snapped. I didn't even realize what I did until I was pulled off her." I spoke loudly, interrupting him on his rant. I didn't want to give him the chance to over think things or piece things together and take Shadow away before I even got the chance to have him. I mean, I told part of the truth; she was trying to chase me out of here like mom, and it did really piss me off.

"Bitch!" he yells and slams his fist on the table. I look up offended. His expression softens when he sees the shock written on my face.

"No, not you; Candy. Seems she got what she deserves. If I had heard her say that I would have fuckin' pistol whipped her. I should have done it to her mother." He slams his cigarette out in the ashtray, pissed.

"I don't think she will be messing with me anymore. I can handle my own battles, Dad." His head whips up at the word "Dad". I didn't realize I even said it out loud; but he is my dad, is it so wrong to call him that?

"I can see that. You're a Devil's Dust Princess." His eyes brighten with a sense of pride as he speaks to me. Is it just me or does the word princess just sound ridiculous? Not that firefly was much better.

"Your mom is going to find out about this; everyone knows. Everyone saw Candy this morning and when asked about it she said to ask you. Candy's mom will be blowing up my phone, I'm sure, and I know your mother is going to be on my fucking back. I think I may just go fishing for the day." He looks over at me and smiles big.

"Good luck, Darlin'." He pats me on the shoulder and leaves the room.

Wow that was close. I don't know how much longer Shadow and I will be able to hide our... whatever we are, from everyone. I push off from the table and notice my palms are sweating; talk about sweating bullets. Before I can leave the room, my mother steps through the door and pushes me back into the room. She slams the door behind her.

"What the hell is going on, Danielle Lexington?" she yells at me while pointing her finger in my face. Wow, she must be pissed; she used my full name. I pinch the bridge of my nose; this is getting really old. I'm sick of her treating me like a child; I'm fucking twenty-one years old. I went with it before because I was so used to her protective ways. I was numb to everything around me; naive even. But now, I am more alive than I have ever been; everything is so clear and I'm done with this, with her. She can't threaten to throw me out on the streets now. I have a place to call home.

I grab her finger and push it back at her, making her stumble. Returning to my seat, I look up and see shock and anger written all over her face.

"I want to know what you did to that poor girl, right now." Her voice is low and trembling with every word.

That poor girl? She never fails to surprise me, taking up for a club whore over her own daughter.

"I beat the shit out of her." She gasps and walks over to my side of the table to look down at me. I can't tell if she's mortified with what I have become or furious.

Testing the waters, I look up at her standing over me and demand smugly, "yes?"

Before I can register what she is doing, she raises her palm and slaps me across the face so hard my teeth chatter. I get up so quick the chair is thrown backward to the ground.

"You bitch!" I yell at her, my hand caressing the sting she left across my cheek. My body instantly fuels with poisonous rage. I want to hit her back but I'm afraid if I lay a finger on her I might not be able to stop.

"Look at you; you are nothing more than biker trash!" she screams.

I smile at her brazenly. "My whole life I've done everything you wanted me to do without question and the only time you were ever there was to tell me what a fuck up I was. Well, no more. I realize now I could have never made you happy anyway. I've always been biker trash to you; that's what pisses you off more than anything. I'll never go back to New York with you."

She charges and slams her body into me. We fall to the dusty wooden floor, knocking chairs over in the process. My head smacks against the floor with a thud, making me see stars. She straddles my body and starts pulling my hair and slaps me in the face. I cover my face with my arms as she assaults me. That's all I can do; if I move my hands to fight back she has full advantage of my face.

"You're just like your father; so ungrateful, so stubborn. I couldn't stand the sight of you past the age of seven! No matter what you did, you reminded me of him!"

My head screams with every strand of hair pulled and every pore in my face stings with each slap; not to mention the pounding that radiates through my skull from our fall. Just when I'm about to fight back, the slapping stops and her weight is lifted from me. I open my eyes to Bobby's hand held out to help me up; when I stand he brushes the strands out of my face.

"You okay?" he asks calmly. I don't answer. I look over his broad shoulder and see everyone in the room; Babs, Bull, Hawk, Charlie, Lips, Locks, even a few other members I haven't met. How embarrassing. Locks has my mother by the forearms, holding her still as she huffs and puffs and tries to pull herself away from his tight grip.

I can feel the burn in my eyes. I blink tightly, trying to hold back my tears. I barrel through everyone and run outside to the garage across the courtyard. I walk into one of the bays and stare at the wall. The white paint is chipped and greasy; the smell of gas and oil surrounds me. My fingers wreak havoc on my lips as I try to calm myself from what just happened.

I may have just lost my mother for good this time, but is she really that big of a loss? Her words are what hurt me the most. It isn't surprising that she can't stand the sight of me, but hearing her admit it is like a knife through the heart. The stinging is becoming too much; I can feel my eyes welling up ready to spill unshed tears.

"Dani? What are you –" Shadow stops mid-sentence when he sees my distraught state. I didn't even see him in here I was so wrapped up in my own turmoil. "What's wrong?"

I shake my head in response.

He pulls me close, wrapping his arms around me. I nuzzle my nose into his grease stained shirt and inhale deep. His woodsy smell mixed with grease is a welcoming scent, it relaxes me on the spot.

"My mom is what's wrong. How can she say those things?" I mumble into his chest, my hands clenching his shirt like a lifeline.

"You would be surprised what a mother can say to her child." He pushes me to arm's length and examines my face.

"What the hell, Dani, your face is all red. Did that bitch hit you?" I can see his eyes dilate with anger, his jaw clenching as he moves my head side to side by my chin.

Suddenly, I hear heavy footsteps coming our way. I spot an open office door and shuffle into the space between it and the wall. Peeking out through the hinges, I see Locks coming into the garage.

"Shadow, you see Dani run out here?"

"Nah, man, I haven't." Shadow acts casual, looking for something in a red tool box.

"She just got into a major fight with her mom; she bolted out of the club running this way. Bull sent me to find her, make sure she was okay." Locks pulls out a red pack and plucks a cigarette from it with his lips, he doesn't light it, just lets it hang loosely from his lips.

"These women, I tell you what; I'm not here to fucking babysit. Not sure what the fuck the Prez was thinking bringing these bitches here."

"I think he thought they are his family," Shadow replies, shuffling through more tools.

"This ain't no place for bitches; that's all I'm saying, brother." Locks pulls out a black lighter from his pocket and lights his cigarette. Shadow takes his focus off the red tool box and looks in Locks' direction.

"Really? What about Babs?" Shadow asks.

"That's different." Locks crosses his arms and widens his stance.

"How so?" Shadow asks, leaning up against the tool box.

"No drama." Locks quips back.

Shadow scuffs at Locks' comment. "Right. Wasn't it about five months back when Babs caught you with your pants around your ankles, fucking Candy?"

Now I get why there is so much tension between Candy and Babs, and what Babs meant by Locks cheating.

"Yeah it was, and I reined that shit in. Babs knew better than to fucking say a word or else." Locks takes a drag from his cigarette.

Did he seriously just say "or else"? What does that mean? Does he hit her? Is that what it's like being with one of them, they can cheat on you and if you say anything they hit you? My chest suddenly feels heavy, the throbbing in my head becomes apparent again.

"I'm not here to have a therapy session with you; if you see Dani tell her to get her ass to the clubhouse." Locks turns and walks away, his heavy footsteps trailing him. Shadow looks at me and nods when it's clear. I walk out from behind the door, and look at Shadow. So many questions to ask, but I don't want to offend him. He instantly cups my face with his greasy hands and looks right into my eyes.

"Breathe, Dani. Some men fuck around on their Ol' Ladies; that's just club life." He says it so calmly, like it's a social norm.

"I don't think I can be an Ol' Lady," I whisper out in confession.

Shadow smiles. "I might be an asshole, but if you were my Ol' Lady, I wouldn't fuck around and I would never raise a hand to you. Just the thought of you being in pain makes me want to kill. Do you understand me?" His tone is austere, his face serious; I know he is telling the truth. How could I think that Shadow would be like that? He claims to be a beast, and he may be with others, but never me.

"I understand."

He leans his forehead on mine and rubs his thumb on my cheek. His touch is so sincere and caring. I could be Shadow's Ol' Lady if he wanted.

"Good. Now come here; I wanna show you something." He smiles the most boyish smile I have ever seen as he grabs my hand. We pass a few motorcycles and proceed to the back corner of the shop.

We stop in front of a black, mean looking car; I have never seen anything like it. I have never seen a car so sexy in my life; it screams muscle.

"It's a 1965 Shelby Mustang; it was my dad's." He pulls a grease rag from his back pocket and rubs a smudge from the hood. I walk around the car, taking in its beauty; its masculinity.

"I like it a lot. It's sexy." I look up and his face lights up even more than it already was. He is so cute with that boyish grin of his. Boys and their toys.

"Man, you keep getting better and better." His grin turns wolfish and he winks at me, making my panties pool with desire. Looking at him and this sexy ass car, all I want is him to bend me over it and have his way with me.

"I see that look in your eye, and trust me I've already thought about it. It's too risky, though," he replies back. It's crazy how he can read my mind so easily after the short time we have been around each other.

"Can you take me for a drive?" Maybe if we get out of here we can have some fun in the back seat. Good God, listen to me; I sound slutty.

"Nah, I've still gotta get a motor. It's an older car so it's harder to find."

Damn.

"Dani! Dani!" I hear my name being called from the clubhouse.

"I better get." I start walking past Shadow and he grabs my hand, stopping me.

"See you at five, Firefly." I just smile at him and walk away. He slaps my ass hard as I pass and I squeal with delight.

Chapter Thirteen
Dani

    I'm sitting in the same chair for the third time today. My fingers pick and scratch at the dips and grooves of the wooden table as I wait for the awkward silence to break. My father is sitting at the head of the table with a bottle of Jack sitting next to him and twirling a shot glass between his thumb and forefinger. On the opposite side of the room, my mother is pacing the floor; her hands on her hips then crossing them in front of her chest. I guess it's time for family therapy; where's our shrink when you need her.

    "These bitch fights are going to stop; I want you two to make amends now. I won't have this happening in my club any further." My dad finally breaks the silence, his voice calm and collected, yet he is staring right at my mother as if he is only speaking to her.

    "Your club; that's all that matters to you, always has been. Some things never change," my mother rants as she continues to pace the floor, not even glancing in our direction.

    "You knew the level of dedication I have for this club when we were together. That's never changed, Lady." His voice rises slightly; I can tell he is irritated with her.

    My mother stops pacing and leans on the table with her hands. She stares directly at my father. "It's Sadie. How many times do I have to tell you that?" she practically screams at him.

    He sighs heavily before twisting the cap off the whiskey and pouring the amber liquid to the brim of the small glass. "I won't have you putting your hands on my daughter ever again." His voice and face are a warning to my mother. He tosses back the shot, letting the whiskey jet back into his throat. He doesn't even flinch.

My mother slapping me isn't the first time; she slapped me a lot when I would go off her path of righteousness. This, however, would be the last.

My mother's face is red, her nostrils flaring with rage. "I'm leaving today; now!" She looks over at me questioningly, silently asking if I'm going with her. I turn my head away, avoiding her inquisitive look. There's no way in hell I'm going with her.

"You can't, we haven't found that douche-bag ex of yours. It's not safe," my father explains, his voice calmer.

"Yeah, well, I'll take my chances," she says with disgusted humor in her voice. "I take it you're not coming?" she finally verbally asks me.

I stare ahead at the wall, avoiding both my father's and my mother's questioning faces. I don't know if my father wants me to stay and I don't want to go with my mother. If my father doesn't want me here, I would rather live like a homeless person than go back to the puppet my mother wanted me to be; not after having just discovered who I really am. She turns on her foot and throws her arms up as if washing her hands of me.

"When I was pregnant with you I thought nurture would win over nature. I should have seen the signs as you grew older, but here I am being slapped in my face for the decision to keep you as my daughter." She turns and looks at me, her eyes swelling with tears. I take it she thought about aborting me when she found out she was pregnant; that really doesn't surprise me.

"I'm staying. I can never be the person you want in a daughter. I never did feel like I fit your mold. After being here, I feel like I know who I am now." The words slip through my lips almost as a whisper. My father hasn't objected so far; he must want me to stay.

"You think you know who you are now, but there are only four things you can become in an outlaw club like this: a whore, a junkie, a prisoner or dead. Don't come running back to me, and don't say I didn't warn you." She glares angrily at me and then at my father. "I already called a taxi. You two enjoy each other. You're both monsters in the same." She turns on her heel and leaves. She just walks out of my life that easy; like I was a used car she no longer wanted.

I feel wet warmth cross my cheek, stinging the cuts Candy left behind. My fingers rub the tears my eyes unknowingly shed.

"Here, you might need this." My father slides the small glass, half full of the amber whiskey, across the table. I toss it back and feel it burn all the way down my throat and into my stomach. My body instantly becomes warm and relaxed. My eyes water and it makes me cough at its lingering assault.

"What now?" I ask, unsure if this is what he wants; if he wants me.

"We'll tie up some loose ends, make sure everything is safe, and get you set up on your feet, Darlin'." His face and voice are sincere; I can tell he wants nothing more than for me to stay here.

"You're my blood. You're always welcome here and always protected, Dani." He pats my shoulder. "Besides, I kind of like you." I look up at a smiling Bull, wrinkles framing his bright green eyes.

I guess this is my home now. With that thought, my pursed lips turn into a smug grin.

I walk out to the courtyard at the appointed time of 5pm to find Shadow already waiting by his bike. He's wearing snug blue jeans, a white shirt and his cut. His dark hair is all messy on top, as usual, and he has the laziest grin when he sees me walking toward him. Just the sight of him makes me tremble with arousal. Every day I feel myself falling deeper and deeper into his web.

He hands me the helmet and revs up his bike. The roar coming from the chrome pipes screams up my spine. I put my helmet on and climb on the back of his bike. He grabs my legs and pulls me closer, making me smile. In a flash, we fly forward and are out of the courtyard and hitting the pavement. His smell is intoxicating; his spicy shampoo mixed with grease. I can tell he tried to wash off all the grease but the smell still lingers. I love it; it's so masculine.

Looking out at the sunset, I see big gray clouds swarming the sky; looks like a storm is brewing. I wonder where Shadow is taking me. This should be interesting. Still, I bet anything he has to offer is better than the blind dates my mother used to set me up with; they always took me to the finest places and threw cash, or their family name, around like it was flattering; it wasn't.

I feel the bike slant off to the side of the road bringing us back to the beach he took me to a week or so back. I'm not complaining. I love the beach and this could be romantic. Then again, Shadow did say he didn't do romantic.

I slide off the back of the bike and hand Shadow my helmet. He takes it and hands me a red and black checkered blanket from one of the saddle bags.

"Go find us a good spot; I'll follow in a sec."

I take the blanket and make my way down to the warm, sandy beach. The breeze has picked up making the waves crash onto the beach. I pick a spot and throw the blanket down. Sitting on a corner, I take my shoes and socks off and dig my toes into the warmth. Feeling the grainy sand squish between my toes is amazing; it is so relaxing. I need this after the last twenty-four hours I have had. The thought of Candy and my mother makes goose bumps rise on my skin. I haven't been at the club long and I have already managed to wreck havoc. What a mess.

I look behind me to find Shadow setting down a red cooler and kicking off his boots and socks.

"What's in the cooler?" I ask, lifting my chin toward it.

"Eh, my attempt of being romantic," he responds, chuckling.

He opens the lid and pulls out a Tupperware dish with sandwiches cut into triangles, then he pulls out another dish with cheese and grapes, followed by two beers. I am in complete shock, my mouth has fallen open and my eyes are as wide as saucers.

"I know it's not a five-star restaurant or anything fancy, but this is about as romantic as I get." He rubs the back of his neck and eyes my reaction. He thinks I hate it; that I'm mortified he would make me sandwiches for a date, but the truth is, I love it. I hate that he thinks I'm some high-class broad from New York that's impossible to please. I bet everyone at the club thinks that.

"It's perfect," I respond, my voice full of emotion.

He scoffs at me. He clearly thinks I'm lying. Jerk.

"I'm not lying," I protest.

He sits down and opens the tub with the sandwiches in it. He takes a beast-sized bite and looks out at the crashing waves. I crawl over and straddle his lap and cup his face so he's looking directly into my eyes. His cheeks, rough with stubble, feel glorious under my fingertips.

"I've been to those five-star restaurants you're talking about; sure they can be nice but anybody can throw money at someone else to cook for their significant other. This takes a lot more thought. You did this yourself; you didn't hire someone else to take care of the hassle. This is way more intimate than anything you might think is considered fancy..." He cups my face back and lightly brushes his lips over mine, so tender and friendly I forget who is holding me.

"So you think I'm your significant other?" he whispers against my lips, his breath smelling of turkey.

My cheeks flush and my heart starts galloping like a horse. Shit, I did say significant other. I know labels aren't his thing. Just taking me out on a date is pushing it and here I am saying "be my boyfriend".

"I... uh... I just mean..." I choke out, not sure what to say; afraid whatever comes out may push him away.

"I'm just fucking with you." He grins, acting amused my by panicked state. Asshole. He can act as if he is messing with me, but it's clear he has trust issues.

Trying to avoid the situation, I reach down and grab one of the little triangular sandwiches and take a bite. It's the most delicious sandwich I have ever had. It is turkey and cheddar with some kind of sauce; it's simple, yet mouthwatering.

"This is amazing," I mumble with a mouth full of food.

He laughs; his laugh so deep and charming it makes me laugh with him. He leans over and wipes extra sauce that has gathered in the corner of my mouth with his index finger. He then places it in his mouth, sucking it clean. My sex clenches wanting those skillful lips on me instead of his finger. The ache in my core starts to throb. I gotta get these thoughts out of my head or I will never survive this date.

He tips his head to the side. "How is a girl like you not taken, or ever been taken for that matter?" he asks, biting into another sandwich.

"Oh, well, it's not like I didn't try, or that I never had a boyfriend before. When I was in high school, my boyfriend and I went back to my place to fool around because my mom was supposed to be working late. She ended up walking in on us right before we were getting ready to do the deed. She was great about always catching me right before I did something she didn't approve of. She dragged him out by his hair; I could hear my mother yelling at him all the way out the front door. He didn't talk to me anymore after that; I'm not sure if it was the embarrassment of my mother throwing him out into the street naked, or what she said to him, but he wasn't the only guy that kept his distance after that. I never had a date the rest of high school. As for college, my mom made it clear I was not to go partying, and that's what college is about, so I didn't really make friends." I look up and see humor on his face.

    He shakes his head. "Your momma is something else," he responds, taking a swig of his beer.

    "Tell me about it. I don't think I will be seeing her anymore after today, though." I feel guilt rise in my throat. I hate that I pushed her away but I feel that if I hadn't I would never be able to live my own life. I sigh heavily, trying to push my mother out of my head; I want to enjoy our date.

    "I heard about it; mothers are a unique breed aren't they?" I look up at him and see his beautiful blue eyes go dark; I wonder what the deal is with his mother. Where is his father? Just as I'm about to slip the questions through my lips, his phone rings. He looks at the screen and sighs heavily; his whole body becomes stiff and his mood shifts completely. He stands up and answers it.

    "You know you're a dead woman, right?" He looks around us frantically; I look around to see if I can spot what he's looking at.

    "Bitch, if I find you, you're fucking dead. Do you hear me?" He looks down at the screen and then shoves the phone in his pocket. Whoever it was hung up on him. His jaw is clenched and his blue eyes look black as night. He runs his hands back and forth through his messy top before looking down at me.

    "Date's over. Get up; help me get this shit." He starts throwing the food in the cooler; his frantic state has me panicking. He grabs my trembling hands as I reach for the blanket.

"Hey, calm down. I'm sorry I'm freaking out; it's just that it's not safe here right now. Your safety matters more to me than anything." He tucks a stray hair behind my ear, waiting for me to respond.

"I understand."

I understand he cares for my safety, but it sucks our date has to end. I want more of Shadow, and when we are at the club we have to hide and sneak. I hate it. Here we can be as open as we want, and don't have to worry about someone seeing us.

"Hey, I'll make it up to you later tonight." He grabs each one of my ass cheeks with each of his large hands and pulls me forward; he towers over my small frame. Leaning down, he bites my bottom lip hard, making me taste blood. The pain is a welcomed feeling; it reminds me how alive Shadow makes me feel.

"Come on, Firefly," he teases as he grabs my hand. The name Firefly catches my attention.

"How could you agree on everyone calling me that?" I ask, smacking his arm playfully.

Shadow pulls me close and looks at me intently. "Because, I can tell you have had it rough and still you have this fire in you." He caresses my cheek with his rough fingertips. "That night you were dancing in the kitchen and singing... the shit storm that was around you and the way I was treating you... never put that fire out."

"You have had it rough, too. I can tell." I say the words before registering them and instantly regret it.

Shadow shrugs. "I have." He looks out at the water with a far-away gaze. "There are many forms of neglect, Dani. Your mom neglects you emotionally; my mom neglected me literally. I, however, have no fire left in me."

Thinking on Shadow's and my stories, I can see why we are so strongly attracted to each other; it makes sense now. We feel the damage in each other, like two wounded animals looking out for each other; for survival. Shadow's past is dark; his name justifies that. My past has also negatively affected me, yes; but hope in a different future still burns bright. I can be the fire; the light that Shadow needs to come out of the darkness in which he lives. Hearing Shadow's reason behind me being called Firefly makes me like the name; gives me hope for us.

  We arrive back at the club just in the nick of time. As we pull into the courtyard, the sky opens up and it begins to pour rain. We both start laughing and run toward the clubhouse. Even with the short distance, we end up soaked. When we walk in Bobby is getting licked and grounded on by some girl I don't recognize. A couple of the prospects are at the bar hooting and hollering at each other. Only Bobby looks our way for a split second before turning back to his female companion. Walking down the hall toward the bedroom, I glance over my shoulder and see Shadow admiring how my wet clothes cling to my body. I turn and walk backward, playing with the button on my jeans. I bite my bottom lip, my wet hair falling in front of my face as I gaze at him lustfully. He's rubbing his bottom lip with his thumb.

  As soon as we enter the room, he slams the door shut and shoves me against the wall with his body. He smashes his mouth onto mine hard, bruising my lips. I instantly wrap my arms around his neck wanting more, as he trails his tongue along my jaw bone to my ear. He sucks my earlobe into his mouth, making me moan lightly. Like a fire has been lit, we start pulling and tugging our shirts and pants off, they're heavy as bricks being as wet as they are. He picks me up and throws me on the bed.

  With horny expectation, I watch as he crawls up me like a slick panther. His head stops at my panties and he tugs on them with his teeth. I bend my knees; the temptation almost too much to handle. He reaches his hands to the side of the panties and rips them to shreds; his muscles bulging in the process. God, he is so sexy. I can feel my body winding up even more just by looking at him. His wolfish gaze shifts from the torn panties to the look on my face. I meet his eyes with my own beastly needs. "Shadow," my voice trembles. I'm not sure how much more anticipation I can take.

Shadow growls and grabs me by the hips; his fingers bruising me with his manhandling grip. He flips me over and throws me on my chest. He pulls my hips up, making my ass stick up into the air. In seconds, he pulls his briefs to his knees and slams his massive length inside of my wet core, making me yell out in pleasure. He reaches his hand around and cups my mouth as he thrusts in and out, his hips jack hammering my delicate sex. I can feel the bed moving back and forth to our rhythm.

He reaches his hand back and slaps my ass; the sting a pleasurable pain. Blood rushes to where he smacked me, making my lower half hypersensitive and making me even wetter. I arch my back and my ass sticks up even further in the air, inviting him to spank me again. I throw my hair to one side of my head and look over my shoulder to peer at Shadow. He's looking right at me; his mouth is hung open in that sexy way.

"Say it," he pants between thrusts, knowing I want him to spank me again.

"Spank me, Shadow." I say, breathlessly. My voice is heavy with lust. I sound so erotic, I don't even recognize my own voice.

He pulls his hand back and slaps my ass again. My head drops back and I moan. I can feel myself trying to plummet over the edge of ecstasy. He reaches down and tangles his fingers in my hair, pulling lightly.

"Fuck yeah, just like that, baby," he grunts as he starts thrusting even harder. I can feel his length pulse inside of me; the fit tight. My body starts to shudder with warmth. I whimper as the heat spreads to my sensitive spots. He moans as I clench around him, pushing us over the edge together. Our simultaneous explosion is so toxic, animalistic and raw. He falls on top of me, causing us both to collapse.

"Fuck, that was great!" he pants. All I can do is nod; I'm so out of breath and instantly feel exhausted. My eyes close; all I can hear is Shadow's deep breathing and my pounding heartbeat, lulling me to sleep.

Chapter Fourteen
Shadow

I lay watching Dani; her silky skin, spotted with sweat beads, rises and falls rapidly. She's breathless. Seeing her dripping wet from the rain was the most erotic thing I have ever fucking seen. The blatant teasing made me want her even more. So I fucked her until I thought she was going to combust at my fingertips, leaving us both gasping for air. Her breathing evens out; she must be asleep. I brush her long, curly hair out of her face; she truly is beautiful; crazy as shit, but beautiful. I lay there for twenty minutes staring at her, wondering what the hell she sees in a fucked-up biker like me. My junkie of a mother threatening me today has me livid. She ruined the alone time I had with Dani.

"So you do have someone special? Better deliver or she's mine."

The simple call replays in my mind over and over. I won't deny that Dani is special to me and just the thought of someone doing harm to her makes me want to burn this whole fucking town to the ground. But I've got to keep a straight head on. There's no telling what this junkie will do. I sit up and see Dani's olive-colored ass is cherry red from spanking her. Who knew she was such a freak in the bed. That shit was hot as hell. I remember trying to spank Candy once and she cried like a little bitch; I barely touched her.

I slip off the bed and notice my briefs are still around my ankles. I was in such a rush to be inside of Dani, I didn't even bother taking them off. I pull them up and start picking up my jeans and shit when I notice a pair of pink, ripped panties. I grin as I pick them up and inhale; they smell of Dani's peachy perfume. I stuff them in my pocket and proceed to put my shit back on. I walk over to Dani and kiss her cheek lightly before heading out the door. I need to go home and get some clean clothes on; maybe even shower. I hate to leave Dani, but being here overnight is too risky.

Walking into the clubhouse this morning, I smell coffee and head straight to the bar. I need something to wake me up after thinking about how to find that bitch of a mother of mine all night.

"Here, Hun, just the way you like it," Babs says, handing me a mug of coffee. She always hooks me up. Love this woman; I don't know why she puts up with Locks' bullshit. She truly is an amazing woman.

"Thanks, babe." I take a sip; it's perfect; straight with two tablespoons of sugar. I go and sit down at the bar next to Bull. He's munching away on toast, getting crumbs all over.

"Got another call last night from the bitch." I blow gently on the hot java in my cup.

Bull finishes the last bite of his toast and looks over at me; he rubs his scruffy jaw in thought. "Let's go, boys. Got shit to talk about." Time for church.

I enter the meeting room and sit down next to Bull, as the rest of the boys follow in behind me. When Bobby comes in, I glance up and see purple spots on his neck.

"What the fuck happened? You look like a God-damned leopard," I ask, not holding back.

He rubs his neck as if he can rub off the hickeys, his cheeks turning red. "Damn bitch was like a fucking vampire. It look that bad?" he asks insecure.

We all start to chuckle. Bobby is always showing up with some kind of out-of-this-world sex story. I have no doubt he probably found some chick who thought she was a vampire. One time, he missed church and we found him in one of the clubhouse bedrooms, cuffed to the bed with a gag in his mouth. He never did tell us who did it to him. That shit was funny, though.

"New business." Bull lights a cigarette and nods his head my direction.

"Junkie mother of mine threatened that if we don't supply her with money or drugs, she's taking Dani"

"Your mom must be tailing you?" Locks speaks up, telling me something I have already figured out. I hate when they refer to this cunt as my mother; it makes my blood turn cold.

"Yeah, I assume," I reply, coldly.

"I don't get why she hasn't done anything; just threatened." Bobby makes a good point. Why hasn't she tried to take Dani, or even show up here at the club?

"Yeah, it doesn't seem right. Just stay close to Dani, Shadow," Bull says. If only he knew how close I was to Dani; he would freak. "Old business?"

"Lady?" Locks asks.

That bitch is definitely old business. She would do good to stay far away from Dani. Something about her is just … off. I don't hit women, but I would make an exception for that one.

"Yeah, I'm pretty sure that bitch is gone. Can't say I'm sad about it either. She ain't the same woman she used to be; she's all kinds of fucked up now. Not sure if I did it or if it was just life in general, but let that be a lesson to all of you and your gals." Bull's face falls; I can see the regret about what went down with Lady.

"Lust like a saint; trust like a sinner," Bulls speaks out in regret. We all nod, knowing Lady was one time he didn't follow his own advice. Lady looked like a saint from afar, making it easy to trust her, but deep down she was anything but a saint.

"So Stevin?" Bobby asks, wondering if he is still a threat.

"Fuck him; he's Lady's problem. She left here of her own free will," Bull says spitefully. His face went from hollow to steel in a split second.

"I got some news for you. You might find it interesting," Hawk chokes out from the back of the table. Everyone's heads turn waiting for the ol' bird to spit it out. "Some locals said they have seen some guys called the El Locos running around town." Hawk's voice is so scratchy, it's often difficult to understand the fucker.

"Makes sense. Bet they were fucking pissed because we declined their shitty service. The drive-by was amateur, and they definitely seemed very amateur," Bobby says, indicating they might have been the ones responsible for the drive-by.

"We take care of this today. Bobby, Shadow, Locks, you're with me. Locks, have Babs get some of the girls, Dani too, to get food and stock up on more booze. When we get back I wanna let loose." Bull lifts his eyebrows in a lewd gesture. Retaliating against the El Locos and then partying all night is a perfect day for Bull, and when he wants to let loose, he really means let loose.

"Hawk, where can we find these El Locos? " Bull asks, smashing his cigarette into the ash tray.

"They are staying at some hotel; about a twenty minute drive." Hawk hands Bobby a map; fucker hasn't heard of GPS apparently.

I walk out of the room and see Dani sitting at the bar eating eggs. She looks over her shoulder and her eyes instantly connect with mine. Every time she does that, I feel like my fucking stomach just went through the floor. That woman makes me feel unspeakable things. She has on a black, fitted tee with blue jeans; her hair pulled up high. She is simply beautiful.

"You boys be careful!" Babs squawks even while Locks is kissing on her and shit.

The ride to the motel takes twenty minutes, just as Hawk said. It is the typical fleabag place with chipping paint and missing shingles. There are about twenty rooms in all. We circle the motel to try to locate which rooms the El Locos may be staying in, but only find a car or two. I look over at Bull and he points to the main office.

"See what you can find out," Bull says to me and Bobby. He always sends Bobby and me after information. Sometimes we can charm the person; sometimes it takes a little more force. I, personally, prefer force over charm. Through the glass doors, we see a young girl with dark hair in a ponytail and thick, black glasses. Even though she's alone in the office, the look on her face is one of fear. God only knows what those fucking assholes have said to her. We push the door open and a bell tinkles.

"Can I help you?" the young girl asks, her voice shaky. She can't be more than sixteen; why her parents would let her work in a place like this is beyond me.

"Why yes, you can, pretty girl," Bobby says, laying on the charm. She instantly blushes; her face of fear turning into a shade of flirtatious red. Obviously Bobby's the charming one and luckily the clerk is, no doubt, a hopeless romantic.

"Cindy is a pretty name," I say, reading her name tag and making her blush even more.

"Thank you." She smiles, showing a mouth full of braces.

"You got any other bikers staying here, Doll?" Bobby asks her.

"Um... I'm not really allowed to give out information like that," she replies, twirling her hair.

I lean over the counter and brush a stray hair behind her ear. "We won't tell anyone, if you don't," I clearly flirt with the underage girl. I would never mess around with a girl of her age, but if flirting with her gets the information we need, then so be it.

"Yeah," she stutters, "we have some called the El... El... Locos."

"What rooms are they staying in?" Bobby asks.

She bites her lip, looking around her before continuing. "Rooms ten through fourteen," she responds quietly.

"How long they staying?"

"I think I've already said too much; I could lose my job." Honestly, if she lost this job, it wouldn't be the worst thing for her.

"I wouldn't ever let that happen, I promise," I wink at her, making her eyes light up. Girls can be so clueless sometimes. I think if I acted this cheesy around Dani she would laugh in my face. Maybe that's what I like so much about her; she's not like most girls.

She starts flipping through some book, trailing her finger across rows of writing. "They don't have a check out date," she responds.

"Thanks, doll," Bobby says, before winking at her.

We walk out to Bull and Locks chatting about something in the parking lot.

"Rooms ten through fourteen; no check out date," Bobby says, interrupting them.

Bull sits there scratching his scruffy cheeks for a second, thinking about what we should do next.

Whistling sounds from behind me make me turn to inspect where it's coming from. A young boy wearing an El Locos' cut comes walking around the corner. The El Locos' logo is some weird-ass eyes that appear to be going around in circles. The eyes represent the crazy that the Spanish word "loco" stands for. I hit Bobby's arm and nod my head toward the boy. Bull and Locks get off their bikes when they see what we're looking at. I pull my pistol from my holster and quietly catch up to the boy. When I'm close enough, I push the head of my gun into his back.

"Don't you fucking say a word or I will shoot you in the spine. You'll be shitting in a bag for the rest of your life. Nod if you get that!" I whisper from behind him; the surge of aggression making me high. He nods his head.

"There anymore of you?" Bobby asks, drawing up beside me.

The kid shakes his head no. He is being compliant, but I want him to fight back. I want to pull this trigger so bad my finger is tensing.

"Take us to your room, now," Bull demands. Bull, Locks and Bobby walk beside me to hide us from passing cars until the guy walks us to Room 13. His body trembles so hard he has tripped twice. He's so pathetic, I think I might actually feel bad if I kill him; then again, probably not.

I'm not programmed like others; things that most people have a conscience for, I don't. Killing and torturing others, makes me feel alive; gives me a control I long for. Growing up with a junkie as a mother, even though she was rarely around, fucks with you. I shut down, I went numb. I've seen things I can never un-see and I have learned to cope with that. The only time I feel alive now, is when shit like this goes south.

Once we are in the room the young guy turns around. The room is filled with beer bottles and fast food trash; it smells terrible. I look down at the boy's cut and notice his name is Chad. What a dip-shit name. I push him down to the mattress with the muzzle of my gun as I check the room to make sure we're alone.

"What the fuck are you guys doing in my town?" Bull asks, his voice deep and smooth.

"Fuck you!" Chad spits. My adrenaline spikes, eager at his defiance. He clearly doesn't know who he is fucking with. He is lucky I don't kill him now.

Bobby, clearly pissed at how disrespecting the little shit is, walks over to the guy and hits him in the nose with the butt of his gun. Blood splatters everywhere. He's lucky it was Bobby because once I get going, I don't like to stop. Bobby knows that first hand. We met in "juvie jail"; he was in for grand theft auto, I was in for assault. I nearly beat a kid into a coma just for teasing me for being poor.

"Fuck. Okay, okay," he yells, holding his nose and making me laugh. Only took one hit to make him rat out his own club; amateur. If he was ours, he would be six feet under.

"Big Jim is pissed you guys disrespected us. He's here to take your business and teach you some respect," Chad sputters out, blood flying all over his arms and hands. Big Jim, must be their shitty president.

"How'd you find my safe house?" Bull asks, rubbing the damn stubble on his face again.

"What safe house?" Chad asks coyly. He knows exactly what the fuck we are talking about. He's starting to piss me off, playing games. The hair rises on my neck and rage floods my veins. I pull my pistol back to hit him; maybe a second hit will remind him.

"We followed you from the pizza joint. Don't hit me again!" he yells quickly, as he winces back on the bed to avoid my gun.

"We sent Charlie out for pizza that night. He must have been tailed back to the safe house, giving them our location," I remind everyone.

"Fucking prospect," Bobby whispers. "He was tailed and didn't even realize it."

"We scouted the house for a few hours and saw there were only three of you; it was easy," Chad says, shrugging his shoulders. Again, my body temperature rises, I grip my gun tighter, and my finger taps the trigger.

"It was easy? One of my men was hit, you fucking turd," Bull yells. The boy just laughs, blood still spilling from his nose. Bull nods at me, "teach him what happens when he fucks with us." I hover my pistol over the boy's leg. "Don't kill him, though. We don't need that kind of heat right now. Just a lesson will do," Bull insists, knowing I will gladly put this fucker under by clipping a main artery.

Chad instantly starts screaming like a damn girl when he sees we are serious. Bobby jumps on the bed behind him and cups his mouth to quiet his screams. Without a second thought, I aim my pistol, cock it, and pull the trigger; all in one fluid motion.

The punk screams louder and his eyes bug out as the bullet penetrates his leg.

"You would think you shot his dick off. What a pussy," Bobby says, laughing.

"You tell your president, Big Jim, to get the fuck out of my town or next time that bullet goes in your head, son," Bull says; and on that note the kid passes out.

"You're kidding?" I laugh.

"I told you, the El Locos are a piece of work," Bobby says, letting the boy fall limp on the shitty mattress.

As we ride back to the clubhouse, I have to admit I wanted the violence to escalate in that motel room. Violence has always been the only thing that makes me feel alive. I've come to crave that feeling. Often in the past, I've hired myself out as a hit man when club business doesn't quench the thirst for blood. Right now, though, all I can think about is Dani. Being with Dani also makes me feel alive. I know I have to be careful. I'm not sure if I can depend on her, trust her, yet. I don't know how she'll react when she learns the full depths of the darkness that lurks within me. If I get too close, if I let her in, her absence could leave me broken and in worse shape than I am now. Oh, hell, who am I fooling? I've already let her in; that's what scares me.

As we pull up to the clubhouse, Bull and Locks head straight in, talking about the party tonight and leaving Bobby and me behind.

"Oh, by the way, Bro, when I got out of the shower this morning I didn't have any clean jeans," Bobby interrupts my thoughts as he climbs off his bike, "so I grabbed a somewhat clean pair from the dirty pile. Come to find out, they aren't mine." He looks at me with a wolfish grin on his face. What the fuck is he talking about? Sharing an apartment with Bobby is becoming a pain in my ass.

"Well, I pulled my phone from my pocket and pulled out these delectable little things," he holds up Dani's pink panties. "I think they have seen better days, though." My eyes widen. "The only girl who could wear something this cute would have to be Dani."

Instantly, my blood boils. I reach out to grab them from his hand but he pulls back, making me miss my target.

"Way I see it, Bull is going to find out about you two and when he does he is going to know I know. I'm going to end up with at least a bullet and I ain't even screwing the bitch. I think it's only fair I keep 'em." He is laughing so hard, I can barely make out what he's saying.

"You are truly fucked up if you think I'm letting you keep those. If you don't hand them over, right fucking now, I'm going to shoot you in the damn foot again!" I quietly growl at him, hoping Bull is inside the club by now.

"Ah, so you did shoot me in the foot on purpose when we were kids." His tone is serious now.

"I'm about to shoot you in the dick!" I yell at him, getting impatient.

He laughs and throws the panties in my face. "What kind of perfume does she use? Smells fucking great," he says over his shoulder walking toward the clubhouse. I have no doubt he has been smelling them; probably jerked off to them. The man is a freak and a dead man. As soon as I get him to myself, I'm going to put my boot in his head. Just the thought of him looking at Dani's panties has me seeing red.

Chapter Fifteen
Dani

I woke up this morning feeling sore in all the right places. Even now, as I help Babs prepare for tonight's party, each painful move reminds me of where Shadow manhandled me; how he took me without mercy and made me his. Just thinking about it starts the flames of desire licking from the tips of my toes, up through the center of my sex, over the peaks of each hard-nippled breast and flushes my cheeks. I hope no one notices as I sweep floors and stock the bar with assorted brands of beer and liquor. Other women have been coming and going, helping to set up trays of dip for chips and all other sorts of finger foods. Babs said my dad wants a party tonight but she didn't mention if there is an occasion or not. Either way, I'm sure he will want me to go to my room. I am not giving in without a fight this time. I look up from stocking bottles and see my dad and Locks walk in. Locks heads into the kitchen to find Babs, I'm sure.

"Hey, what ya doing?" my dad asks as he ambles up to the bar.

"Just helping out Babs," I reply. "Hey dad, I was thinking I can help bartend tonight," I word vomit, not even thinking before speaking.

"No way, absolutely not." He answers shortly.

"Oh, come on, Bull. She's going to see what goes on in the club eventually, especially now that she's staying," Babs interjects, coming in from the kitchen.

"Whats going on?" Shadow is standing next to my dad looking confused. I didn't even see him come in I was so wrapped up in asking my dad to willingly desensitize me.

"She wants to bartend tonight for the party," my dad tells Shadow, as he rubs his scruffy jaw. I love when he does that; it reminds me of the sound of sandpaper.

"I don't think that's a good idea," Shadow says quickly, his face as worried as I have ever seen it. His expression takes me by surprise for a second. Is he afraid I'll see who he really is at the club's most carefree moments? Will the beast he claims to be come out? It can't be much worse than licking coke off a whore's nipple, come on.

"She can get paid; help get her out of the club. Bet she would do great in tips," Locks says. I turn and glare at him, he just wants me out of the club. I remember him bitching to Shadow about me and my mother staying here.

"Yeah, alright, but don't make me regret this, Dani." My dad gets up from the bar. "You got anything good to eat back there, Babs? I'm starving," he enters the kitchen with Babs and Locks on his tail.

"Can you get me a beer, Firefly?" Bobby asks. I reach down and grab him a Bud Light. When he reaches for the beer, I see dark red blood spattered across his hand and I feel all my own blood drain from my face.

"Shit!" Bobby says, swiping the beer from my hand and rushing toward one of the rooms down the hall. I look up at Shadow and see concern written all over his face. I know I'm getting a peek at the monster under the mask now. What I don't think he understands is that getting a glimpse behind his mask might give me a better idea of what exactly I have hiding behind my own mask.

"I'll be fine; everything will be fine," I assure him, whispering so nobody can hear me.

He nods toward the hallway, gesturing for me to follow. Once we are in my bedroom, he locks the door and turns to me. "I don't want you out there tonight, Dani." Even when he's mad, he's gorgeous.

"Yeah, well, I want to be out there. Are you afraid I will see this beast you claim you are?"

"You think being out there tonight is going to give you a glimpse of my demons? Ha! Maybe a little, but most of my beast lies closer to the idea of what was on Bobby's hands, Dani."

I'm completely taken aback by his comment. Does he think he's a beast because he has killed? Is he a murderer like my mother says; like the news articles said? The thought that he has murdered is a little scary. I'm sure he could kill me in a split second if he wanted to.

"Tonight will just be guys trying to pick you up and get you drunk to have their way with you. Not everyone will back down just because you are the president's daughter," he says, snapping me from my thoughts.

"Like you?" I smile.

He laughs as he runs his hand back and forth through that messy top. "Yeah, like me."

By 6pm there are tons of bikers at the clubhouse; some I have never met before. There's also a sea of half-naked girls. I can't see where Shadow went off to because there are so many bodies and I am being yelled at left and right for shots or bottles of beer.

I am pretty busy, but every once in a while I look out into the crowd and see things I have never seen before. In the corner is a guy from another club who has his head thrown back in ecstasy while a girl is bobbing up and down in his lap giving him a blow job. It turns me on, surprisingly. There are multiple people sniffing coke off the coffee table with rolled up dollar bills. The half-dressed girls are now running around completely naked. After an hour, I have pretty much seen it all. The club becomes thicker with the smell of smoke and cheap perfume; and louder with the cacophony of voices and blaring music. To actually hear what anyone is saying, I have to be face to face and sometimes just lip read.

"Well, look at you," yells a guy with a black bandanna and black beard grown out into a braid. "You must be new. I would remember a gal like yourself." He has a black shirt on with a cut that says he is one of our own; his name, 'OLD MAN', sketched on his worn patch. I haven't seen him before, but there are plenty of the members I haven't met personally.

"What can I get you?" I yell, before taking a sip of the beer I have setting under the bar. His attempt to charm is lost on me; everyone has been flirting. Everyone except Shadow, that is. Where is he?

"How about you on your knees?" he yells back and flicks his tongue out at me. I can only laugh. Seriously, is this a line they use on girls?

"Something funny, bitch?" he sneers, puffing his chest out.

"Yeah, the fact that you think you're God's gift to women. Either tell me what you want to drink or get the hell out of the way so I can help someone else," I yell back at him while sipping my beer again; this being my third one, I can feel my nerves ease and my confidence rise.

"You little cunt!" All of a sudden, he jumps over the counter to grab hold of me with his meaty hands. I instantly grasp the neck of my bottle, ready to wallop the man in the head with it. Before he can make contact, though, his arm is ripped backward. I look past him, following the tattooed arm holding the dirt bag, to find Bobby shaking his head at the man. He leans in and whispers something in Old Man's ear. Old Man's face nearly turns pale, then serious.

"Your dad should get a hold of you before that mouth of yours gets you into trouble," he sneers as he's walking away.

"You are a brave woman talking shit like that to a biker; and what the hell were you going to do with that bottle?" Bobby asks amused; his face full of laughter.

I look at the bottle I'm still clutching in my hand. I'm a little stunned that my first instinct was to fight back.

"You're different," he says, trying to size me up.

"How so?" I ask, taking a swig of the beer.

"Most women don't mouth bikers," he says, laughing. I shrug in response and grin.

Looking out into the crowd, a swarm of people move as one and I spy Shadow standing in a circle of boobs and legs. The sight makes me slightly gasp and my palms sweat. I hate how jealous I am and that just makes me even more pissed. A girl just looking at Shadow makes my claws come out and he isn't doing anything wrong; he is just talking.

Suddenly, in my line of sight, I see a pair of dainty fingers snap. They belong to a woman I haven't seen before. Her short hair is black with streaks of blond slicing through it. Her smoky eyes and bright red lipstick have been meticulously applied. A black leather jacket is covering a red tube top but the counter blocks my view below that. She is quite fierce looking; nothing like the other girls I've seen around here.

"Can I get two beers here!" she yells at me, her voice like silk yet sassy.

"Yeah, sorry," I respond, snapping from my embarrassing gawking episode. I reach down into the cooler and bring out two beers. She rolls her eyes as she snatches them and walks off. I can't help but watch her walk away; her black leather pants are skin tight, showing off everything her mother gave her. I watch those swaying hips walk right toward Shadow and his circle of babes.

"That's Chelsea; she's a hang-around. She's been trying to become Shadow's Ol' Lady since she laid eyes on him," Bobby, now behind me, whispers in my ear.

"And Shadow?" I ask, curious about what Shadow thought of this Chelsea.

"Shadow doesn't do relationships. That's what he tells her, anyway. He has fucked her a couple of times but sent her packing when he was done. She's trouble, he says. I don't think you have anything to worry about." He holds a small glass of clear liquid in front of my face, "here, have a shot with me."

I watch Shadow's face light up when Chelsea hands him a beer; instantly the other girls leave. Are they scared of her? Am I going to have to stake claim of Shadow like I did with Candy?

"Put this salt on your wrist and lick it. Shoot the shot and then bite this lime." Bobby pushes the glass into my hand, snapping my gaze. He turns my other wrist and shakes salt on it. "Lick it."

I dart my tongue out and lick up the grainy salt. He lifts my hand with the tequila, and I shoot it back. I wince visibly, making Bobby chuckle.

"Hurry, bite this. It helps," he says, handing me a lime wedge.

I bite it and feel the sour tingle overcome the burn of the alcohol. My body instantly feels warm.

"I have never done that before. It was awesome!" I yell at him, making him double over in laughter.

I glance over at where Shadow and Chelsea stand and see her lean in and kiss him on the lips. Those are my lips, bitch!

She turns and nestles herself right in front of his body, her back to his chest, claiming him in front of everyone. I literally feel my heart beating through my chest. My fists clench, making my nails cut into my palm. Shadow puts his hands on her hips, not even fighting her off. That just hurts. My eyes sting from the sight happening before me. Chelsea turns and runs her hand down his chest and over his groin. What the fuck?

I start to exit the bar, ready for a throw down, but Bobby grabs my arm and leans into my ear. His frame, large like a football player, overshadows mine.

"Breathe, Dani. If he pushes her away, it's going to raise a lot of fucking questions. If you go over there and make a scene, it's going to raise even more questions. Come drink with me, and breathe." His words make sense but the effects of my heart shattering still run cold, making the hurt vibrate through my limbs.

"Come on, I'm not that bad to be around, am I?" he teases.

I smile and grab three empty shot glasses, slamming them on the bar with a thud.

"Hit me!" I yell at Bobby.

"That's my Firefly!" he yells back proudly.

He grabs a bottle of tequila and fills all three shot glasses to the top. I shake some salt on my wrist, feeling the small crystals coat my skin. I lick my wrist and shoot back the first shot, then the second shot, and finally the third; the burn still not easing any. As I slam the third glass down on the bar, Bobby hands me a lime wedge and I bite it hard. My body temperature is rising rapidly and I start pulling on my shirt.

"It just got really hot in here!" I yell at Bobby.

"Keep your shirt on. Your dad will beat your ass if you flash all these bikers!" He tosses back three shots as well.

I look over at Shadow and see Chelsea whispering into his ear. His face is masked with an unfamiliar look.

"Hey, can I get a shot of Jack!" a voice yells at me from over the bar. I grab a clean shot glass, fill it and hand it over to an older lady.

"Try this; it's called a lemon drop." Bobby hands me another shot glass. "Chicks dig it," he says as I down it without question. It is delicious and comes with less kick than the straight tequila.

"That is so yummy!" I say dramatically, rolling back my eyes and feeling slaphappy. The liquor is clearly taking over.

"We should dance. I could totally dance right now," I say, grabbing on Bobby's arm.

"Eh, how often do you drink?" Bobby yells in my direction, trying to be heard over the loud music of Buckcherry.

"Never. Well, I mean I have had wine here and there, and a shot with my dad the other day," I explain, slurring my words. Bobby's face goes a little pale.

"I'm cutting you off," he yells at me, putting up the tequila bottle.

"What? Why?" I yell in protest. I was just starting to have fun.

I grab Bobby's arm and drag him out on to the dance floor. If Shadow can be a slut, why can't I?

Bobby hesitates and tries to pull out of my grip as I drag him to the few dancing bodies in the center of the room. I start moving my hips in front of his, lowering my body as the song "Crazy Bitch" by Buckcherry takes over.

"You're gonna get me killed, Firefly," he whispers in my ear as he grabs my hips and pulls me close.

"It's fine. My dad went in the back a little while ago with some girls," I assure him.

"It's not your dad I'm talking about."

I try to look back over at Shadow and... what was her name again? All I see is a swarm of people; fuzzy people, I might add. Suddenly, my stomach feels queasy and the room starts shifting.

I look up at Bobby. "I don't-" I stop mid-sentence, choking on my tongue which now feels like it's too big for my mouth.

"Run! Run to the bathroom!" he yells, pushing me in the small of my back toward the hallway. The floor is rolling like the waves at the beach and I am pretty sure I'm stomping because I can't tell if it's on its way up or on its way down. My foot somehow catches on the floor and I go tumbling forward. Bobby catches me just before my nose lands. His hands are huge and hold my frame easily as he picks me up and throws me over his shoulder. The room spins even faster.

"That really didn't help!" I choke, trying to hold back vomit.

"Don't fucking puke on me, damn it!" He rushes down the hall with my body bouncing on his broad shoulder. I clamp my hand over my mouth to hold the bile that's rising.

He slides me down on the floor, right in front of the toilet, just in the nick of time. I lean over and spew a mixture of lime, beer, and tequila.

"Oh, wow, that smells," he says, pulling his shirt over his nose. I glance up at him; he truly is beautiful. His blond curls and blue eyes would make any girl swoon.

"You're so pretty," I pronounce before expelling more vomit.

He leans down and pulls my hair back as I continue to heave into the toilet.

"I have never held a bitch's hair while she vomited. This is really gross," he says in disgust. "And I'm not pretty. I'm handsome, rugged and good looking."

My fuzzy thoughts go back to Chelsea. She is so pretty and seems so secure of who she is, while I'm in here puking my guts out. Not so pretty right now.

"I am pretty!" I yell in a drunken state.

"What?" Bobby asks, laughing.

"I could look hot in leather, right? She was not hot," I cry, vomit dribbling down my chin. I am truly a mess. Never again!

"Chelsea?" Bobby asks. I nod my head more than necessary.

"She is hot in leather and so biker, and I'm not so much. I, ugh... I hate this. I hate this feeling, I mean. No. yes." I am not making any sense. Then I vomit in the toilet one more time, making Bobby laugh again.

"Shadow's a fucking tool. You would be way hotter than Chelsea in leather," Bobby says quietly. Feeling a little better I lift my head up at Bobby.

"Really?" I ask, still insecure.

"Well, maybe not right now," he chuckles and grabs some toilet paper to wipe my chin. All I can manage is a snort in response.

"Besides I've slept with Chelsea before and she's not as hot as you think." He scrunches his face in distaste. "That skank gave me crabs." We both start laughing, even though I'm sure the situation wasn't funny.

"Don't tell anyone I told you that!" he hisses. I nod my head in understanding and slide my fingers across my lips as if I'm zipping them.

"Shit, how much did she have to drink?" Shadow asks, barreling into the bathroom. My sincere gaze at Bobby turns into a sinister grimace toward Shadow. I stumble up, pulling on Bobby as I try to stand. I hold onto the wall as I make my way toward the door frame where Shadow is. There is red lipstick on his neck. The sight of it makes me sick to my stomach, well, more than usual right now.

"You –" I stumble on my drunk tongue. "You have a little slut right there," I say, pointing toward his neck. He steps around me and peers in the mirror, confused.

"Fucking Chelsea!" he mutters under his breath.

I stumble toward the bed. It is literally only six feet from the bathroom but it feels like twenty.

I can hear Bobby and Shadow whispering heatedly at each other, but I cannot make out what they are saying. All I can focus on is the spinning room and it's making me feel like I might vomit again.

"Make the room stop spinning!" I yell out to nobody in particular.

I look over and see Bobby leaving the room. He looks angry. Shadow comes at me from the bathroom.

"Hey, drink this," he demands as he hands me a glass of water. I take a small sip and almost gag.

"No, drink a little more; you'll thank me in the morning." He tips the glass up making me take a bigger sip. I glare at him and wipe my mouth with the back of my hand.

"I'm sorry, Dani," he says sincerely, running his finger over the rim of the glass. His voice is deep and smooth, warming me with every syllable. Maybe it's the liquor talking, but I cannot be mad at him. I didn't like what I saw, but what was he supposed to do exactly. I feel like making him squirm just a little longer, though, so I say nothing.

"I was in a tough spot; everyone knows I mess around with Chelsea. If I told her to get lost everyone would have wondered what was up." Hearing him confess that he messes around with that slut-cake doesn't make me feel any better.

"Then just go be with her," I yell at him. I'm sure it would make everything a lot easier.

"Will you stop acting like that? I don't want her, I want you. It's just complicated," he whispers, his admission that he actually wants to be with me stuns me out of my hissy fit.

"You weren't fighting her off very hard," I whine, not sure if he can understand my words slurring together.

"Well, she's pissed now." He raises his eyebrows. "I told her it wasn't happening." My eyes shoot up and I look at him skeptically. "Like really fucking pissed," he says, laughing. "But, I was worried about you, I've been watching you all night and I knew you had more than you could handle" his voice is heavy with emotion, "and, at that point, I didn't care what others were going to think. Fuck 'em." I'm shocked, I didn't think Shadow was watching me at all, I wonder if he saw me dancing with Bobby?

"Well, Bobby agrees that I would be hotter than Chelsea in leather anyway," I slur.

"Bobby better learn to keep his opinion to himself," Shadow mumbles, while gently guiding me the rest of the way to the bed.

The alcohol takes me down into a deep, dark slumber. I try to open my eyes but it's no use, I'm passed out and I don't even have my shoes off.

Chapter Sixteen
Dani

I wake up to a slight throbbing in my head and the sunlight shining through my window feels like a laser beam. I pull the blankets over my head to block out the light and hear something slide off the bed. I peek over the side and see a large, white gift box on the floor. What the hell is that?

I reach down and grab it. It's heavier than it looks, so I drag it onto the bed with me. I open the lid and find a crisp, white note setting on top of black tissue paper.

"I told you that you would hate me more than like me, but you're mine and mine is the hottest bitch in leather. -S"

A small grin spreads across my face as I reread the note. I rip the tissue paper open and uncover a jet black leather jacket folded up. I run my fingers over the leather as the smell of it overtakes the room.

The door opens and Shadow steps in. "Do you like it?" he asks with his hands in his pockets. He's nervous; how cute.

"I fucking love it!" I respond, making him laugh. "Nobody has ever given me anything like this before." I pull out the jacket to admire it. The only time I've ever been given anything was when it was expected, like a birthday.

"Well, I have never given a gift before, so it's a first for me, too," he says quietly and sits down next to me.

"Do you remember anything from last night?" he asks me, shifting his body behind me on the bed. I lay back and nestle myself on top of his hard chest; his masculine smell makes my senses instantly wake up.

"Some," I reply back.

"Don't ever think that you are not as hot as someone else, don't ever stoop that low again," he whispers in my ear. His tone is dominant and not to be messed with.

He grabs my chin and lifts it so I'm staring right into scorching blue eyes "Don't ever drink that much again, either." He leans in and grazes his lips across mine.

"Let's get you in the shower and brush your teeth, babe," he says laughing and pushing me off his chest. I'm sure I smell of vomit and stale liquor.

Getting out of bed, I notice for the first time that I have been stripped down to my red bra and panties. Shadow must have taken my clothes off after I passed out. Ugh, red. After that girl last night, I can't stand the color of red. Just the thought of her has me all pissed off again. I head for the bathroom with Shadow right behind me. When I reach the sink, I place my hands on the counter and glare as he's turning on the shower.

He sees me staring at him; I'm sure my face radiates my hatred.

"Who was that girl last night, Shadow?" I finally ask.

"Chelsea," he answers flatly.

"Who is she to you?" I wonder if she's actual competition, or just another bed notch like Candy.

He grabs the hem of his shirt and pulls it over his head; my eyes immediately dart to his toned abs and happy trail. He's not playing fair. I can't be pissed and focus on our conversation when he takes his shirt off and looks like that.

"She started coming around when Bobby and I became prospects. I started sleeping with her here and there. She got clingy, though; wanted more, wanted to be my Ol' Lady. That shit wasn't happening, though. I just didn't see her for anything more than a good lay." He spoke matter of fact. I nodded my head in understanding, somewhat. I hated that he had slept with her; she was beautiful, not trashy like Candy.

He walks up behind me and starts kissing my neck lightly. My skin flutters with goose bumps in response to his tender lips.

"She's just another club whore to me; she's not you. Nobody can be you." He whispers against my skin, his breath so warm and sticky on my neck I turn my head, inviting him deeper.

The scent of Shadow in the bed permeates my brain before I'm fully awake. I've gotten used to waking up like this over the past week. It started that day Shadow made love to me in the shower. Our hands slipped and slid all over each other. Our mouths nipped and sucked at every inch of wet skin we could reach. The shower stall filled with heavy moans and loud panting. My body molded to Shadow's perfectly; like I was made for him. Every time he touched me, whether it be his mouth, hands, or scruffy jaw scraping my delicate skin, I could feel our relationship flourish.

I felt my emotions becoming deeper. Some would call it love, but how can you love someone you've known for just a short amount of time? Telling Shadow I am falling in love with him would surely scare him away. A guy who doesn't do relationships would piss himself at the three little words a normal guy just dreads. I won't say it until he does; when I know it won't push him away.

The rest of the week went by much like what unfolded in the shower that day. We made love multiple times and even fucked a couple. Of course, we had to sneak and hide. Watching over our shoulders at every second was exhausting, but Shadow said it was necessary. Go figure, the first time I fall in love it has to be in complex terms.

A few club whores flirted with Shadow over the week, but I just bit my lip and made myself busy.

Afterwards, Shadow would come find me and fuck me into ecstasy like I was the only girl in the world.

Shadow only stayed the night a couple of times. When he didn't, he was all I thought about. We even texted like teenagers to help the emptiness we felt when we were apart. I can feel the affection from Shadow growing deeper, but he hasn't said I love you yet; not even close. He has, though, become even more possessive. He doesn't want me to talk to the other guys, and he's telling me what I can and can't wear. I know he cares even if he doesn't come right out and say it.

Shadow left my bed early this morning. He had to go take care of some club business; said he would only be gone for a couple of hours. I don't know what he's doing, but according to Babs, you never ask the guys what they are doing. I get up and follow my usual routine of getting a shower and brushing my teeth with Shadow's toothbrush.

I grab my last clean bra and panties set and a not-so-dirty pair of shorts. In the closet I find the last clean tee, too. I need to do laundry today, and that will help keep my mind off Shadow for a while.

I walk to the back of the kitchen to a little nook off to the side; it holds a little white washer and dryer. I throw my clothes in the washer and grab the laundry soap bottle. It's empty. There must be more around here somewhere. I search the cabinets in the small room but don't find any soap.

I walk through the kitchen, into the main area and find Babs cleaning as usual. "Hey, Babs, where can I find a new bottle of laundry soap?" I ask.

She waves me to follow her. In the kitchen, she pulls a door open that leads to a pantry. Shelves are filled with cleaning supplies, paper products, everything needed to run a clubhouse. "Shit, we're completely out of soap. Have to go get some." She says shaking her head.

"I can go. I need to get out of here anyway; getting cabin fever," I offer.

"I can get Charlie to take you," she says, leaving the pantry. When we get back into the main area, Babs yells for Charlie who comes running in from outside. As loud as Babs is, I'm not surprised he heard her.

"Hey, babe, go get some laundry soap and take Dani with you. Girl could use some sun," Babs says, handing Charlie some cash. "Just go up to the Mom and Pop's store." He nods his head in agreement.

I grab my new leather jacket and my phone before running out to the courtyard.

Charlie climbs onto a bike similar to Bobby's. As soon as I'm settled on the back, I feel uneasy. I feel like I'm doing something wrong by climbing on the back of the bike with Charlie. I place my hands on the side of the seat and lightly on his hip, trying to make as little contact as possible. If Shadow saw this, he would be pissing fire, I'm sure. That's why I feel so uneasy about this; as protective as Shadow has been, this would be sure to throw him in hostile territory.

Charlie starts the bike and takes off. His bike is fast but he doesn't go near as fast as Shadow. The sun feels great on my skin and the smell of the water is breathtaking. After about fifteen minutes, we pull up to a little white building that strongly resembles a gas station. A sign reads 'MOM AND POP'S' above the door frame.

"I'll go get the soap. Be right back." Charlie says to me and heads inside.

I take my helmet off while I wait; it is suffocating me. Suddenly, I hear a weird noise. I climb off the bike, helmet still in hand, and listen for where the sound is coming from. It sounds like there's a hurt animal behind the building. I look over at the doors Charlie had gone through to see if there is any sign of him coming out; there's none. I move closer to the side of the building and the noise gets louder. When I'm nearly behind the building, I see a black puppy with its leash caught on a bush.

"Aw, you poor thing," I coo, trying not to frighten it. I grab the leash and pull fiercely, breaking limbs in the process. When it's free, the puppy looks up at me for a split second then cowers down, lets out a distressed howl and takes off like a bat out of hell, leash and all. What the hell? I take a step after it and I'm suddenly pulled back with force. I drop the helmet as a hand grabs me by my forehead and holds me against a strong body. While I try to pry the hand off my head, a white cloth is slammed over my mouth. I open my mouth to scream, causing me to inhale whatever is on the cloth. Everything becomes numb. Blackness swamps my vision.

My head is throbbing; throbbing so bad that I can feel it in my neck. I need to get up and get some pain reliever. I must have slept wrong. I open my eyes and see an unfamiliar wall. I sit up on a stained, queen-sized mattress and in a flash everything comes back to me. The puppy. The cloth. The darkness. Ah, my head. I reach up and touch my head and feel something thick and moist. I bring my hand down and see blood on my fingertips; why in the hell am I bleeding? I look around the room; it's just empty. I feel my heartbeat accelerating; my blood rushing like the Nile. I'm panicking. "Breathe, Dani, breathe," I whisper, trying to calm myself. Panicking will get me nowhere.

Looking around the room, I see two rectangular windows near the ceiling. Wondering if I can reach one, I climb out of the bed and instantly feel an excruciating pain in my ankle. There's a metal clasp around it, attached to a chain. Forget panicking, I am on the verge of a heart attack. I run for the door but the chain stops me short, slamming me backwards to the floor.

"Help! Can anyone hear me?" I scream, frantically.

My voice trembles with fear; my spine stiffens. "Hello?" I yell and scream for help, but nobody answers. The voice making blood curdling pleas for help sounds like it is coming from someone else; someone scared that she might die. I have nearly lost my voice and my throat screams for something cool to ease the fire burning within.

I curl up on the bed in a fetal position; the smell of leather from my jacket surrounding me. Just then a glimmer of hope strikes: my phone. I've been so panicked I forgot I grabbed it before we left the clubhouse. I feel around the pockets of my shorts; nothing. I look in my leather jacket; nothing, no phone. They must have taken it. Of course, they did; that's kidnapping 101.

"Shadow," I whisper. Tears begin to caress my face, dripping off my lips onto the soiled mattress. The jacket reminds me of him; more tears hurdle themselves over the rims of my eyes. Does Shadow know I am even missing? Who kidnapped me? What do they want? Are they going to kill me? The last thought feels like I've been stabbed in the heart. The thought that I may never see Shadow again, that I may never live a life free of manipulation, has me holding my breath.

I hear a commotion beyond the door, breaking up my pity party. I try to quiet my sobbing and slow my panicked breathing so I can listen.

"This is so fucked up, Cassie, I can't believe we did this," an unfamiliar, scratchy male voice echoes through the wall.

"Well, it's not like I had much of a fucking choice, Ricky," an unfamiliar female voice ridicules.

"They're going to be pissed. You think you're in shit now, you wait. This is not how they go about things!" the male voice says back.

"Hey, you are in this as much as I am, asshole! We've got someone they want. Adrian will either give us the cash or the drugs and then we split town."

Adrian, who the hell is Adrian? They have the wrong girl, I don't know an Adrian.

Chapter Seventeen
Shadow

 I hate leaving Dani, but Bull insists I need to check out the warehouse with him. Got a call that some unfamiliar bikers have been around the area. I have no doubt it is the El Locos, but I can't point a finger of blame unless we have proof. Well, Bull can't. We pull up to the old warehouse where we keep a lot of our merchandise; not everything, we're not stupid. We keep our drugs and weapons in different warehouses around the state under different handles. That way if we ever get busted they won't get everything.
 "Car tracks!" I point to the dirt road as I slide off my bike.
 "Yeah, that's not good, brother," Locks chimes in. Someone has been here. If it was a rival club there would more than likely be motorcycle tracks; but that's not always the case. Especially seeing that the only rivals we have right now are the El Locos, and let's face it, they are dip-shits.
 "Looks like someone tried to break in, but failed," Bobby says, inspecting the locks on the door.
 "I'm sure they'll be back to try again. Let's get this shit moved. We need to start watching our tails, someone's following us." Bull says, climbing back on his bike. "Considering we still got heat rolling on us, we can't rule anything out."
 I climb on my bike for the ride back when Bull's phone rings. "What's up, Charlie?... Calm down, calm down. I can't understand a fucking word you're saying!" Bull yells. For some reason the hair on the back of my neck stands on end, and an arctic chill roars up my back.
 "Are you fucking kidding me?... Where are you?... Get to the club now!" Bull demands into the phone, his

hand trembling and his face the darkest shade of red I have ever seen.

"What's up?" I ask.

"Dani's missing. Charlie thinks someone took her." Bull starts his bike without further explanation. My heart stops beating; my blood pools to my feet. My Dani was taken; the girl I live and breathe for is missing. I start my bike instantly and head toward the club. The speed I'm driving leaves everyone in my dust. The whole time my heart hammers against my chest; my hands grip the handlebars so tight my knuckles are white. I will kill whoever took Dani. I will seek their blood and piss on their corpses when I find them. I will show no mercy.

We pull up to the courtyard and Charlie is outside pacing. I park my bike, throw my helmet to the pavement and start toward him; seeking some kind of clue as to what has happened. How was Dani even taken? I didn't even have to ask, he started spilling his guts instantly.

"We needed laundry soap. Dani wanted to ride with, so I took her. I went inside to get the soap. She waited outside. I came back out and she wasn't on the bike where I left her. I yelled for her, but nothing. I circled the building and found Dani's helmet on the ground." His eyes glassed up and his face went soft. "I fucked up."

The rage filling my very existence is at its breaking point. Why in the hell would he leave her outside? Why was she even on the back of his fucking bike? Without another thought, I rear my fist back and crack Charlie across the jaw. He stumbles back but doesn't go down. This fucking prick took my girl on the back of his bike, breaking a club law, and then didn't even protect her? Hell no! I grab him by his shirt and crack him in his mouth again, blood splattering across my fist as it collides with his mouth. I am going to kill him with my bare hands.

"You took her without permission and then didn't even protect her, you piece of shit!" I grit out between my teeth.

"Calm down, Shadow. Let him go!" Bobby yells, coming up from behind me and pulling my death grip from Charlie.

Bobby leans his head next to me, "you better get hold of yourself. I know you are a fucking mess, but everyone is going to wonder why you are taking this so personal."

"Let them think what they want," I huff. I don't care anymore. All I want is to know that Dani is safe, and who has her. A part of me knows he's right, though. I lost my cool with the thought of her on someone else's bike and the fact he didn't protect her. It's like she's my Ol' Lady; that I have subconsciously claimed her. I know the last week with her made me feel for her on a whole different level, I just didn't realize how fucking deep 'til now.

Dani

The voices on the other side of the wall have gone quiet without revealing any usable information. What the hell would anyone want from me? Whatever it is, I won't go down without a fight. I will cut, claw and kill whoever I need to to survive. Ha, listen to me, I sound so bad-ass. The Dani in New York would never have said that. She would have let them do whatever they wanted, and would have given them whatever they needed. That was when I was weak and I molded to whatever form my mother wanted. I'm convinced my mother saw the evil lurking within me, even before I did. I can see now why she shielded me from anything that would have provoked the darkness within. Shadow and my father's club lures the savage out.

Enough of this sitting around. It's time to fight and survive.

I climb off the bed, the chain rattling as I walk over to the door. It stops me about a foot short, so I lean over and start slamming my fist against the old door. My heart hammers with adrenaline and the fight to live.

"Let me the fuck out!" I scream, my voice crude and every bit of rude.

"Sounds like the priss is awake," the male voice says. I hear footsteps coming toward the door. I back up, ready to pounce on the first person that comes through. When the door opens, I see the man that took me against my will. His brown hair shags down to his eyes; it's oily and unruly. He's wearing a flannel shirt with the sleeves ripped off and stained blue jeans. He smiles; his teeth rotting out; his thin colorless lips snarling. His eyes are dull like someone who should be in rehab or in a casket.

"Well, well," he rasps. The sound of his voice is infuriating, making him my target. I pull my fist back and connect it with his oily face. He stumbles and falls to the dirty floor; curses flying from his mouth. I start toward him, the chain rattling behind me, to kick him in his stomach but, he grabs me by the foot and pulls me to the ground with him.

"You little bitch!" he yells, his breath permeating my space. I can feel my stomach protest at its rancid smell. He punches me in the face with no warning. His knuckles collide with my mouth, making my teeth sink deep into my lip. I immediately taste blood. My face screams out in pain and I see stars. He jumps to his feet, rears back his black boot, and connects it with my ribs. My eyes water to the point I have to close my eyes. My breath stolen from my lungs, I gasp for air. He leans down and grasps me by the throat, squeezing tightly. His muscle no match for mine, he brings me to my feet. My eyes pop open and stare at the man who is killing me by refusing my lungs air.

"Put her down, Ricky," the raspy female voice sounds from behind me. "We can't use her if you kill her."

Ricky's eyes squint and scowl at me, but his grip releases and I fall to the ground. I instantly reach for my throat and take in the sweet air I was deprived of. I choke and sputter as my lungs inhale that first shaky breath. I was stupid and naive to think I could overpower him. I will need to be smart about this if I ever want to see Shadow again.

"You would do well not to do that shit again," the woman says, walking over and squatting down in my line of view.

Her jet black hair is tangled into a rat's nest; her body nothing but bones. She is wearing a ratty red t-shirt; her arms stained with needle marks from drug use. I look into her eyes and see dull, lifeless blue eyes, the corners etched with wrinkles. She smiles and her teeth are rotted out, her breath sneaking out and stealing mine with a rancid tide.

"I'm Cassie. This is Ricky. Next time you wanna play boxer, I'm not going to stop him. Got that?" she asks, her forehead gathering wrinkles.

How dare she. I wouldn't have to play boxer if they didn't take me against my will. My beast wants to be released again. I grit my teeth at the bitch.

"Fuck you!" I whisper, my eyes never leaving hers.

She nods her head as she stands. "I can see why Adrian likes you. You're feisty." She laughs, taking joy in my displeasure. Who the hell is this woman?

"What do you want with me?" I ask, my voice cracks from the assault from Ricky. I try and stand, wincing at the burn coming from my ribs, the pain so hostile my vision becomes blurry. I wonder if the fucker cracked my rib; as bad as it hurts it wouldn't surprise me. Cassie sees my pain and tries to help me to the bed. Her touch repulses me and I slap her hands away. "Get the hell away from me!"

"You Adrian's Ol' Lady?" she asks as she sniffles. Ignoring my comment, she sets me on the bed.

"I don't know an Adrian," I yell, frustrated, making me wince again.

She sniffs loudly again; taking the back of her hand she wipes her nose with it. Suddenly it all makes sense. This junkie is Shadow's mother. Is Ricky his father? Is Adrian, Shadow?

Shadow

I sit at the same wooden table we do every other day. Usually, though, we are discussing shipments and payments. I never thought we would be talking about the fate of someone I care deeply about. Care deeply about; listen to me, I am pussy whipped beyond repair. I instantly regret pushing Dani away, holding out on her. The short time I had with her wasn't enough, and in my world I wasn't optimistic Dani would come back the Dani she was when they took her. Thoughts of her being raped and abused surfaced, making my stomach curdle with gut wrenching regret.

"Bobby, see if that store has surveillance," Bull says.

"Got it, Boss," Bobby responds, rising from the table.

"I'll go with him." I need to clear my head. Sitting here thinking of shit that could be happening to Dani is not helping me. I know who has her; just have no idea where they've taken her.

We walk out onto the courtyard. Grabbing my helmet off the ground where I threw it earlier, I start putting it back on my head. The simple gesture sparks a memory of when Dani had such a hard time with her helmet. That was her first ride; the thought makes my lips curl into a smile. A smile I hadn't had all damn day, not since I last saw Dani anyway.

"You going to be alright, man," Bobby asks, climbing on his bike. I don't answer because the truth is that if something happens to Dani, it will be earth shifting.

We pull up to Mom and Pop's store. Once inside, the smell of candy and bread invade my nose. I see Ma and head toward her. The club helps support this little shindig, so they know us well.

"Hey, Ma, you got your cameras on?" I ask her politely.

"I always got my cameras on, son; you can't trust anybody these days. Why you ask?" she asks, her voice shaky with old age. Ma had to be in her late seventies, her and Pa have had this place since I could remember. I am pretty sure only Devil's Dust comes here, I haven't seen anybody else.

"Just got a situation that took place earlier. I would like to see them if that's alright." I lean up against the counter, trying to control the urgency of my voice. I take a deep breath.

"Sure, follow me." She walks into a door behind the counter, leaving me and Bobby to follow. She sits down in a rusty metal chair with a computer monitor sitting on a desk.

"What do you need exactly?" she asks, looking up at me.

"Go back to around the time Charlie was here," I tell her. She knows who Charlie is because we send him after a lot of crap; bitch work. Considering what went down today, if he isn't kicked in the fucking ground, he'll be doing a lot of bitch work for a while.

Ma starts rewinding and then stops. I see Dani and Charlie pull up to the parking lot. The sight of her makes my heart gallop. I'm determined to find her. Yet I see red and want to blow Charlie's head off for having her on the back of his bike. When you have a girl on the back of your bike, she is your responsibility. Her being the president's daughter should make that more than a rule; it's law. Instead he treated her as if she was Candy on the back of his bike. The thought makes me high with anger; this shit isn't over with me and Charlie.

    I see Dani walk to the side of the building.

    "You got cameras on the back lot?" Bobby asks.

    She presses a button and an image of the back lot pops up. You can barely see Dani's head at the bottom of the screen; the camera pointing toward the parking lot instead of her. Within seconds, I see Dani's hands flailing around and a rusty blue, older style Maxima pull up into the view of the camera. I see a man with a mask on carrying Dani's lifeless body toward the trunk. The thought makes me swell with anger. The man is having trouble putting Dani in the trunk; he seems familiar to me. Then I see a person getting out of the car to help the man.

    "That's the junkie; my mother. I fucking knew it!" I yell. She threatened to take Dani, I just never thought she'd have the balls to do it. That bitch is as good as dead.

Dani

    "What's your name?" Cassie asks. I just look at her, her body completely taken by drugs long ago. I wasn't telling her my name, screw her.

    "Fine. I don't need your name," she says flatly. "Tell me about the club; they run guns? I know they have drugs being an MC, right? You being Adrian's Ol' Lady, I'm sure you know." She fires the questions rapidly, sitting on the stained mattress with me.

    Why does she want to know this; telling her would make me a rat. Images of the articles on the computer I had found that night flicker through my head. The club takes care of rats in a way I didn't want, they kill them. Even if I'm the president's daughter, being a rat wouldn't go unpunished; even I know that.

"She ain't going to tell you shit," Ricky rasps. Their voices are making my head hurt. The pain from my head, my busted lip, and sore ribs makes me see double. I just want to sleep, sleep in Shadow's arms; just one more time.

"Doesn't look like Adrian is showing up with drugs or money. Now what?" Ricky asks, making me aware of Shadow's absence.

"We could call Poppy," Cassie says, her smile so disgusting it rips at my skin.

"Ah, Poppy. I bet she would go for a pretty buck!" he says in astonishment, his smile mimicking hers.

"Who's Poppy?" I ask, the name making my skin crawl as it slips from my lips.

"Now she wants to talk," Cassie says, proud of herself.

"Poppy buys girls and sells them to men with lots of money. A girl like you, I bet, would go to a high bidder." Ricky raises his eyebrows.

If I don't tell them what they want to know, they are going to sell me into sex trafficking, but if I talk, I am sealing my fate with the club. My heart thrums with alertness. I feel cornered; no way out. Why hasn't Shadow come for me? He should have noticed I was gone by now. Sex trafficking means being abused, drugged, raped, and my soul branded into an object. I wouldn't be a human; I would be owned. Shadow is not the beast he claims he is. This bitch he calls a mother is a beast. Men like Ricky and Poppy; they are beasts.

"I'll give him a call," Ricky says, leaving the room.

I jump to my feet, pain ripping through my body and making it hard to think clearly. "Wait!" I yell.

Ricky skids to a halt at the door frame.

"How is Shadow, er, I mean Adrian supposed to give you what you want if he doesn't know who has me?" I reason, trying to think on my toes at where I am going with this. I am merely trying to stall them.

"What do you mean; he knows who has you. I told him what would happen if he didn't give me what I want. I've given him plenty of time," Cassie says, as she lifts off the bed to join Ricky.

"He is in a Motorcycle Club. I have had plenty of threats of being taken, sweetheart. He has no clue who has me," I say, my tone flat and shaky. As far I know only she has threatened to take me, but maybe if I play my cards right I can make contact with Shadow so he can pinpoint exactly where I am.

"What's your point, bitch?" Ricky asks, irritated.

"Call him; tell him where I am? Take a picture of my face?" I say, pointing to my busted lip and my head. If it looks as bad as it feels, it will make Shadow blow his lid for sure. "Show him you're not messing around," I pronounce, matter-of-fact.

"And what happened to my head anyway?" I ask, as it throbs loudly.

"I couldn't get you in the fucking trunk," Ricky says, laughing. So glad my pain brings him pleasure.

They both look at each other, both wondering if I had a point.

"Go get her phone," she orders Ricky. He rolls his eyes and mumbles off into the other room. He comes back with my phone and starts trying to figure out how to take a picture. I look around the room to see if something can help locate where I am, but even I don't know where I am.

"Maybe you should take me into the other room; the lighting in here sucks. He will never see my busted lip with the lighting in here," I say, trying to play them over. Night is coming on and the two little windows did nothing for light. Maybe in the other room there is a larger window and something out the window will place my location. I have to be quick with night approaching so fast.

"Nice try, bitch. I worked hard on that chain. You're staying in here where you can't escape," Ricky says, pointing the phone in my direction. My gut wrenches; Shadow will never know where I am. They will give a drop location and never deliver me. They will sell me to Poppy and I will never be with Shadow or my dad again.

"Shit, she's right. This damn lighting in here sucks. We are going to have to take her to the other room," Cassie says, looking at the picture. My heart resumes beating; a flicker of hope springs to the surface.

"Shit," Ricky says, agreeing with her after looking at the picture. He walks over to me and pulls a key from his pocket. He leans over and takes off the metal cuff suffocating my ankle. Once released, the relief makes me moan in gratification. He grabs my forearm hard, his fingers bruising my delicate skin.

"Don't fucking try anything," he hisses in my face, his breath so deadly it brings bile to my throat.

He pushes me into the other room. My eyes sway around the room taking in anything I might be able to get my hands on to help my escape. The floor looks like it has never seen a broom or mop, the only furniture is an old ripped blue couch and an oval kitchen table with two rickety chairs around it. Ricky pushes me in front of the table with used drugs littered across it. His grip tightens making the circulation difficult in my arm. I wince. I notice behind the table is a window; it has a blind halfway torn down and I can see pink and blue lights illuminating the dark sky through the window. It's not much, but maybe the odd, "Miami Vice" looking building will give Shadow a clue as to where I am.

Ricky stands behind me. His arm snakes around the front of me and grasps my throat tightly. I wince from the harsh contact, my skin still sensitive from when he choked me earlier. I can still breathe, but his grip makes it difficult and my panic rises. His dirty fingernails cut into my skin and I can feel my blood rush to the small nicks he is causing.

"Yeah, I think we should still sell her to Poppy. Give some poor bastard an early Christmas," he snarls in my ear while thrusting his hips into my lower back. His erection is evident and I gag. I look up at Cassie, wondering if she is seeing this, but she is messing with my phone and not paying attention.

This is it for me. I'm going to die in this shit hole. I will never see Shadow or anyone again. I feel a tear slide down my cheek, making me feel vulnerable. Ricky turns my head to the side and snakes his tongue out of his dry cracked lips. I whimper and try to pull free but he grips my throat tighter forcing me in place. His cold, slippery tongue darts to my fallen tear and licks its presence, leaving behind his slimy trail of an existence. I look into his eyes; the eyes of an empty shell with no remorse or regret.

"Yeah, I bet he would pay more than Adrian; would get us a lot further," she answers Ricky as she points the camera in my direction and takes a picture. Looking at these two, reality sets in. What if Shadow doesn't come quick enough and this Poppy comes to get me? I can see some Cuban man named Poppy smoking on a cigar, laughing in excitement at how much I would sell for. I have to try and fight. I can't just let these junkies sell me into sex slavery so they can run from whatever it is they can't face.

Without thinking, I rear my head back and bust Ricky in the nose. He bellows out in pain and stumbles back. I see my chance to run for the door and take flight, not thinking about Cassie. As soon as I round the table, she grabs me by the hair, "Oh, no, you don't, bitch!" she snarls, halting me in my run for safety. The door only feet away from me, I can almost taste my freedom. I can't stop fighting; I have to get out of here. I bust my elbow in her nose, making her scream out in pain and she lets go of my hair. I push her bony body away from me and run for the door.

    Just as my hands grab for the door's golden handle, I feel my body push toward the door unwillingly. Before I can look back at what is happening, my forehead bashes into the door. I whelp in pain, grabbing my forehead. Ricky snatches me by the hair, pulling so tight I can feel my hair snapping and breaking and my new injury bursts with pain.

    "Let me go!" I scream, my hands clawing for his hands, my nails scraping and tearing at his arms.

    "You're not going to sell well if you're all beat up, I hope you fuck as hard as you fight, princess." Ricky whispers in my ear. His hot, sticky breath makes my spine stiffen in alert. With his dirty fingers tangled in my hair, he throws me to the ground like a wet mop. My ribs scream out in the most excruciating pain imaginable. My body can't take anymore. My vision is blurry and my body screams from every angle in pain.

    "You stupid bitch. I can't wait to sell your sorry ass to Poppy!" Cassie yells, holding her nose up high to stop the bleeding. She stumbles over to me and kicks me in the ribs. Her blow is not as forceful as Ricky's, but it's enough to make me see black spots. I try and fight the darkness invading my vision, scared of what Ricky might do if he gets the chance.

    "Shadow will find me and he will kill you." I whisper, delirious with pain. They both start chuckling at my response.

    "Oh, honey, you're a hoot. Once we get our money, your ass is sold and we are gone." Cassie laughs between each word.

    "Then I will find you and kill you myself." My voice trembles, revealing how scared I truly am. The darkness finally pulls me under, the pain is too much for my body to tolerate.

In my darkness, I see Ricky's nasty tongue swimming around like a serpent. Cassie's raspy laugh cracks black walls. My mother's face telling me, "I told you so". I'm swimming in a darkness that's my hell; no Shadow. Where is Shadow? He has to come. He wouldn't leave me here; my dad wouldn't leave me here, would they? Is this my fate; I'm either going to die or become a slave. The darkness that swims within me is weak and hiding, giving up and wanting to die before it's dealt a fate it has no control over.

I open my eyes. My vision still blurry, I see Shadow's face. His blue, smoldering eyes are blazing with fire and rage. His cheeks are full of stubble and his jaw set to worry. His lips part to allow his harsh breathing. His black hair, thicker on the top and shorter on the sides, make my fingers itch for it. He's so handsome. Clearly this is just a dream, my pain induced state making me see things. I reach out, trying to feel for his face, as I sob.

"My beast," I breathe, still lying on the dirty floor where Ricky and Cassie left me.

"Dani, I'm here, baby. Nobody is going to hurt you anymore." His voice is full of emotion; he seems so real I can even smell him. He wraps his bulky arms around my frame, picking me up from the floor. I yell in pain as he lifts me.

"What is it, baby? What's wrong?" he says, worry etching every word.

I can't speak so I just point to my ribs; my eyes squint shut with such pain. He gently pulls my shirt up and I not only hear him gasp, I can feel his chest rise and fall rapidly.

"Fuck. Okay. Just wrap your hands around my neck. I'm going to get you out of here. It's going to hurt, but I'm getting you out of here." He places my hands above his head and cocoons my body with his arms. My head falls into the nook of his neck. I feel safe; my body relaxes knowing Shadow has me. If this is hell, I want to live here forever.

"Are you real?" I sob.

"Yes, baby, I'm real," he whispers into my hair and then gently kisses my head. He turns toward the door; my prince charming rescuing me.

"What the fuck?" Ricky hollers. My body immediately tenses; images of him thrusting his pelvis into me and his slithering tongue make my spine go straight. I lift my head to see him and Cassie entering the front door. Bobby is standing next to us, along with Bull and the crew. The whole gang came to save me.

"Hold on to my neck, Dani," Shadow whispers. I tangle my hands together and try my hardest to hold my weight as Shadow reaches for something behind him. In a millisecond, he is stomping toward Ricky. He points an unforgiving silver pistol and without a second thought, pulls the trigger. Brains, skull, and blood spatter across the room. Gun powder and something metallic, caress my senses. Cassie screams and runs from the house.

"Shit!" Bobby yells, running after her.

With a deep sigh, I replace my head in Shadow's neck. I think I just saw the beast that masks him from being normal.

He climbs in the back seat of a car, never letting me go. I wince with pain as he adjusts us; his hand brushes the hair away from my face. His thumb planting circles on my cheek, he leans in, "don't you leave me again." I just nod, my head thumping with pain as I do so. Did Shadow save me? Is this real? I try to open my eyes and look at Shadow, but blackness snakes its way around and takes me into a deep, unforgiving pool.

"I... I fucking love you, Dani," Shadow whispers in my ear.

This clearly is a dream; Shadow doesn't love.

I'm sitting in my bed at the clubhouse; the sight and smell of the old place makes me feel at home. I wonder if they ever caught Cassie; the question makes me uneasy. Fear rattling my cage, I gulp a dry swallow, trying to stomach it all.

"Doc's here, Dani," Shadow says, brushing my hair away from my face. I have never seen such a caring side of Shadow. I turn, wincing from just the slightest movement.

"Hey, Dani, you can call me Jessica." The blond beauty struts into the room wearing white scrubs and carrying a black bag. When they said Doc was coming, I envisioned an old, bald guy with nasal hair.

"What hurts, honey?" she asks, pulling out a stethoscope from her black bag.

"I have a headache and my ribs," I rasp. Just talking makes my head throb and my ribs bite with torturous pain.

"What about your neck?" she asks, nodding toward my neck.

"My neck?"

"It looks like you were choked; were you raped?" she asks with sensitivity.

"What?" Shadow steps up next to Jessica.

She stands up and places her arms on Shadow's shoulders pushing him back. Just the simple gesture makes me jealous.

"I need you to go stand outside, Shadow. All of you need to give us some privacy," Jessica says, still pushing Shadow toward the door. For the first time, I see Bull and Bobby standing in the doorway.

"Yeah, I need to talk to you and Bobby anyway, Shadow," Bull says, grabbing Shadow's shoulder roughly.

Once Bobby and Shadow leave the room, Bull pops his head back in. "Uh, Doc?" Bull asks roughly, his voice full of authority and hostility.

"Yes?" she answers, sitting back down on the bed. She looks at my dad over her shoulder.

"When you're done with Dani, you may want to stick around."

"Hmm, I wonder what that's about." She looks at me with her left eyebrow lifted.

Shadow

When I received the picture of Dani beaten within an inch of her life and saw the way Ricky had his fucking hands on her, the beast was released without thought. I'd know that ugly pink and blue lighting in the background of that picture anywhere; it's a bar Bobby dragged me to years ago. After finding the bar, it was only minutes before we found the house. I had my head so wrapped up in Dani, I didn't even wait for Bull to give orders. I just went in, ready to blow anyone's head off that stood in my way. When I saw Dani on the floor beaten, I lost all thought. I felt like I had no control; hopeless, afraid, and in love.

I still can't believe I told Dani I loved her. I didn't realize the feelings that had been stirred up were ones of actual love. Can a guy like me love, is it possible? Is it possible to love a guy like me? After saying the words without meaning to, I know I feel deeply for Dani, but I just don't trust her, not fully anyway. In the world I live in, trust is harder to earn than love. Take me sitting here at this table, all my brothers eyeing me, because I broke the law of trust among us.

"You fucking Dani?" Bull asks, his voice bitter and cold.

Not all that happy to give all my brothers images for their spank bank, I grit my teeth and answer, "yes."

"You know about this, Bobby?" Bull asks. I feel regret wash over me for bringing Bobby into this, but I tried to warn the fucker.

Bobby looks over the table at me, his stare held straight. We were brothers before this club, and I knew he had my back to the grave.

"Yes, I did." He speaks with courage but we both know we are only minutes from pissing ourselves. Bull is not one to be messed with, especially when it comes to trust. One time we had a prospect get arrested and all the boy did was mention the club was having a party, that Bull had lined it up for us to have some coke and whores to relax with. Thankfully, we had the cop in our pocket so nothing came of it. Sadly for the new prospect, though, he was put six feet under, but not before Bull tore his tongue out with an old rusty knife for ratting.

"Trust like a sinner," Bull mutters under his breath.

"I'm not someone you would normally trust; hell, I'm the biggest sinner there is, but I thought this club had a circle of trust. You broke my trust, boys, something that's not easily earned." Bull speaks with primal authority.

"You think Dani is tough enough to live in this world? Her mother wasn't. What makes you think I want the likes of you being with my little girl? I know the fucked up world you live in. The darkness that rattles your cage is not something I want around my daughter," Bull roars as he pounds his fist into the table. I forget that Bull knows a lot about my shadows; shadows I will have to reveal to Dani eventually.

"She hasn't been here a month, and just a piece of you nearly gets her killed, maybe even raped. She may leave, my daughter I just met, might leave because she can't stand to be around you, one of my best men. What am I supposed to do about that?" Bull asks, his voice calm and smooth. It was as if he was bipolar, one minute yelling and slamming tables, the next quiet and cool.

Dani is a big girl, maybe for once she would like to make her own choices and her own life. Sadly for her, if she is mine, that will never happen.

"I think-"

"You don't get to think," Bull yells, cutting me off, "thinking has you fucking up my club and having brothers lying for you. You broke a law!" he screams. "Fucking with the president's daughter and lying behind my back!

"Candy the other day, was over you, wasn't it?" I don't answer; I know it's a rhetorical question and nothing I say will help anyway.

"Bobby, Shadow, outside," Bull snaps, standing up, his chair skidding across the hardwood floor.

"What? Why?" Bobby asks.

"You boys broke laws, time for justice," Bull clarifies, "and I don't want blood on my fucking floor, that's why," Bull hisses.

The last thing I will do is be sorry for wanting to be with Dani. If Bull kills me, it was worth it. Dani is the best thing that's happened to me; she's brought me out of the shell I lived in, brought me fire to show me a path I have never known. She may even be able to bring me back from the shadows that follow me, my shadows that lurk in the dark.

Bobby and I are standing out on the courtyard as Bull walks up to us, the rest of the boys come in from behind him. I'm curious at what his next move may be; he wants blood for betraying him, that's obvious. Is he going to kill us? Nah, if he was going to kill us he wouldn't do it here in the open, would he? I suddenly feel regret consume me; betraying my only family for a bitch is not something I would ever do. Yet here I am, and dragging a brother down with me in an ocean of betrayal.

Bull pulls out his pistol. Tapping the barrel on his leg, he looks up at me, "arm or leg?" I guess I am lucky he's giving me a choice and not aiming at my skull.

"You better choose fast before I pick both, or change my mind and aim for your head," he says, raising his voice.

"Ar-" Before I can say the word he fires a round straight into my arm, the same arm that was shot in the drive-by. The shot echoes in the quiet night.

"Fuck!" I yell out in pain, grabbing at the wound barking at my flesh.

The pain radiates up my arm and into my neck; blood starts gushing. The blood is a symbol of the betrayal I have shed on my family, a reminder at how I took Dani's innocence. The blood that was on my hands then, makes me pay with my own blood now.

"Bobby, arm or leg?" Bull asks.

Bobby looks up at me, his eyes show that he's clearly pissed that I dragged him into this shit. To be fair, I tried to tell him to butt the fuck out the day he saw blood on my hands.

"Fuck, arm," he says, closing his eyes and waiting for the assault.

A shot rings out into the night air. Bobby groans deeply and grabs his flesh wound.

"I let you boys off easy. I think of you as my own, but mark my words, Shadow, you fuck this up with Dani, and the next bullet won't be in the arm or leg.

"You bring her into your bullshit again, I will bury your ass," Bull yells, pointing at me as if I am a disobedient child. I would tell him to fuck off, that I warned Dani about the man I was, but he was the one holding the gun.

"Oh, and she will be staying with you from now on," he says wolfishly, making the rest of the boys laugh.

"What?" Bobby yells, saying exactly what I am thinking.

"I can't have her staying at the club, I don't need another Candy episode. I live here, so she can't stay with me and seeing how you were so kind to take her under your wing, she's staying at your place." Bull turns toward the clubhouse, leaving me and Bobby bleeding and dumbfounded.

"You fucking owe me big time!" Bobby smarts off at me, gritting his teeth to bare the pain.

I just look at him. I do owe him big time, but I won't admit it.

I walk into the clubhouse tightly holding onto my wound to stop the bleeding as much as I can. Actually, that's a lie; I squeeze as hard as I can so that I do, in fact, bleed on the floor. Fuck Bull.

"Good thing I stuck around," Doc says, eyeing me and Bobby as we stumble in.

"Me first; it's his fault I'm shot in the first place!" Bobby mumbles, pushing past me. I sit down on the couch and watch as Doc assesses Bobby's wound.

"It's a through and through; just some stitches is all," she says, reaching into her bag. "Why did Bull shoot you guys anyway," she asks, smartly.

"Shadow fucked around with Firefly," Bobby says sarcastically.

"Oh!" She stops and looks at Bobby and me. "That's kind of sweet, Bobby." She says, examining his wound to start stitching.

"Sweet?" I scoff.

"Yeah? Yeah! Yeah, it was. I thought it was romantic. I knew they were perfect for each other so I put my life on the line for them. That's just the kind of guy I am; a secret romantic." Bobby says, clearly lying through his teeth. Fucking cheesy as hell; If Doc ate that up she was weaker than I thought.

I grabbed a couple of shots to help with the pain while I waited. Hearing Bobby turn my messed up situation with Dani into a way to get into Doc's pants was more than I could stand. The man was more sappy over Doc than I thought.

After about twenty minutes it is my turn.

"Yours is a through and through, too," she says, eyeing me.

"How's Dani?" I ask, trying to take my mind off the pain. I am worried about her injuries and if that bastard did anything to her. A gun shot to his head was too gentle; I should have waited for Bull to give the word. I could have had a good time torturing him, something I have wanted to do since I was a kid.

"Bruised ribs, possibly cracked, and maybe a slight concussion," she says, darting a needle into my arm to numb it. Finally!

I sigh in relief; the twisted, gut-wrenching pain is starting to subside.

"She wasn't raped, if that's what you're asking. She can't remember much with the concussion, but I'm sure she will have some post traumatic distress. You may get more out of her with time, but she just needs rest really. I wouldn't let her sleep for a while, but that may be harder said than done."

As Doc stitches up my arm, I contemplate what exactly I'm going to say to Dani. She's going to have questions; more than I'm willing to answer. Not fully trusting her is going to be a problem, and who her daddy is makes for a bigger problem. If I don't make her happy, all it takes is her crying to daddy before another shot is fired off in my direction. Bull ordering her to stay with me pisses me off. If this whole situation shows me anything, it's that I just need to stay away from her before both of us are dead.

Chapter Eighteen
Dani

Laying on the bed listening to my iPod, "Demons" by Imagine Dragons is roaring in my headphones when Shadow walks in holding his arm. Dry blood is swirled around his arm and his face is grimaced with pain and confusion. I yank the headphones off and try to sit up, but the overwhelming pain makes me lay back down.

"What happened?" I ask, pointing at all the blood on his arm and the big bandage wrapped around it.

"What happened? Let's just say your dad didn't take me being with you under his nose very well," he says sarcastically, laying on the bed next to my feet. The fog starts to show face in the corners of my vision; I blink tightly trying to push it away.

"Oh." What can I say? He just took a bullet to be with me.

He turns his head, still lying flat on his back, to look at me. "Oh?" he says mockingly, making my dazed state breed anger. His mother did this to me. He said I was safe, but how safe was I when that Ricky guy nearly fucked me with his tongue.

"I mean- to be fair, I am like this because of your mother and–" I pause not sure who Ricky is. Is he Shadow's father? Shadow just glares at me, knowing my next question.

"Are you fucking kidding me?" he barks at me while lifting from the bed. "I tried to warn you from the day you pounced on me like a dog in heat!"

Really? He's turning this all on me, acting as if it is my fault this happened.

"Excuse me?" I yell back, my ribs and head howl with savage pain. I gasp and continue my rant. "I didn't see you putting up a big fight, asshole!" I wince, and hold my head. My whole body stiffens at the karate kicking in my skull.

"You broke a law climbing on the back of that fucking bike with that dick weed, Dani, not me!" he says, his chest puffed out in anger.

I look up through my lashes and see his face etched with worry. He is so confusing. I don't remember much from the kidnapping, but I remember the tone and how caring Shadow was when I thought he was a dream. Now that I'm here and he knows I'm safe, he's back to demanding Shadow again.

Fury drowns my pain. How dare he act as if this is all my fault; does he have any idea what I just went through? Trying to remember everything is hard; I have lots of questions, I just can't remember all of them.

"Who is Ricky?" I whisper, curious. That is one I do remember. I will never forget him; the way he made my skin crawl. I would need a shower of acid to be rid of him.

Shadow sighs deeply, and throws his hands over his face.

"Is he your dad"? If he was indeed his dad, then maybe Shadow was more messed up than I thought. He just killed him without so much as a blink of an eye.

"No, he was not my father," Shadow says flatly, clearly irritated I would even insinuate that.

I bite my lip at his tone. When I was in that shit-hole of a room, all I could think about was Shadow. I realized that I love him and sadly that I don't even know who he is.

"Maybe I wouldn't get that idea if you would share with me, Adrian." I say his name sharply, his head nearly snapping off at the sound.

"How do you know my name?" he asks, astounded.

"Your mother, if she is indeed your mother, kept calling you by that name," I say sarcastically, the fog and blurry visions washing over my senses like an eager wave.

Shadow sits up on the bed and runs his hands through his hair. His body is stiff; when he looks at me, his eyes are unreadable.

His hesitation gives me the feeling he doesn't trust me. I don't know why, I haven't done anything for him to question my loyalty.

"This will never work if you don't let me in," I sputter, feeling hurt. The pain in my head and ribs don't compare to the hurt he just inflicted on my soul.

"You don't trust me," I say. The way his eyes glaze over confirms the accusation, sucking the breath from my lungs. He winces at the hurt dilating my eyes, his face softens.

"I don't trust easily. I want to trust you, I do, but then I don't," he says, looking down at the comforter. I can see he's uncomfortable with his trust issues. I can't hate him for not trusting me; not when he wants to but he just doesn't know how. It's not that he can't trust me, I just simply need to earn it. The ache in my chest lessens at the thought.

"Then talk to me, Shadow, damn it"! I cry as the pain radiates through my head like fire.

"Damn it, Dani, calm down. You're hurt." Shadow climbs up the bed and envelopes my body into his. My nerves and mixed emotions, as high and thick as the evening tide, relax as my body molds to his. The smell of sweat and woodsy body wash lick my senses, making me feel at home in his strong arms.

We lay that way for a while, just listening to each other breathe. Our heartbeats become one and our breathing syncs with one another. I hate that I'm so head-over-heels for Shadow when he may not feel the same.

"My father joined the Army when I was a kid," Shadow says quietly, his breath whisking into my hair as he speaks.

"After a while, I guess my mom needed more than love letters and the occasional military leave from my father. Apparently, I wasn't enough either. One day she left and didn't come back for a few days. When she did, she was different; she wasn't my mother. I never saw my mother again," Shadow sighs heavily. I can literally hear all the sorrow in that single sigh.

"She used to have such bright, blue eyes, but after that first time she left me alone, they were dull and pathetic. Then she would be gone for weeks at a time; her thick body was slimming down to skeletal and her teeth were rotting.

"When I did talk to my father, I never told him what was going on. My mother and I were his lifeline over there. I think he knew, though; he kept asking for her and I always had to make up an excuse. She quit writing him back when his letters came.

"Then she started showing up with Ricky. I could hear them fucking through the night." I hear Shadow grind his teeth. "I hated that fucker, he used to call me 'Champ'. I just wanted to kill him." Shadow spoke with such hurt and remorse, his body tense. I wanted to roll over and hold him, but I was afraid to move; afraid he would close up. So I laid there listening.

"One day I got the news my dad had been gunned down in Iraq. My mother had been gone for a week. When she finally came home, she showed up with Ricky. I told her the news and she laughed; she didn't even go to the funeral. She just took off with the money that was donated to us by 'Fallen Soldiers' and left me. Eventually the electricity, water, everything was turned off. I had no food, no father, and no mother. I was fourteen years old." Shadow pauses, rubbing his hands over his face. I want to turn and see his expression, his eyes, but I don't have it in me to see the man I'm in love with hurt so much.

"All I have of my father is his dog tags and the car we would work on together when he got leave," Shadow says in a whisper, making my own eyes water. The car in the garage; he said it was all he had from his dad. I can see a little boy working on a car with his dad when I close my eyes, making the water that drenches my eyes spill over.

"When I was younger I got thrown in "Juvie". That's where I met Bobby. He was in there for stealing a car. We ended up getting the same release date, and I went home with him. His parents invited me in with open arms; they never judged Bobby and I. They provided food and a roof over my head without asking anything in return. They both died in a car crash our last year of high school," Shadow sighs. "Bobby and I dropped out and found the club."

I thought my life was messed up, but I had nothing on Shadow. His past clearly has done some damage. Is this what he has been so scared to tell me? Or is he just telling me this to get me off his back? I roll over and look into Shadow's eyes, digging down into his soul. He tenses under my stare, aware of the unspoken connection our souls share, and breaks eye contact with me.

There is more; more he wants to tell me but can't. I can sense it.

"You don't have to tell me anymore tonight. I get that you just shared a fuck load," I say, reassuring him that I am happy he shared with me. I am greedy and want more, but I won't push for anymore tonight.

My body protests its cruel and unusual punishment. I need rest, but not yet. I want to bask in this moment of feeling safe and somewhat trusted.

"Ever since I can remember, my mother worked. Whether it was waitressing or dancing, which I recently learned was actually stripping, she worked. She didn't show up to my school plays or talent shows. She always had an excuse; she was always working.

"She would find the worst sitters when I was young. One sitter she hired would lock me in my room with a chair against the door. The only times she would let me out was for food and right before she knew my mother was coming home. I tried to tell my mother but she never believed me.

"As I got older, her distance from me got worse, but when she met Stevin, the distance became hostile. When she was home, we fought badly. I didn't do anything right in her eyes, and she would always say I was abnormal and needed help." My head throbs with the effort to remember, causing me to pause.

"My mother was very precise about my future. I was just as trapped in my life with her as I was in that locked room," I share with Shadow, trying to give him a glimpse at why I was a naive little girl when I showed up. A Tit-for-Tat, if you will.

"Why didn't you just move out?" Shadow asks, as if it was so easy.

"I tried, she forbid it. She took all the money out of my bank account and threatened the girl I was going to move in with. I was stuck with the bitch," I explain. My mother didn't want me, but didn't want anyone else to have me either. That's why it doesn't make sense that she left me here so easily.

"Enough sharing for tonight, we have a busy day tomorrow. Seems you're moving in with me," Shadow says, getting comfy behind me. My eyes snap open wide, nearly popping a blood vessel.

I can't breathe; the air is thick and demanding as it fills my lungs. Everything is dark. My eyes dart around trying to find light, but it's pitch black. I'm lying on my side and have no idea where I am. I try and move my hands to get up but when I pull my hands my feet tug; I'm hog tied. No, not again! I've been taken against my will. I feel my heart race; panic cascades down my spine. My lips tremble with fear as I try and listen to the surrounding noise, the thumping from my heart making it hard. It sounds like a car engine. Suddenly my body is thrown up and then slammed back down and red lights illuminate the area. I'm in a trunk. How did I get here? I don't remember being thrown into a trunk. I hear car doors open and shut and then whistling as footsteps make their way to the back of the car. The trunk pops open. The sun is shining so brightly behind two people I can't make out who they are, just silhouettes.

"Oh, yeah, she will sell well!" one of them says.

A dark, tanned hand reaches in and rubs my cheek; it's soft and silky and smells of cigars. I shake my head violently back and forth.

"No. No. Please, no!" I cry, trying to pry my hands from the bindings, only to have it cut deeper into my skin.

"I wanted to sample her out for you, but wanted your permission first, Poppy," a familiar voice says, rough and husky. The silhouette leans in and I realize it's Ricky, his tongue darting out of his mouth to lick his cracked, dry lips. I thought he was dead; what's he doing here?

"Yes, by all means go for it," Poppy says. I still can't see his face from the blinding light.

"I knew you wanted that slut!" a female voice sobs. The voice is familiar, but I can't put a face to it.

Both guys throw their hands up in surrender and step back from the trunk. Why are they doing that? I can't see from laying in the trunk, so I try to lift my head and see over the rim. A small silhouette appears in my line of view, but all I can focus on is the gun pointing at me.

"Die!" the voice yells. It's Cassie!

"Noooo!" I scream.

"Dani! Dani, wake the fuck up!" I hear Shadow yelling at me, his hands shaking me by my shoulders.

I open my eyes, running from the dreadful terror behind closed lids. I'm soaked with sweat and my breathing is so spastic I feel I may stroke out at any moment. It was just a bad dream... just a dream, I chant silently to myself.

"Calm down and breathe," Shadow coaxes me as he rubs my back to help soothe me.

"Damn, that must have been a hell of a dream," Shadow whispers, his voice sexy and rough from sleep.

We lay there in the dark room in silence. I'm too afraid to go back to sleep. I can't sleep. I need a shower. I need Ricky's mouth off of me.

I throw my legs over the bed only to jerk them back up again. What if he's under the bed? No, Shadow killed Ricky; he can't hurt me anymore, right? I put my legs back over the edge of the bed, hesitant. What about Cassie though? My mind haunts me, making me pull my legs back up onto the bed.

"Where are you going?" Shadows asks, his voice full of sleep.

"I have to get a shower. I need to," I say, sobbing. I feel so weak, so vulnerable.

"I'll help you," Shadow says, rising from the bed.

"No, I got it. I can do it myself," I respond, more spiteful than intended. I can't help but feel a little hurt that he doesn't trust me, even after all the shit his blood put me through.

"No, you can't do it by yourself. I'm helping, end of discussion!" His tone is harsh and demanding. I risk looking at Shadow, our gazes holding a new energy than when we fell asleep. The air seems angrier and more hostile than before. But why?

I lift off the bed and feel like I weigh a thousand pounds. My belly is yelling in hunger and my mouth is parched, but all I can think of is cleaning myself off with an iron sponge.

I hunch over and start making my way toward the bathroom. Once there, I look into the mirror as Shadow turns the shower on. I can't contain the ungodly gasp that escapes from my mouth when I look at my reflection. I have dried, caked blood on my forehead; a split lip that is all purple and black with more dried blood; my throat has a ring of purple around it; and I haven't even looked under my clothes yet.

Shadow grasps the hem of my shirt and pulls it over my head. He unhooks my bra letting the cups dangle from my chest; I slide the straps down my arms and let it fall to the floor. He unwraps my bruised ribs that Dr. Jessica wrapped tightly to help with the pain. Shadow turns me and fiercely sucks in a breath at the sight of my ribs. My sides are the darkest hue of purple I have ever seen; borderline black. Just trying to bend my head to look at them makes me cringe with pain; they look terrible.

Shadow grabs me by the hips gently, rubbing his thumbs across the tainted skin. "Fuck, Dani," he whispers, his voice dripping with sympathy and concern.

"It actually looks worse than it is," I admit.

Shadow looks at me with hooded eyes. His arctic blue digging deep into my emerald green and tugging on my soul. My panties instantly wet at the sight of him mourning my injuries.

"I know that look and the answer is simple; no." The worry and concern are gone from his voice, replaced with cold restraint. His whiplash behavior has me confused as hell all over again.

I walk up to him and trail my nails down his clean cut abs, feeling his skin explode with goosebumps under my touch. My touch affects him.

"We can be gentle," I sigh, trailing my hand to the waist of his jeans. Shadow growls deeply.

He grabs my wrist, stopping my touch and the vixen spell. He clamps his eyes shut for a moment before staring again, guns blazing.

"The feelings I had when you were gone, they were deep. I lost control. Someone took something of mine and they hurt what was mine. I'm way past pissed that you got on the back of another brother's bike; a brother that didn't protect you. You should have never been on the back of his bike, especially without permission." Shadow throws my hand back at me. I gasp with shock; how was I supposed to know getting on the back of that bike was breaking a so-called law? I open my mouth to yell at him, but am stopped short when he leans in and nips my earlobe painfully. It borders on pleasurable. Flashes of him spanking me and pulling my hair fly through my closed eyes, reminding me that the dark is not such a bad place when thoughts of Shadow consume it.

"I will fuck you, spank you, claim you, but only when I'm good and ready," Shadow whispers into my ear, his breath hot and humid against my skin. The sudden throbbing that sweeps into my swollen clit makes my legs wobble. I grab onto Shadow for support and he grabs me by the nape of the neck.

"Now that your dad knows about us, you're more than mine, and everyone will know it." He says it like it's a bad thing; his change in demeanor now makes sense. My body bemoans at the sudden realization that Shadow is protesting against me because my father has ordered me to live with him. I look at his bandaged arm; his price for being with me. I want to tell him I don't have to go with him, that we can do this at our own speed, but we both know that's not true.

"How did you get beat up so bad?" he demands.

I close my eyes trying to think; everything is still blurry in places. Did I ask for this or did they just enjoy inflicting pain on me? My head swamps with images of being kicked and thrown into the door; but why?

A prick of sensation flares to life, reminding me of the overwhelming urge to fight that day. I felt reckless, manic, furious, and ominous; my blood was pumping so hard I could feel my heartbeat pounding in my toes and fingers.

"I felt an overwhelming rage to fight," I respond. "So I fought; I fought to live. A dark side of me roared through my reason." Looking back, I could have been killed. That is exactly why I fought; it was kill or be killed.

"I wanted to kill them!" I whisper, remembering the overwhelming feeling of helplessness. How I would have loved to have found a weapon to seal their fates; to end the domino effect they had on other people's lives. How I would have loved to get even for Shadow.

I sat on the bench, outside of the Principal's office, swinging my feet as I waited for my mother to come out. I knew I was in trouble; my mother never seemed happy with me anymore, but this was sure to put her over the edge. I got in a fight with Sophie. I hated her. She was ten, just like me, but she was a bully; pulling my hair because I didn't have long, blond hair like her and her friends; dumping paint over and blaming me, she even managed to ruin any art I made in school; pinching me 'til I bruised, she always left marks on me and sometimes she even drew blood; teasing me because I didn't have a dad, her dad was a lawyer and rich; kicking me in the ankle as she walked by my desk, I couldn't walk right for a month after the last time. The teacher and my mom never believed me when I told them what she did, or that she started it. Today wouldn't be any different. She was every suburbia mom's wet dream; long blond hair, perfect grades, and perfect parents. She was just perfect. I hated her.

My mother came busting through the Principal's door and grabbed my hand to leave. Her grip was so tight I thought she would break my fingers. Once in the car, I knew all hell would break loose; I would be out of the public eye.

"You want to explain to me what happened, Danielle," she asked, looking at me like I was the biggest mistake she ever made.

"The Principal said you pushed a girl causing her to fall down and hit her head on the pavement. Then... then..." My mother started to sob, making me feel regret for what I had done. I wasn't sure why I decided to fight back that day; I never had the courage to fight back before. Something snapped, something dark inside of me called me out of my scared shell. I had the fury of a black panther, and Sophie was my prey. If the teacher hadn't pulled us apart, I would have killed Sophie.

"Then you yelled that you wanted to kill her? Who are you? You're not normal," my mother yelled at me, making me feel ashamed. I should have just let Sophie throw the ball at my head. I should have done nothing about it, then my mother wouldn't hate me even more than she had. I don't know what came over me, but I would never let it happen again.

"Dani? Dani! Where did you go?" Shadow says, slightly jarring me from my flashback.

I shake my head, not wanting to talk about it. Apparently this darkness has lived with me my whole life; my mother just did a good job making sure it was rarely triggered.

"Tell me," Shadow says, grabbing the nape of my neck roughly and making our eyes lock.

"When I was younger, I fought back a bully. I even told her I wanted to kill her. My mother called me abnormal. That feeling I had when I yelled I wanted to kill that bully, came out when I was kidnapped. Seems I've always been screwed up." I whispered the last sentence, feeling ashamed of my own darkness.

Shadow's nails dig deep into my skin, grabbing my attention. "Don't be ashamed of your darkness. It's a part of you and it's easier to deal with it than to try and believe it's not there. You are your father's daughter; you are bound to have some darkness swimming in your veins. You are only dark when you have to be, when you're at your breaking point. That's understandable." Shadow pauses, holding back. I can feel he wants to relate, but when he looks into my eyes I can see he just isn't ready to tell me. He is sheltering me; protecting me. His hot and cold attitude is tormenting. He is trying to be cold and withdrawn but it lacks full potential when he shows caring attributes. I understand that my father crossed a line, but is there something else making Shadow act like this?

"Be glad it's only in drastic circumstances that your darkness wants to be released, Dani," Shadow says with such emotion; his voice so raw and deep. Looking in his eyes, I can see my darkness is nothing compared to what he lives with. I wonder if I really want him to tell me what darkness he possesses.

Shadow undresses the rest of my body then leans against the wall looking off at nothing in particular.

"Aren't you getting in?" I ask, confused, since we have taken showers together many times.

Shadow doesn't speak or make eye contact, he just shakes his head no.

Climbing into the hot jets of streaming water, I instantly feel it washing away the repugnant touch of Ricky. I grab the shampoo bottle and squirt soap into my palm. I raise my hands to my head, stretching my ribs, and yelp with pain.

"Shit," I mutter. How am I supposed to wash the blood away if I can't even stretch my arms out?

"Damn it, Dani," Shadow says, concerned. He rips his clothes off quickly and climbs in. Squirting soap into his hand, he says, "I got it."

"No, I can do it. I don't want you to take the role of caretaker," I respond. I don't want Shadow to feel like he has to take care of me, especially if he is trying to push himself away from me. Just the mere thought guts me. While I was in that shitty-ass house I became hopeless, much like when I was a kid. I was weak, vulnerable, naive and feeble. No one saved me then, but when he delivered in rescuing me this time, Shadow crashed the remaining walls of protection I had, making me ultimately his. What hurts is that now he doesn't want me.

"Just go. Don't do this. You don't have to take care of me," I mumble, trying to salvage what dignity I have left.

"I want to take care of you. Don't ever think otherwise." Shadow plunges his soapy hands into my wet hair; his dexterous fingers work magic on my scalp. My body comes alive from every nerve ending. Internal warmth licks up my spine; gone with insecurity and alive with want. My lips part, my eyes close, as I take in the nurturing affection Shadow inflicts. I have never felt so cared for, so cherished before. Shadow pulls me closer and inhales deeply, I can feel his excitement flick against my lower back as he growls. His hands leave the soapy mess on my head and travel down my shoulders to roughly grab my soapy breast. I moan loudly; his hands igniting my need into a blazing fire.

"Just the sight of your soapy, flushed body has me ready to blow my load all over you," Shadow whispers against my neck, his confession my undoing. I throw my arms over his neck, ignoring my screaming ribs and roll my neck onto his shoulder, inviting him to take me.

Shadow's moan thunders through his chest, sounding like a man-eating beast. He pushes me off his body. "As much as I want to take you right here in this shower, as badly as I want to paint your ass red right now, it would teach you nothing." His voice, full of restraint and hostility, has my mind overpowering my body. I have had enough of his alpha male ego.

"Excuse me?" I ask, turning around to look at him; my eyes seething with anger.

"You heard me." His words put out my arousal and light an internal rage.

"You are not to pleasure yourself either. I will know if you do and you won't like the consequences." Shadow looks right into my eyes, promising me that if I disobey his wishes I will be punished. He's pushing sanity over the edge, yet making me about to cum at his words.

"I will do what I want, you don't own me!" I yell, my fury so strong my vision goes blurry. My darkness is trying to rise. It seems it's wanting to appear more often here lately.

Shadow grabs my wrists and pins them down by my waist. He holds my body against the shower stall. "I do own you. You are mine"! Shadow places his knee in between my legs and spreads them wide. My heart drops at his words; who is this man? I have never seen this side of Shadow before. My body wiggles to try and make contact with his knee; it's desperate for anything.

"Do you want to run now? Do you want to deny that you're mine"? Shadow asks, his voice gruff. This is wrong; I'm not a possession, I'm not a submissive. It's not fair that he is playing with my mind. He says he wants me, but acts differently.

I'm too weak to say anything. I want Shadow; he made me want him. My body is on high alert wanting more of Shadow's touch. My folds, dripping from kindling arousal, disagree with my mind; wanting to be owned and loved by Shadow. Giving Shadow everything, maybe he will see how much trust that takes from my side; maybe that will open his mind to trust me. My internal battle has me confused, but my body speaks volumes over my mind.

"No, I'm yours." I don't realize I've spoken the words out loud until Shadow's lips turn up into a wolfish grin.

"Good." Shadow smashes his lips on mine hard, opening the cut on my lip, demanding and imprinting his mark to seal the deal. Making it official; Shadow is my kryptonite.

My eyes widen at his behavior; I'm confused but intrigued nonetheless.

"I'm not any different," Shadow asserts, reading my facial expression. "I demand control; I don't do well without it. I have always been like that. When you were taken against my will, I lost control. I never knew another person could have such an affect on me until you were taken." Shadow steps out of the shower, leaving me with a confusing amount of feelings. He's trying to prove to himself he doesn't need me; the reaction he felt when I was taken is new to him. I shouldn't be okay with this; I shouldn't be turned on by this, but I am both. My lips turn upward into a grin. I will prove to Shadow he needs me as much as I need him.

Chapter Nineteen
Dani

I wake up in bed alone. I'm sure Shadow has church again this morning, seems like I will have to get used to waking up alone if I want to be with him. I know church is important to the boys; I bet they have a lot to talk about after the kidnapping.

I sit up and my ribs wake with pain. They're not as sore as they were yesterday, maybe the hot shower helped. My head feels a lot better, too. Everything is not as fuzzy, and it doesn't feel like a rock band is playing in my skull.

I climb off the bed and realize I'm naked. I don't even really remember going to bed after the shower. I do remember Shadow, though. He was… different; stubborn, distant, dominant, pissed. Pissed? I don't think pissed is the accurate word to use; he was beyond that. I knew getting on the back of Charlie's bike was a bad idea; I just didn't realize how bad.

I walk over to my suitcase to find some clothes. Everything is clean and folded and sitting on my suitcase. Hmm, I wonder who did that. I grab some black leggings and a gray tunic. I love this tunic, it is wide and loose at the top, hanging off my bare shoulders, and tight and stretchy at the bottom as it hugs mid-thigh.

I make my way to the bar where everyone always seems to congregate and smell food immediately. My stomach kicks in high gear, pissed that I haven't fed it in twenty-four hours.

"You must be hungry, doll. Here, have some eggs and toast, and this cup of O.J. It will make you feel like a million bucks." Babs slides a plate over the bar.

"Yes, please. Thank you." I scarf down the eggs, toast, and juice like a starving child in a third world country. I could barely taste the food I ate it so fast.

From the corner of my eye, I see my dad sit down next to me. He sips on a cup of coffee and I can feel the tension radiating off of him. He is still pissed about me and Shadow. I avoid eye contact and finish my food; our silence thick and heavy with unspoken words is enough for me.

"Thanks, Babs. I'm going to go pack up my things. Looks like I'll be staying with Shadow for a while." I push away from the bar, trying to flee from the talk I didn't want to have with my dad.

"Aww, you are more than welcome. I cleaned your clothes for you, by the way," she takes my dish and puts her hand on her hip, waiting for my thank you.

"You didn't have to do that, Babs. Thanks." I start to turn.

"It was a breeze; a lot easier than washing these dirty bastard's clothing. Anyway, you going to help me bartend after the Bike Rally in a couple of weeks?" Babs shifts the plate in her other hand and eyes my father, asking him more than me.

"What Bike Rally?" I ask, looking at my dad.

"It's something the town does every year. MC's and bike enthusiasts come from all over; we go every year. If you want to help bartend you can, as long as you keep your hormones to yourself and don't fuck any more of my men." He looks up from his coffee and cocks his eyebrow.

I scoff and go to my room. How dare he talk to me like that; acting as if I was sleeping around with the whole club. I sit down on the bed seething with anger and play with my bottom lip. Have I worn out my welcome here? Maybe I should have gone with my mom.

"You ready?" Shadow asks, opening the door to the room.

"Yeah, that's my-" Shadow zips up my suitcase and walks out of the room before I can even finish my sentence. My heart feels like it's being chipped away at.

My heart aches with the harshness Shadow is displaying toward me.

I grab my purse and walk behind him; exiting the clubhouse.

"Get in, I'm driving you there." My dad yells from the front of the black SUV.

Fucking fuck, fuck.

I climb in the passenger side of the SUV and look out the window, praying Shadow doesn't live far and my dad doesn't utter a word to me.

We make our way out onto the road, the sound of the wheels on pavement filling the silence. Shadow is following us on his bike. I miss riding, but I know my ribs are in no condition.

"I don't approve of this, Dani." My dad finally speaks, his words slicing through the thick tension. I keep my eyes out on the passing buildings, the taste of salt becoming thicker. We must be headed toward the beach.

"My brothers have been dishonest; they lost a part of my trust, something not easily earned." His tone drips with harshness, his wisdom about earning trust not going unheard. I nod.

"Shadow, he's no prince charming. He has his..." he pauses, "his shadows, but he will protect you. I know he wouldn't go under my nose if he didn't really feel for you. He's like a son to me; he wouldn't jeopardize my trust for just anyone." He speaks like a wise old man.

"I ordered you to stay with him. I can't have you staying at the club; having cat fights and my men fighting is not something I am willing to tolerate." I could feel him look over at me, looking for a reaction.

We pull up to a building that is as tall as my eyes can see. I would have to stick my head out the window just to see the top floor. The front is redbrick and covered with balconies. Palm trees with spotlights at their bases scatter the front entrance. It looks expensive. How can Shadow afford such a beautiful place? In fact, he seems to have lots of very nice things; the nicest bike, name brand clothes, and now this apartment in an obviously upscale neighborhood.

My dad stops the vehicle and turns to look at me, his face etched with worry lines. He looks much older than usual. "Just remember, Dani, our world is different than what you're used to. Don't go running before you truly understand it." He's acting like I'm a frightened animal ready to flee at any moment; like my mother.

"Lust like a saint, trust like a sinner," he chants as he puts the vehicle in reverse. My door opens abruptly with Shadow holding my suitcase and waiting impatiently for me to get out. I look at my dad one more time before climbing out, curious what the hell that last comment meant.

In the elevator, Shadow hits the button for the fourteenth floor. The ride is silent. He doesn't even look at me; he just stares at the digital screen showing what floor we are passing. When we finally make it to Shadow's apartment, it is a typical bachelor's pad. To the left of the entrance is a brown leather couch and matching recliner with a huge, bulky coffee table between them. On the far wall is a large flat screen TV littered with game consoles and games.

If you walk straight, there is a small kitchen with stainless steel appliances and an island with barstools to separate the living room from the kitchen. To the right of the living room are double glass doors that lead out to a patio. I will be checking that out later. To the left of the living room is a guest bathroom and two bedrooms, both with their own private bathrooms. The apartment is littered with pizza boxes, fast food bags, beer bottles, soda cans, and dirty clothes. I walk into the kitchen to get a feel for the apartment and see a condom sticking out of the overflowing trash can. I look at Shadow in disgust, my mouth gaping open at the thought. So much for me being his and him being mine. I can feel my skin flush with anger as Shadow rounds the bar and sees what I am staring at.

Shadow looks at me and cocks his brow, daring me to ask him.

"Goddamn, my arm hurts," Bobby's voice interrupts as he enters the front door. Not aware of the war developing in the kitchen, he walks toward us with a smile.

"Oh, hey. Welcome to our humble abode," Bobby show tunes, sweeping his arm around like a game show host.

Wait, does he live here, too? Bobby and Shadow are roommates? Maybe that's how Shadow can afford such a beautiful apartment; they split rent.

Bobby looks down at the trash can that both Shadow and I are staring at. "Oh, sorry about that; been meaning to take out the trash. It's going to be different having you live with us, Firefly." Bobby pushes the trash down to hide the used condom.

"Yeah, looks like I'm not the only one with trust issues." Shadow shakes his head and walks down the hall.

"Shit!" I mumble under my breath.

"You, ah, you guys okay?" Bobby asks, leaning up against the island.

I shrug and walk to the balcony; I can use some air. Truth is, Shadow and I are far from okay. I can feel him getting farther and farther away from me and it's killing me from the inside out, starting with my heart. As soon as I open the double doors, the salt air hits my nostrils like a freight train. The building is so tall, you can see the ocean. On the deck sits two sun loungers; I can easily curl up with a good book and get my tan on. If Shadow keeps acting the way he is, I will be out here a lot, I'm sure of it.

"Yeah, the bitches love the scene," Bobby says, walking up behind me.

"The bitches?" I ask, laughing.

Bobby nods with a boyish grin.

"I can see you two are having problems," Bobby declares as he takes a swig from his beer.

I ignore the accusation and stare out at the ocean.

"He's different, Firefly. I don't know what is going on between you two, but know this: I have never seen him the way he is with you, especially when his fucking mom took you. He fucking lost his shit." He looks at me with focused eyes. "That has to count for something, right? Don't let him push you away." He drinks the last sip from his beer before turning toward the doors. "Even if his ass doesn't deserve you."

His words sink deep, confirming my belief of why Shadow is acting the way he is. I make him feel hopeless and weak; hell, I make him feel, period. Now to make sure he never hurts like that again or loses control. Can I take the push and push back, am I strong enough?

Shadow ignores me for the rest of the day. He plays video games with Bobby, asking me to get him a beer or make him a sandwich here and there. To pass the time, I wash the dishes, take out the trash and pick up the dirty clothes. The balcony doors have been open to let the place air out. It looks great, but my ribs are hurting to the max. I sit down on one of the sun loungers, exhausted from all the hard work. My ribs are pushing my pain level past bearable and my head starts to throb. I am in need of a break.

"Dani!" Shadow yells, laughing at Bobby about something. "Get me another beer!" He's still playing that fucking video game. I bite my bottom lip and don't budge; who does he think he is.

"Dani!" Shadow yells again. His voice grates on my nerves, my anger begins to seethe through my pores.

"Dude, go get it yourself. What the fuck?" Bobby sneers, his voice lowered in an attempted whisper so I won't hear.

"Dani!" Shadow yells again, ignoring Bobby.

"Goddamn it," he curses and stomps all the way to the balcony doors; his eyes like daggers at the back of my head.

"Did you hear me yelling for your ass to get me a beer?" Shadow asks, pissed off I didn't jump at his beck and call.

I turn my head and glare at him. I don't mind getting him a beer, but he could, at least, ask nicely. If he is trying to push me away, treating me like this is a great way to do it.

"Go get it your damn self," I snap back, returning my gaze to the ocean view. It is beautiful with hues of purple and pink as the sun goes down.

Shadow grabs my chin and yanks my vision from the ocean.

Staring into his icy, blue eyes, his soul renders me speechless. It shows anger, lust, confusion and darkness. He is angry and I don't know why. I have given him everything I possibly can, including my heart, and he still is not happy. I'm exhausted in so many ways; my heart is literally shattering.

Shadow turns and walks away, leaving me on the sun lounger to watch the sunset by myself. I feel my heart crash and burn. My chest feels like it is on fire and I gasp for air. I hate the effect he is having on me. I have to be stronger than this and push back if I want to keep him. Prove to him I'm not going anywhere. Can't he see that he makes me feel, too; that he takes the control I need away, as well?

At midnight I can't keep my eyes open anymore.

"Hey, I'm going to bed, you coming?" I ask Shadow, who is still playing video games. He doesn't even acknowledge me; just keeps his eyes on the screen. That's all he's done all day, even through dinner.

When I open the door to Shadow's bedroom, it is very masculine. The bed has black sheets with a black, gray and white comforter and is covered in fluffy pillows. I came in here earlier to grab dirty clothes and beer bottles, but I didn't stop long enough to really appreciate the room. There is a huge floor-to-ceiling window that looks out over the city and there are black sheer curtains on each side. The dresser is black with a huge mirror. The room is sin in its own right. How can Shadow afford all this?

I go to the closet and pull down one of Shadow's white MC shirts; my black one got ruined by Candy. As I grab it off the hanger, a whoosh of air assaults my senses. It smells of Shadow. God, I miss him.

'You don't think just because you're sweet and innocent that he cares about you, that you can tame him, do you? As soon as he's done with you, he'll come running back to me.'

Candy's words fly at me like a bullet. I remember Shadow hiding in the closet as she verbally accosted me. The thought she might have been right makes my mouth go dry.

No, things are different between me and Shadow; I know it.

I put the shirt on and climb into the huge sleigh bed. It feels cold and lonely laying in it by myself.

The door across the hall slams, knocking me from my self-pity. Little school girl giggles and deep smooth laughter from Bobby muffle from the room next to me.

Then it goes quiet. Hmm, odd.

"Oh, Bobby, don't stop!" a girl moans loudly. This cannot be happening.

I can hear her moaning incoherent things, and Bobby rutting like a beast. This is more awkward than I ever thought imaginable. Where is Shadow? I climb out of bed and pad my bare feet to the living room. Shadow is asleep on the couch with a blanket and pillow. I sigh loudly; looks like I will be sleeping alone tonight. I pad my way back to the bedroom; rejection and loneliness weighing on my heart.

I climb back into the bed; the moans from the other room becoming louder. I can feel their bed slamming against the wall. I can't handle this anymore; I have more built up sexual tension than anyone right now. I climb off the bed and grab my iPod, maybe music will drown them out. I climb back in bed, place the headphones on my ears and fire it up. The first song that plays is "Is This Love" by Whitesnake; the song Shadow and I listened to the second time we made love.

I yank the headphones from my ears and throw the iPod to the end of the bed. As soon as the headphones leave my ears, Bobby and 'Moaning Chick' fill them with animalistic sex noises.

"Are you kidding me?" I yell, flopping onto my stomach and covering my head with as many pillows as my flailing hands can grab.

I wake up to the sound of giggles from the next room. My head is still buried deep under a mound of pillows. I have no idea what time I finally fell asleep last night; Bobby and "Miss Moans-A-Lot" had me up all night. Every moan and growl coming from the next room made me think about climbing on Shadow and humping him into tomorrow.

I roll over on my back and look up at the ceiling. I don't feel like getting up, or showering, or eating. I just want to lay here and stare at the ceiling. So I do; thoughtless and emotionless for at least a few hours.

My stomach yells and screams at me to get out of bed. Giving in, I climb out of bed and throw my hair up in a messy bun. I walk out of the room in just the big MC shirt and panties; maybe showing a little skin will bring Shadow around.

I walk into the living room and Shadow is sitting on a stool at the island. He looks sexy as hell in just a pair of gray sweatpants. He looks up from his bowl of cereal and his eyes go wide at my appearance.

I round the island to pour myself a bowl and spot Bobby whispering sweet nothings into a blond's ear. She throws her head back and laughs; her voice is familiar. She looks up at me and my breath is stolen from my lungs.

"Doc?" I think out loud.

"Oh, good morning, Dani. How are you feeling?" she asks, jumping straight into professional mode. I nod my head avoiding eye contact; a little embarrassed I heard her climax twice last night.

"Can you take me to the book store? I would like to buy a few books," I ask Shadow, who is still looking at me like he wants to eat me.

He gains composure and goes back to his cereal.

"How long are we going to do this?" I ask him, pissed with the childish games he is playing. "I don't think this has anything to do with me getting on the back of someone's bike; something I didn't even know was a law. So, what is it?" I nearly yell, ready to drown his ass in his cereal bowl.

"Don't push me, Dani," Shadow says, grimly.

"Fuck you!" I yell, grabbing my cereal bowl and stomping back to the room. Fuck him. Fuck him and his arrogant ways. Fuck me for falling in love with him, even when I was warned.

I eat my cereal then lay down looking out the window; people who live normal lives walking the streets. Families, laughing and smiling, walk together. I hate them all.

I wake up with my head pounding from all the sleep. Sitting up in bed, I see a black box with a red bow attached to it at the end of the bed. I grab the box and open it up.

"What the..."? I ask myself out loud.

It's a Kindle Fire. What the hell was he getting at? Treat me like shit, then reward me with gifts? I love it, but he isn't going to know that.

I look at the clock and see it's 6:30pm. All I have had is cereal and I'm starving for some actual comfort food. I toss the Kindle on the end of the bed and go in search of food, still in just a t-shirt and panties.

Shadow is watching a movie instead of playing video games. I glare at him and walk into the kitchen.

I grab some angel hair pasta and pull some meat from the fridge. I look in the cabinets and find some pasta sauce; spaghetti it is.

After about an hour of cooking and burning myself with boiling pasta sauce, dinner is done. I have watched enough cooking shows, being locked down in my house in New York, to pick up some tips and I have to say my sauce is tasting pretty yummy tonight. I start throwing some spaghetti in a bowl when Shadow enters the kitchen.

"Hmm," he says, dipping his finger in the sauce.

He opens the freezer and pulls out a tub of chocolate ice cream, grabs a spoon from the drainer and flips the lid with his thumb onto the floor.

"Yeah, I think I'll just eat this," he says, snidely. My eyes bug out and my mouth drops open in disbelief, did he just dis' my cooking?

My face turns into a scowl as my blood begins to boil hotter than my pasta sauce.

"Damn this shit is thick. Dani, grab me a beer," Shadow demands as he spoons another scoop of ice cream.

I bite my cheek and nod my head. I'm so pissed I can't even see straight. I open the fridge and grab a beer bottle by the neck. "You want a beer, huh?" I say coyly. "Here, have a fucking beer!" I throw the beer bottle at him.

Shadow ducks just as the bottle collides with the wall and shatters into a million pieces.

"What the fuck?" Shadow hollers, looking at the wall of glass and beer. "I'll eat the fucking spaghetti."

"Oh here, let me get that for you, too." I grab the bowl of hot spaghetti and throw it at him as well, spilling some on the counter. He ducks again, just in time, as the bowl and noodles join the beer and glass on the wall.

"You fucking crazy bitch!" Shadow yells as he drops the ice cream and makes his way toward me.

"Fuck you, I'm not someone you can just walk all over," I yell back at him, angry that he is right. I am acting crazy, but he did this to me; he made me crazy.

Our eyes of blazing blue and venomous green meet; souls of abuse and torment meeting in a ring of fire. Shadow grabs the nape of my neck harshly, pulling me closer. I bring my hand back and slap him across the face, his tongue snakes out and licks his bottom lip.

Our eyes locking once more, anger floods our judgment. He grabs me by the hair and pulls my head back. His body is screaming alpha and his temper flares like a beast.

Without warning our mouths crash together in need. Shadow grabs me by the thighs and slams me on top of the counter. Spaghetti and sauce go flying all over us and the counter. Shadow nips my bottom lip as his hands dive into my hair. Pulling my head to the side, he licks and nibbles some sauce from my neck.

"God, I fucking love your temper," he whispers against my skin. He thrusts his hips into my hypersensitive folds causing me to grind against him for friction. He slides his hands up my shirt and grabs my breast greedily. I grab at his bare back to pull him closer. My body is begging for more as he kisses me. Our lips those of anger and passion. He tastes of chocolate and sin; together becoming an addiction on its own. He bites my bottom lip harshly, causing me to moan. My pain becoming my pleasure. I lock my legs around his waist and return the bite on toned pecks. He moans and grabs my head back to look into his stormy eyes.

"Is everything okay?" Doc asks, coming in the front door as it opens.

"What the fuck happened to the wall?" Bobby asks, walking in behind her.

My eyes snap to Shadow's; his face of lust and anger replaced with something unreadable. He pulls away leaving me cold and confused. I slide off the counter of spaghetti and see Doc and Bobby confused and staring. Shadow grabs his cut off the chair and walks out, slamming the door behind him.

Chapter Twenty
Shadow

I woke up yesterday pissed at myself; pissed I have let myself become so weak, pissed that I've allowed Dani to have this kind of control over me, pissed at myself for loving her. I'm also pissed I almost let her get killed because I didn't take that junkie of a mother seriously.

I lost control when she was taken; lost control with the thought of her on Charlie's bike. She is right, I am trying to push her away. I am trying to protect her from the beast that I am. But, I can't let her go, my body is addicted to her. I live and breathe Dani. When I think about her not being with me, I feel hopeless. She has shown me a light; she is the heaven to my hell.

"Firefly is asleep," Bobby says, as I sit down next to him on the couch. I needed to get out of here earlier. Dani in the kitchen cooking in that shirt was torture, but when she defied me and went fucking crazy, I couldn't hold back anymore, I had to have her. When I realized what I was doing, it became clear to me that I couldn't push Dani away even if I wanted to. She is mine, and I am hers.

"Go ahead, baby, I'll catch up," Bobby says to Doc, dismissing her. "What the fuck, man? Talk to me," he demands of me when she's gone.

"There's nothing to talk about, leave it." I get up and make my way to the kitchen for a beer. The spaghetti mess is still present. I look at the counter and see a clean spot from Dani's cute little ass.

"I took a fucking bullet for you to be with that girl and now you are pushing her away. Why?" Bobby yells at me, that boy has balls talking to me like that.

"She fucks with my head. That day she was taken, my whole world fucking shifted, Bobby, and I lost control," I fess up.

"Love has a funny way of fucking with you. I get it; you think pushing Firefly away will keep you from feeling that helpless again," Bobby says, getting up and walking over to the island.

"Yeah, and I don't trust that she won't leave when she finds out what I really do; how I stay alive." I take a swig of my bottle, regret of the fucked up numbness I call my life and the way I cope with it, swallowing me into a black abyss. If Dani is anything like her mother, she will run far away from me. Pushing her away now is better than after I completely give myself to her, or so I think.

"She's Heaven and I'm Hell. When we're together angels cry and Hell freezes over." I look at Bobby, "It's no shocker we are from different worlds."

"Nah, I don't see her running, Shadow." He takes a drink from his beer. "You push her away, she will find someone else, and when you see that, it will be the worst kind of hell. Trust me, I have lived it," Bobby looks down, his voice full of shame.

"Fuck you." I yell at Bobby. Just the thought of Dani with someone else makes me angry.

Bobby laughs, "Yeah, Firefly has you by the balls."

"I'm about to cut yours off, you keep talking shit!" I walk right in front of Bobby, testing him to say something else.

"I'm trying to help, man. Calm down." Bobby throws his hands up in surrender.

"I fucked this up too much anyway, she won't ever forgive me." I say to Bobby, finishing off my beer. The thought of Dani showing off some new guy to Bull, has me nearly crushing the beer bottle in my hand. How could I think pushing her away would make me feel better? Pushing her away was a weak move.

"Looking at you two on that counter earlier, I think different." Bobby cocks his brow and lifts his chin toward the kitchen.

"So take her away; shower her in love. Earn each other's trust; find out what each other likes and hates," Doc says, stepping into the room, clearly eavesdropping.

Bobby's face lights up when he sees her; and he has the nerve to say Dani has me by the balls.

"I know nothing about that," I reply to Doc, sitting down on the couch.

"He's telling the truth. He's never been in a relationship, ever," Bobby says, seriously.

"Man, what the fuck? Really?" I ask, throwing my hands up pissed off that he would just spill my life out to some chick.

"Aww, that's cute," Doc coos. "From what Bobby has told me about Dani, she hasn't either, so don't sweat it."

It pisses me off that Dani and I are their choice of topic for pillow talk. I would tell her to fuck off if I didn't need her help. I know nothing about romantic getaway trips; or anything romantic for that matter.

"You said I should take her away somewhere. Where?" I ask, rubbing my bottom lip with my thumb, something I do when I'm deep in thought. Truth is, I just want them both out of my and Dani's relationship; getting to the bottom of this quickly should do just that.

We all sit thinking, silently.

"Oh! A surgeon I work with said her husband rented a beach house. It was just them and some staff occasionally. She said it was super intimate and romantic. It sounded awesome from everything she told me. You should do that." Doc's voice is perky and damn near annoying. I don't like in-love Doc.

"You know you can afford it," Bobby says, sarcastically.

I can afford it, I know that. Money is not a problem. The problem is whether Dani wants to go with me now that I have been such a dick.

I reach into the end table and pull out the laptop. I was taking Dani whether she wanted to go or not. Getting her away from danger, and these two love birds, would help ease some of my tension.

"Tell her everything, I don't think it will make her run. She's a tough one. People are going to hurt you, break your trust no matter what. It's up to you to decide which ones are worth risking that," Bobby says. He has clearly been around chirpy Doc too long.

"Where did you hear that?" I ask him snidely.

"I don't know. I've had enough chicks break up with me. I'm sure one of them said it to me," Bobby says, laughing, looking at Doc who is clearly not amused. Doc gets up and stomps out of the room, pissed at Bobby and his confession of being with lots of women.

Dani

I step out of the shower. Washing the spaghetti and shame off of me was harder than I thought.

The bedroom is dark. There's just enough illumination from the moon to allow me to navigate. I look out the window to watch the pedestrians scramble like ants. It still makes me wonder what a normal person's life feels like. Hands slide over my bare back, startling me and causing my heart to race.

"It's just me. It's okay," Shadow whispers into my ear. I didn't even hear him come into the bedroom.

"I fucked up," he confesses, removing his hands from my skin. His lips kiss below my ear, trailing down my neck to my collarbone.

"Forgive me?" Shadow asks, his voice rough and sexy. My head spins with the many emotions Shadow has me in. We're so up and down; I don't know if I can play these mind games anymore.

"Come away with me," his fingers twirling my hair as he asks.

I turn around abruptly.

"What?" I ask, confused about what he means by away.

"Just me and you; away from the club and everyone we know. I want to get to know you better." He leans in and pecks my lips but I don't return the kiss.

"Are you fucking kidding me?" I ask, furious he would think I would just forgive him so easily.

"I'm not fucking kidding you," he mocks.

"I get it, I fucked up; I was a dick. I admit I tried to push you away. The way I feel for you, the way you make me feel, scares the shit out of me. I don't know what else you want from me." He looks right into my eyes and cups the back of my neck bringing me closer. Our lips brush against each other. "I love you, Dani," he whispers, his lips teasing mine.

His confession has me stunned. I should tell him I love him, too, but I can't move my lips to form anything other than a question: "You do?"

Shadow bites my bottom lip gently, "I fucking do, and it scares me."

I smash my lips into his; his tongue dancing with mine. He tastes of beer and sex, making me wrap my legs around his waist. He walks us to the bed, laying me on my back, my legs never breaking contact.

"I love you, too, Shadow," I reveal breathlessly.

"This is scary for me, too. I have never loved anyone before, "I say, running my hands through his tousled hair. Saying the words makes me feel like a lioness. Finally being able to say the words is a relief. I love Shadow; bad, biker-boy Shadow, beast and all.

"Does that mean you'll go away with me?" he asks, pecking little butterfly kisses along my neck.

"Yes, yes, I will go away with you," I reply.

"We leave tomorrow," he whispers as his lips make love to my delicate skin and his hands snake around to grab my ass.

This day has already been a whirlwind. Shadow woke me up with the sun this morning, he had made pancakes and we ate on the balcony watching it rise. It was the most personal time I've had with Shadow in days.

Last night was a long night. Bobby and Doc were up having sex all night again, keeping us up with their intense howling. Shadow and I laid next to each other, our bodies silently apologizing for the last few days.

The kidnapping had given us both a violent reality check, I get it, but I still can't shake the way Shadow tried to get rid of me so easily. Getting away with Shadow is just what we both need. I'm hoping to truly forgive Shadow for his dickish moves and I hope to learn more about who he is.

After breakfast, Shadow took me shopping. He said our trip was to a beach house, so I bought three bikinis; a red and white one, a green one, and secretly, a black leather one. I can't wait to strut my stuff in the leather one; Shadow is going to have a stroke. I got a couple of big, floppy sun hats, and a few cute lightweight cover-ups, and finally, a couple of pairs of sandals. Shadow paid for it all. When I told him it was too much, he threw random stuff on the counter and cocked an eyebrow at me.

"Really, this is too much, Shadow, you have to stop buying me things," I protested, pointing to the bags hanging from my arms and his.

Suddenly, he drops the bags and grabs a fist full of my hair, pulling me harshly toward him. He might have felt bad for pushing me away, but his alpha dominant male ego is still there.

"I want to buy things for you; I was an ass the last few days and want to make you happy. Let me spoil you.

You're mine and mine will have whatever she wants." He brushed his lips against mine; not caring about the passersby eyeing us in shock.

After packing up all of our purchases, we climb into Shadow's Mustang and head out. I didn't know he'd put the motor in until this morning. The car is loud and fast, making me ache with sexual tension. Shadow takes my hand and tugs on it. I look over at him and he tugs my arm again. His playboy smile indicates he wants me to climb on his lap.

"Seriously?" I ask, looking out at the road lined with traffic; knowing it's dangerous and against the law.

He smiles wolfishly and nods. Not being able to resist, I climb over and sit across his lap, my back facing his door, and throw my arm around his neck. He wraps his left arm around my waist and pulls me close, "A man could get used to this," Shadow says, kissing my collarbone and steps on the accelerator making us race forward with a roar of the motor.

I wake up just as we arrive at the beach house; the loss of vibration waking me. I slowly start to open my eyes and feel Shadow brush a stray hair behind my ear. He grabs me by the thighs gently and picks me up off his lap. He sets me in the passenger seat slowly and lightly, not realizing I'm already awake.

He climbs out of his seat and quietly closes the door, then makes his way around the car. I stretch my legs into the floorboard and stretch my arms into the ceiling. My body aches from the cramp of sleeping on Shadow's lap the whole way.

"I see you're awake now. I tried to let you sleep," Shadow says as he opens my door.

"Yeah, I woke up when we pulled up."

Shadow looks out behind us. Hearing another car, I turn in my seat to see what he's looking at. A white

Bentley is slowly pulling up behind us. I climb out of the car and stand next to Shadow, wondering who it is. The windows are darkly tinted so there's no way to see in.

The passenger door of the car clicks open and a white cane presents itself on the asphalt. Two fancy, white shoes follow. Like a scene from a movie, all I can see is under the door.

"Hope you guys weren't waiting too long?" a scratchy voice sounds as an older man steps around the car door. He has thin, white hair, dark eyes and pale skin. The total effect is topped off by a white suit.

"Not at all," Shadow says, bringing his hand out to shake the older gentleman's. "I'm-"

"You must be Adrian Kingsmen?" The gentleman asks, cutting Shadow off. Hearing Shadow's last name throws a dagger in my heart; I'm in love with a man whose last name I don't even know. Geez, I'm pathetic.

Shadow smiles politely as he grasps the older gentleman's hand firmly and shakes it, "Yes, I am, and you must be Harold White?"

"Indeed I am," the man confirms before freeing his hand from Shadow's and leaning on his cane. Harold looks over at me and smiles, his face flabby and wrinkled from age.

"This must be your wife?" he asks, as he comes my way.

"I, um, I'm..." I hesitate. I'm not sure what I am to Shadow. I know I'm not his wife, but I don't even think I'm his girlfriend at this point.

"This is Dani; she's my girlfriend," Shadow explains for me, his label making me smile.

"She's quite stunning, isn't she?" he asks, lifting my hand and pecking it gently.

My eyes never leave Shadow's. "Very." He smiles as he admires me.

"Sorry, Uncle White, I didn't realize what time it was."

I turn to an unfamiliar male voice. There stands a man, no a boy, with brown hair that breezes down into his eyes; eyes of brown. They are pretty, but not nearly as vivid as Shadow's. This new guy is just a little taller than me and of a smaller build than Shadow. He is wearing a white, button-up shirt with khaki shorts.

"Ah, yes, my belligerent nephew; late as usual," Harold sneers, his teeth gritting as he speaks.

Turning to Shadow, he continues, "This is Rudy. He will help with whatever it is you may need. He will cook for you, bring you drinks while on the beach, whatever you choose. Please use him from cleaning the toilets to fluffing your pillow." Harold commands, his face twisted in disgust as he eyes Rudy.

"Rudy here is paying me back for his little escapade last month. Rudy thought it would be a great idea to get drunk and do drugs with his buddies. He crashed his mother's car and left it at the scene. Getting him out of jail was not cheap as this is something we like to do often, isn't it, Rudy?" He eyes Rudy up and down. "Yes, this one is used to getting things handed to him, but not anymore. He'll be staying in the guest house, so no worries." Everyone stands in silence; the energy becoming awkward. I head toward the car to grab some bags and my luggage.

"Yes, anyway, down to business, Mr. Kingsmen," Harold chirps. "Rudy, help the missus with her things while Mr. Kingsmen and I take care of the last minute details."

With my hands full and Rudy ahead of me, we walk down a pebbled trail. The area is definitely secluded and it's a long walk along the path to the gorgeous house. Its walls are the color of dark green sandstone and its roof is of dark brown shingles. There are green vines that grow up the sides of the house, entwining with each other. It seems cozy and small, but elegant at the same time.

Walking in, my mouth gapes open at the luxury. To the right of the doorway is a cute little kitchen with stainless steel appliances and an island in the middle. To the left of the doorway sits a small living area with an overstuffed tan couch that has green and white pillows thrown on it. Next to the sitting area is a bathroom that looks huge from where I'm standing.

But what catches my eye is the bed in the middle of the room. As soon as you walk in, a bed sits in the middle as a centerpiece. It's a big, sand-colored, metal four-poster bed. White sheers hang elegantly along all four sides. I drop my bags and luggage and make my way to it. The comforter is white and fluffy and when my fingers touch it, I feel feathers inside. There is a sea of white pillows of every size and shape thrown all over it. In front of the bed are two floor-to-ceiling double glass doors that lead out onto a patio and beyond that a beach and the ocean.

"Yeah, everyone loves the view." I snap my gaze from the bed and the double doors to find Rudy; who is standing way too close. I smile sweetly and brush past him, making my way back up the trail to Shadow. I see him taking a black bag from the trunk of the car and walking toward Harold. Harold opens it up and pulls out a stack of cash. He then looks in the bag and nods before closing it. He shakes Shadow's hand and makes his way back to his Bentley. The question that has been plaguing my mind for days resurfaces; where does Shadow get all this money?

"The things I'm going to do to you on that bed," Shadow says, entering the house. His eyes are hooded with sinful promises.

Shadow grabs me mid-thigh and throws me over his shoulder. My ribs flinch in pain, reminding me they are not quite healed.

"Shadow, I want to see the beach first," I yell, half serious.

"It's a beach; you've seen one, you've seen them all. I'm fucking you on this bed right now, Dani, and nothing is stopping me," he says seriously. He drops me on my back on a cloud of blankets; my landing soft and plush.

"I do believe I have been an asshole to you Dani, and I'm going to make it up to you." He grabs the hem of his shirt and lifts it over his head; his pecks and ripped stomach flexing with his movements.

"And how do you plan to do that, Mr. Kingsmen?" I ask innocently.

Shadow starts to unbutton his jeans as his eyes penetrate mine; his jaw clenched and face serious. "By making love to you like you deserve; like you're my queen and I'm your king."

He throws his jeans away from the bed and climbs on top of me, his lips claiming mine possessively. He grabs the hem of my shirt and pulls it over my head slowly. I lay flat on my back as Shadow palms the crevice between my breasts with his calloused hands. His hands move down my bruised ribs to my stomach. As he kisses the tender trail behind his palms, I arch my back wanting more of him.

Shadow bites the zipper on my shorts and pulls it slowly down as his fingers unbutton them. His lips kiss my stomach as he removes my shorts. He throws them over his shoulder and pulls himself up on his hands. Lifting himself slightly off of my torso, he lightly kisses the elastic hem on my panties. Making his way upward, he dips his tongue in my navel. His hands trail up the side of my body at the same time; his hands large and greedy as they claim me.

My body vibrates with ecstasy as Shadow takes his time claiming me; admiring me, making me forget everything bad that has lived between us. I dive my fingers into his dark hair, bringing his lips back to mine and nipping them as he searches for the hook of my lacy bra.

My nipples pebble from the cool air coming in through the double doors. Shadow leans down and sucks one into his mouth attentively as his fingers find the sides of my panties. Finding his mark, he trails them down my legs slowly, his blue eyes never leaving mine as he does so.

"So beautiful," he whispers. "I don't deserve you."

He nudges my legs apart with his knees, his length insistent against his boxers. He presses his excitement against my swollen sex, making me throw my head back and gasp for air. His tormenting has made my body come alive with sensitivity and desire. If he doesn't give me what my body craves, I'm afraid I might cum at his next touch.

My hands grab the back of his thighs, pushing his clothed cock against my more-than-ready entrance. "Now, Shadow," I moan, half coherent.

With the simple words, Shadow urgently pulls his boxers off, his eagerness heightening my arousal. I pull him to kiss me, needing some kind of contact. Without warning, Shadow plunges his hard length deep inside me. My head instantly lolls back, my back arches bringing my nipples to tickle across his chest, and my nails dig deep into his shoulders. He slowly pulls back and then forcefully thrusts forward again; his thrust delivers a sensation of warmth and butterflies throughout my body. I moan loudly.

Shadow grabs the nape of my neck and pulls my head from its lolled position to look up at him. "Eyes on me, Firefly," he demands. His brow furrows with exertion as he continues to thrust in and out of me; beads of sweat assault his forehead and threaten to drip. I slide my hands down his damp back to his chiseled buttocks and hold on as I feel his thrusts becoming faster and harder. Our eyes never break contact.

I wrap my legs around his thighs, my nails dig into his firm cheeks, and my breath becomes spastic as I feel the rise of warmth head toward my core. I feel the build-up teetering on the edge of climax as Shadow thrusts hard and deep. His muscles bulge as his fists dig into the sheets beside me.

He leans down and kisses my lips before plunging his tongue deep into my mouth. His tongue fucking mine is my undoing. My legs tighten and my fingernails dig deeper. I moan and rock into his thrusts as the tingle of sensations battle with the overwhelming feeling of warmth.

"That's it, baby." He reaches back and grabs my hand off one of his butt cheeks. He pulls my arm above my head entwining his fingers with mine. His body stiffens and he drives himself deep. Low moans fill his chest as I feel him pulse inside me, filling me with his own release.

Shadow falls to the side of me and grasping me by the hip, pulls my body half on him. Our chests heaving and demanding air, we lay in silence looking out the double doors. The ocean waves crash onto the beach; the sound fills the beach house competing with our loud panting.

"I love you, Shadow," I whisper as my fingers trace the wound my father gave him. It brands Shadow as mine; a reminder of the price he paid in claiming me

Chapter Twenty-One
Dani

I wake to the sound of waves crashing and my stomach growling. I sit up, resting on my elbows, and look out the double doors at the setting sun. We must have slept for a few hours, at least. The bed is bare of any blankets or sheets and only a few pillows are left after Shadow made love to me. He was so caring and showed so much emotion. I rub my fingers over his cheeks, the stubble scratching against the pads. He looks so relaxed and carefree when he's sleeping; so lovable and far from anything beastly in this moment.

"Are you going to keep staring at me, because it's kind of creepy," Shadow slurs with a deep, sleepy voice.

"Sorry, you look so cute when you're sleeping." I smile, earning a scoff from him.

"Yeah, well, this bed is really fucking comfortable." Shadow sits up with sleepy eyes and looks out the double doors. His body is still naked and as delicious as ever. I can't help but sweep my eyes over it. I look back at Shadow and he has the sexiest smirk on his face. Caught in my eye-fucking, I smile and turn my gaze out to the sunset.

"Yeah, it is very comfortable. This whole place is really nice." I'm still unsure how Shadow can afford it. Where did the stacks of money he gave Mr. White come from?

"But what?" Shadow asks, sensing my tension.

"How can you afford it?" I look over at Shadow who is rubbing his hands over his face in irritation.

"I saw you hand that cash over to Mr. White outside," I admit. Shadow drops his hands and looks at me with shock and confusion.

He looks out at the ocean again. His body, once relaxed and carefree, is now as stiff as a board. I sense that he doesn't want to tell me. He may love me, but he doesn't trust me.

"Ah, you still don't trust me."

"It's not because I don't want to, Dani." He looks at me, brushing a hair behind my ear. "If it means anything, I trust you more today than I did yesterday. It's just going to take time." He cups my face and brings me close.

"You have to let me in to trust me, Shadow," I release with a heavy breath.

"I promise I will tell you everything before we leave. I just... I just want to enjoy this week with you, in case the truth does make you leave." His face grows with sorrow and uncertainty. Why does he think I'm going to leave him, is it that bad? The thought that it's something dangerous, or even enough to put myself in danger, scares me because I know no matter what that I won't leave Shadow. I'm too in love with him. I would rather fall into the flames of hell with him, than be without him.

I grab the back of Shadow's head and bring his lips a hair's breadth away from mine. "I'm not going anywhere, Shadow," I whisper, my lips brushing his.

"That fire the lives so deep within you, that fire that makes you my Firefly, I'm afraid my darkness will snuff it out; take you under and make you someone different." His lips brush against mine in confession, his eyes digging deep into mine.

"Fireflies can't live without the dark," I respond.

Shadow crashes his lips with mine; both of us on our knees and naked. The sea breeze wisps in and surrounds us, making us whole.

"Oh, shit, so sorry!" Rudy's voice sounds from the double doors. I jump out of Shadow's embrace and scurry to the floor for sheets. Shadow chuckles at my embarrassment, so confident he doesn't even cover himself.

"What do you want?" Shadow asks Rudy.

"I'm here to make dinner." Rudy looks out to the patio, trying to avoid Shadow's naked ass.

"Come back in the morning; my girl's making me some of that spaghetti of hers."

I look up at Shadow from the floor, a smile wide across his face. I could get used to this.

The night went just as beautifully as the day. We stayed naked all night, even while I cooked spaghetti. Dinner was delicious and Shadow admitted my sauce was the best.

"Goddamn, this is so good," he said between bites.

"I thought you didn't like it?" I tease, taking a small bite.

"Oh, I loved it that night just as much as tonight," he confesses, taking another man-sized bite.

After Rudy came and made breakfast, I decide to go for a quick shower. Between the heat and the sex with Shadow, I need it. The bathroom is big and beautiful. The counter is a shade of green marble that matches the house, and the garden tub is big enough for a family. Although a soak in the tub calls to me, I climb into the separate stall for a quick shower.

I leave the bathroom and look for Shadow. "Shadow?" I yell into the beach house.

I hear a curse come from out front and make my way up the path toward the car.

I hear the hood of the car slam and watch a greasy Shadow turn.

He's wearing torn jeans that hang low on his hips and that's it; no socks or shoes, no shirt. He has grease on his chest and all over his hands. His body is glistening with sweat and his muscles are flexed. My mouth instantly parts; his dirty state playing havoc on my senses.

Shadow wipes the sweat off his forehead with his arm and causes a streak of grease to spread. Dear God, give me strength.

"Hey, I was just messing with the car. The timing seems off to me." He walks toward me, his muscles dancing with sweat and grease. As soon as he's in reach, I jump on him, wrapping my legs and arms around him tightly. His grease spreads across me. I claim his lips with mine, begging him to take me right here on the hood of his car.

"Shit, sorry!" Shadow turns us to confront a red-faced Rudy on the pathway. This guy is really starting to get annoying.

"What?" Shadow yells at him.

"I was just wondering if you guys had any preference for lunch today." He says, eyeing me.

"No." Shadow declares, turning his back on Rudy and dismissing him.

"Is it just me, or does it seem like he is purposely interrupting us"? I ask as Shadow slides me down his body to my feet.

"No, it's not just you." Shadow looks back over his shoulder to where Rudy was standing a moment ago, his face dripping anger.

"I think I'm going to jump in the shower, babe." He brushes past me, his anger vibrating off him. Thanks, Rudy; thanks a lot.

In the bedroom, I dig into my bag and find the green swim suit. The top is barely enough to hold the girls in place and the bottom is tight and snug. Maybe this will get his mind off of Rudy and onto me.

Shadow

I wrap the towel around my waist and shuffle out of the bathroom to find Dani. The weather is warm and humid as it blows through the double doors; it smells like rain. Since Dani and I arrived everything has been peaceful; no club, no junkie mother, nothing annoying except for this Rudy fucker. He clearly has a thing for Dani as every time he's around he just stares at her. It's not lost on me that a guy like Rudy is probably more of Dani's type, even closer in age. The mere fact of it pisses me off.

I want to make this trip meaningful for Dani; show her I can care for her at least. Trusting is a little more complicated, but even if it kills me, I'll show her I can trust her, too.

I find Dani sprawled out on a sun lounger; her body glistening with beads of sweat and the smell of coconut fills the air. She's wearing a small bikini and fuck me if I'm not hard as a rock. Her breasts are playing peek-a-boo with little green triangles, and the bottom is so tight I'm dying to see her ass in it.

"Fuck me," I breathe out in admiration.

Dani's eyes shoot open and she smiles devilishly.

"Why me, Dani?" I ask, the insecurities playing with my mind. Fuck Rudy.

She looks stunned by my question.

She looks out at the view then back at me, "Why not you, Shadow?" Her words make me feel like I'm just as good a person as any.

"Because of my lifestyle; because of who I am." I sit in the sun lounger next to her.

"You haven't told me everything, but what I do know of you, I love." She smiles. "But most of all, it's how you make me feel. You knocked down my walls of suffering, showed me how to live, helped me figure out who I really am inside and out."

I fake a smile for her. Her confession is endearing, truly, but it doesn't mean shit. Not until I tell her everything, then we'll see if she's singing the same tune.

"The things I have done and felt since I have been here are all new to me, yet feel so familiar." She looks back out at the horizon, the clouds of dark gray fighting with the sky of light blue.

"Shadow, since we're being honest, why did you push me away?" Her question knocks the wind from my lungs. I know why I pushed her away, but my explanation makes me sound like a pussy. What do I say; because it hurts more to be without you; that I was trying to prove I didn't need you to live freely, to feel; that I was trying to protect you from the fucking beast that pounds at my chest when it needs a fix?

"And why did you change your mind and bring me here?" she asks deeply.

"Because I'm selfish." Her eyes go wide, then scowl. It's the truth, though.

"If I cared at all about you, I would have pushed you away in the beginning. I wouldn't have let you get involved with a guy like me, but I'm selfish. I want you to myself; I want to make you mine." I bite my bottom lip in frustration. "Your innocence attracted me, your defiance tempted me," I confess.

Dani straddles my lap, cups my face and kisses me passionately. "I love you and I'm not going anywhere."

After laying out in the sun for a few hours, thunder roars from above and dark clouds threaten to pour rain.

"Let's get inside," I tell Dani.

"Hey guys, looks like a storm is coming in," Rudy says, stepping onto the patio. "Sorry about lunch. I forgot and figured you guys could make do." He winks at Dani as he eyes her body in her barely-there bikini.

On top of him looking at my girl, his ignorance and shitty service have finally hit my last nerve. I want him nowhere near Dani. "Go home, Rudy, we don't need your services anymore." I throw my hand out at him, dismissing him, as we make our way into the beach house. Thunder roars above, the light around us dim from the dark clouds.

"Excuse me?" he asks, stunned.

I stop in my tracks and turn to glare at him. "I said fuck off!" I say with force.

"You think you scare me?" he quips. Apparently this fucker has a death wish. If he knew what I was capable of, he would be smart to be scared of me.

He puffs his chest out, "I saw the bruises on her ribs." He points at Dani. "She deserves better than you."

Reaching my limit, I stride over to him. The shithead trembles under my stare. I know I will never be good enough for Dani, but what really pisses me off is that this Momma's boy thinks he is. He thinks he has the right to judge me.

"You're just-" before he finishes his sentence, I slam my fist into the side of his mouth. The force drops him to the ground in one steady motion.

"Shadow!" Dani yells from behind me.

"Go inside, Dani." I point toward the doors; she has to learn when to keep her mouth shut. If this was a situation within the club and she spoke out of turn, it could get her killed.

I flex my fist; the sting from the impact radiates through my bones.

Rudy looks up at me through teary eyes, cupping his jaw.

"You'll live if you stay the fuck down!"

I grab Dani's hand and take her inside. I throw her on the bed as the darkness consumes the room. I lower my body over hers, our passions as fierce as the storm.

She grabs me by the shoulders and rolls us over to where she's on top. Her action to take charge makes my dick so hard it hurts. I untie the dainty strings holding her bikini top together. The room is so dark, I feel it fall rather than see it. I find her hips and untie those as well.

Her hand trails down my stomach to my shorts. She shoves her hand in them and forcefully fists my dick. She leans down and starts pecking my stomach with those sweet lips; her nipples gliding across my abdomen. My dick can't get any harder than it already is.

I start to shuffle out of my shorts, the urgency to be inside of her taking over. Lightning strikes and lights up the room briefly; enough for me to see the lustful state Dani is in. Her long hair is pulled to the left side of her shoulders; her bottom lip is sucked in beneath her teeth; her tits are perky and ready for my rough hands. I grab her breasts, greedy for contact, making her head fall back. I grab her by the hips, lift her and impale her with my throbbing erection.

"Oh, Shadow," she moans loudly, her sweet voice making me groan. Her pussy is wet and warm, hugging my dick tightly.

She starts to rock her hips, but I can't take the painfully slow rhythm she's taking. I have to have her now; all of her. I grab her hips and lift and lower her body into my thrusts. She plants a hand down on my chest to steady herself as the other grabs one of her nipples. The image of her playing with herself makes me about to bust a nut. I dig my fingers into her hips and throw her under me. Taking charge, I piston my hips in and out of her trying to find that sweet release she brings.

Her nails dig deep into my shoulders as her pussy clenches with pleasure, her body's warning that she's on the brink of orgasm.

I grab her thighs to pull her closer, wanting to be deeper inside. She lifts her leg from my hip and puts it on my shoulder, letting my dick slide deep inside and hitting the back of her. She sighs loudly with every blow. I feel my balls squeeze as my release begins to stack within. My thrusts become harder; my breathing harsher. My energy makes it hard for Dani to hold on and she takes her leg down to wrap them both around my waist. Lightning strikes again, giving me a glimpse of Dani's beautiful face; her face nothing but an image of pleasure. The prickling sensation enters the head of my dick; the warm vibration radiating through my balls. I moan as my orgasm hits its peak. She moans with me as her pussy clenches hard. I feel a sudden sting on my shoulder as Dani bites down, making my release heighten. The sensation is almost too much to take. I bite down on her shoulder to return the favor.

 I watch Dani sleep; confused at how this girl has me feeling things I have never wanted to feel for another. It would kill me if she left. It's in this moment I realize I need to make Dani mine permanently. If I own her, she can never leave, even if she wants to, thanks to the laws of the club.

Dani

 I wake in the middle of the night to an empty bed. Sitting up, I see Shadow standing at the double doors as the storm continues.

 "Shadow?"

 He turns and smiles as he brings his naked self back to the bed. His blue eyes meet my green eyes with a flare of intensity.

 "What?" I ask, sensing something is off.

 "Be my Ol' Lady," he asks, throwing me for a loop. I hesitate.

 "I want to give you the opportunity to say yes, but it's not needed." His tone is serious and somber as he says the words. What does that mean?

What does being his Ol' Lady entail exactly? I have seen the things Babs goes through, but I know she is treated different than others. I haven't really seen any other Ol' Ladies around the club, yet, to get a feel of what they do exactly.

"I'm not sure what an Ol' Lady does. I don't know if I would be a good one," I confess.

"It means I protect you; that the club protects you. You're my family, as well as the club's. You'll wear a cut that says you're my property and as long as you follow the club laws, you'll be fine," he says, kissing my forehead.

"Laws?" I whisper. I have heard of these laws here and there. I've even broken one and didn't know it.

"Yes, laws." He runs his hands over his jaw pausing at his mouth and running his thumb over his bottom lip.

"As a motorcycle club, we have our own laws, our own way of life. We make and follow our own rules. Those who break the rules deal with our way of justice. The laws for Ol' Ladies: a brother decides who his Ol' Lady is; the woman doesn't get a say. Some women become property against their wills. The woman is not allowed out of her role as an Ol' Lady until a brother says he's done with her." He stares at me, trying to read my expression. He chants the words as if he is reading a bible ingrained in his brain.

"You'll learn them as you go; it's common sense really."

I sit on the bed taking in everything he says; laws, property, against their wills. It is all reeling through my head, making me second guess the excitement of being an Ol' Lady. Is this why Babs puts up with Locks; because she can't leave?

I'm suddenly ripped from my thoughts when Shadow crawls up my body like a sleek snake. He bites, nips, sucks, and kisses his way up my torso until we are face to face.

"You're mine, Dani. You knew that already, don't over think it." Before I can say otherwise, he smashes his lips onto mine, his sinful mouth claiming his property. What would arguing do anyway? He's made it clear the woman gets no say. I know Shadow is different, though; when Locks went on his woman-hating rant at the garage, Shadow assured me he was different.

Chapter Twenty-Two
Dani

The next two days are erotically, sinfully sweet. Shadow and I don't leave the house in two days. More like, Shadow won't let me leave the house. In-between fuck sessions is eating, sleeping, or showering. It is animalistic, sexy, and beyond the most pleasurable thing I have ever experienced.

Shadow confirming I am his Ol' Lady set a fire in his eyes I haven't seen before. Finally sealing the deal of me being his property seems to make him more at ease; he is playful and less dark, yet more sexual.

I don't let myself think too deeply on becoming his property and the laws of it. I knew I was owned by Shadow when I fell in love with him. I feel the walls surrounding our trust breaking down. I give my body in every way he wants it in these two days; not asking why, not caring why. I am his, he is mine.

Having cabin fever and with Shadow in the shower, I slip on a robe to go out onto the patio.

I let out a squeal when greedy hands grab my from behind, dragging me to the bed. My body comes crashing down on Shadow's.

"Mmmm," he breathes in. "Where do you think you're going?" His voice, sexy and deep, vibrates off my neck as he nuzzles his face deep within.

"Shadow, my body needs rest," I laugh.

"Rest is for the weak."

"We only have today left; let's go eat breakfast on the deck, go swimming," I whisper against his temple.

"Mmmm, fine," he says, kissing all over my face. I laugh and start heading for the door again.

Shadow grabs his trunks and shuffles into them, his bronzed skin looking immaculate. His muscles bulge and flex as he ties the string on them. My tongue darts out and licks my bottom lip, he is sexy as sin.

"You keep looking at me like that, I'm keeping you in here for two more days."

How I have the urge to keep going after two days of sex is beyond me. Then again, looking at him, no woman could tell him no.

"I think you might be going for a world record if you do that," I reply jokingly, walking toward the dresser.

Shadow chuckles and grabs me before I'm out of reach.

"Well, I'm always up for a challenge," he says arrogantly, sliding his hand down my belly. My body arches into his touch; I can't help but be weak when it comes to him.

Shadow leans in and bites my collarbone, making me throw my leg around his waist.

"Up for a challenge, huh?" I whisper, my arousal making it hard to speak.

Shadow pulls back and looks at my expression; amused.

"I bet you can't keep your hands off of me for the rest of the day," I taunt, knowing he won't take the deal and I don't want him to anyway.

"Hands only"? he asks, his voice borderline sneaky. I could see him now fucking me with no hands; he wouldn't be breaking the rules and he would be proud of that.

"As in, no having sex with me all day," I say, making the terms more clear.

Shadow sucks in his bottom lip and looks to the floor deep in thought.

"Deal," he says, reconnecting our gaze, his words surprising me. Shit, how will I live a day without him touching me? I wasn't thinking when I made this deal.

I open the drawer with that, wondering how I am going to keep to my own terms, when my eyes spot the bikini I had as a surprise. Maybe getting Shadow to lose this challenge would be more fun than I thought.

I grab the bikini and go into the bathroom, afraid that if he sees what I am putting on he will make me take it off before he is slammed with the full effect.

I slip the top on; the thin little triangles cover my breasts, but barely. I reach for the bottoms, slide my legs in, and tie the strings at my hips.

"I'm going to get a drink, babe." I hear Shadow call out. I hurry and open the door and walk out, throwing my hair over my shoulder casually.

"Huh? Yeah, okay," I say, acting as if I don't look like a piece of fuck-me candy.

"What. The. Fuck." Shadow bellows, his mouth hung open in astonishment.

"You play dirty, Bitch," he says, sexually. He walks over and brushes his fingers across the material on my breast. I look down and watch.

Shadow smirks. "Mine looks fucking sexy as hell in leather." He continues admiring me .

When I saw the black-as-sin leather bikini, I knew I had to have it. I was sure it would buckle Shadow at the knees.

He grabs me by the hips with a growl and throws me on the bed.

"What about the challenge?" I plead. He can't give in this easy; I have all kinds of taunts and teases in my head.

"Bets off"! he says, pulling his trunks off and releasing his massive erection. It was so hard it looked like it would explode.

"But-"

Shadow pulls my bottoms to the side, not taking them off, just giving himself enough room and slams his erection into my wet heat quickly. My head is thrown back as his hand slides to the small of my back lifting my torso slightly off the bed. Arching my back gives him that angle where he rubs my g-spot and he goes in deep.

After another round of hot, mind-blowing sex, I lay next to Shadow panting and staring. He has been so playful lately, will he go back to being an ass when we get back to the club? I know he will never leave the club and, to be honest, I don't want him to, we just need to find a balance. I wonder if he always wanted to be part of a motorcycle club.

"What?" he asks.

"I was just curious, what did you want to be when you grew up?" I play with the skull being crushed tattoo on his back, the club's insignia.

Shadow sits there for a second, pondering. "I wanted to be like my dad," he says with sorrow, making me regret my question.

"What about you?" he asks.

I smile at him, knowing my answer will shock him.

"A ballerina."

Shadow snorts, making me laugh.

"So why didn't you?" he asks seriously.

I shake my head. The thought of why I wasn't a ballerina causes my chest to constrict with anger. I sigh loudly.

"I started ballet young; I loved it. I did it almost every day. As I got older and my mother became the bitch she is today, it became my escape. I felt like a princess, ya know?" I look at Shadow, his lips turning into a smirk. "As I got older, I got good, too, really good. My instructor wanted me to help teach younger children, maybe even get a scholarship. When I told my mother, she was anything but excited. She told me acting like a princess wasn't a career choice for her daughter and to stay in school. She made me not only decline the offer, but drop out. She said I needed to focus on school. She drained my bank account so I couldn't pay for the classes anymore, in case I tried to go behind her back." A tear escaped my swollen eyes as I retold the hurtful memory. I remember it as if it was yesterday, but in reality it was only a few years ago.

"If it wasn't for your mother, would you still be doing it today?" Shadow asks quietly, his thumb brushing off the lonely tear.

I look into his blue eyes. "Absolutely." There is no doubt in my mind I would still be doing ballet if it wasn't for her. She would never listen to what I wanted, even if it made me happy. She wanted the status of what others would think of her, even if it made me miserable.

Shadow shakes his head in agreement, his thumb that brushed my tear away now rubbing his bottom lip.

"Your mom is gone, when we get back you're starting ballet again." His tone is serious and dominant.

Before I can tell him no, he interrupts me.

"You're not getting out of this, I can see how much passion you have for this. She's not here to weigh you down anymore. You're doing this and you're going to be amazing, I can't wait to see you teach little girls how to be princesses." He says every word with a big goofy grin.

I can't help the smile that creeps up on my face, his caring words infuse themselves into my soul.

"We leave tomorrow," I state. I don't want to go back to the club and the danger of Shadow's escaped mother.

"Yeah, probably going to leave early. I bet they need help setting up for the after party." Shadow sits up on the bed, his hair sticking out in all directions. The man is more sexy when he has bed hair than ever.

"For the bike rally thing?" I ask.

"Yeah, it's usually fun. But there have been problems in the past," he says, running his hands back and forth through his hair.

"What do you mean?"

"Oh, cops are usually swarming the place, waiting for a biker to fuck up; get a chance of probable cause to dig deeper; rival clubs going at it and shit," he says, rubbing his hands over the stubble on his cheeks. It has grown out a little over the last day or so and gives his face a darker look.

"Nothing has happened in a while, but stay close to me," he says, eyeing me .

"Thanks for bringing me here, Shadow. It really has been great." It has been a big step for us, getting away, but I still need to know more. I need to know everything about Shadow.

"What you said you would tell me, are you ready?" I state, frustrated.

Shadow climbs from the bed throwing the sheets off him and onto my lap. His cute butt cheeks greet me, causing me to stare.

He grabs some boxers out of the drawer and slides them on, blocking his cute buttocks from my view.

I look up and see him glaring at me, trapping me with his intense stare.

He breaks his glare and looks off toward the beach.

"I kill people," he mutters.

I know that. I saw how he killed Ricky without a second thought. He told me he killed people, was that what he was so afraid to tell me.

"Yeah, I know that," I respond.

"No, I mean I kill people for a living," he replies, his tone alarming.

My heart stops beating briefly. "What?" I gasp, in dismay.

"What, not the prince charming story you wanted to hear? You wanted to know this shit, so here you are. I kill people for money!" he shouts at me, angry.

"Like a hit man?" I ask, my voice timid.

"I guess you can call me that," he says, sitting on the bed. His elbows rest on his knees as he rubs his thumb back and forth over his bottom lip.

"Why?" I ask.

He turns and looks at me. He seems to be gathering his thoughts.

"Growing up the way I did, I had to learn how to ignore things to live. I eventually became numb, just a shell of a person." He pauses, staring at me before continuing.

"When I joined the MC, Bobby and I were instructed to kill a potential witness, a rat. Bobby wussed out, so I did it. When I killed that person was when I realized how numb I had become over the years. Suddenly, I felt alive, raw and powerful for the first time, finally in control of something.

"Bobby and I were sent to take out a lot of threats after that. When I would kill, for a brief second, I would feel something other than the numbness that had become my tomb. The recoil brought back a high that no drug or pussy could offer. It became an addiction." His vivid blue eyes go gray. "I was good at it and I enjoyed it."

Shadow pauses, looking at me for something, but I am dumbstruck with the information he is giving me. He enjoys killing people; his dark shadow is something I can never compare myself to.

"Word got out how good I was and I did jobs for local clubs. They said I was the kid that lives within his Shadow, no soul, no remorse. Eventually, word got out further and I did side jobs for civilians." He looks at me, his eyes penetrating down to my soul.

I don't know what to say; he is a hit man. I didn't think for a million years that the man I love would enjoy killing people and get paid to do it. That it would be the only way he could escape his demons. If I feel deep down, I feel sorry for him. I feel like I could stab Cassie a million times for what she did to him, what she has made him.

"Say something," he says, snapping me from my thoughts.

"That's how you're so rich?" I ask, in a trance.

"What? I'm no millionaire. I get paid; I get paid well. I don't use much of it, so it has piled up over the years," he says, standing.

"When was the last time you did it?" I ask.

"Not since before you showed up; I don't feel the need to. You bring me out of my darkness. When I tried to push you away, I felt the need to do it; helpless and out of control." He walks up to me and grabs my cheeks and looks into my eyes.

"So, you won't do it anymore?" I ask, hopeful. Shadow sighs and runs his hands through his hair back and forth before looking at me.

"I won't do it out of the club anymore, no. What Bull and the club need of me, is out of my control," he says. I shake my head in knowing, as my eyes sting to hold back tears.

I look up at him, and see him staring at me, needing me to accept him. I love Shadow, even if it comes with a darkness. Who am I to judge, I have dark shadows as well. Who's to say mine aren't as messed up as his.

"Why didn't you trust me to tell me this sooner? Were you afraid I would run to the cops or leave you?" I question.

Shadow shrugs.

"Kind of both," he answers truthfully.

Given my mother's history of running off, I can see why he would get that assumption. Truth be told, if I were not completely smitten with Shadow, I probably would have run far away from him before.

I look around at the house and the clothes he bought; all paid for by blood. The blood of innocent people?

"What kind of people did you have to kill?" I ask. His jaw ticks, he's getting frustrated with my questions.

"I don't know. I never asked why I was hired, I just did it and got paid," he says sternly before looking at me.

"Well, there was one time I asked why. When I received my info on the hit, I saw it was on a female minor. I have never had to kill a minor." Shadow stops and looks at me. I can tell he is uneasy about giving me this kind of information. I take his hands, so big they swallow mine, and give a reassuring squeeze.

"You can trust me," I whisper.

"When I asked the reasoning for the termination, I was told the girl was a babysitter the family had hired since the child was born. One day the girl was caught hitting the baby. It was so bad the child was sent to the hospital. She hit that baby to make it stop crying, they said." Shadow looks up at me, darkness swimming in his eyes.

"I took the bitch out with pleasure," he says.

I look back at him, in understanding. If my child was hurt under someone else's watch and was a minor looking to slide under the system for her actions, I would have hired Shadow, too.

"Don't look at me like I'm some fucking hero, I doubt everyone I killed was in the wrong," he says, snapping me from my fantasy.

"Look, I know it's a lot to take in. I would understand if you wanted to leave-"

I cut Shadow off. "I'm not going anywhere," I say quickly.

"I was going to say, if you wanted to leave, too damn bad, you're my Ol' Lady now." His lips come up into a sinister smirk, reminding me I am his, until he says otherwise.

Chapter Twenty-Three
Dani

We arrive at the apartment after our week of luxurious bliss and sinister truths to find it trashed and foul smelling.

"Oh, my God, what's that smell?" I ask, covering my face with the crook of my arm.

Shadow comes in behind me without luggage and winces at the smell.

"That would be Bobby, man is a fucking pig," he mumbles, not pleased.

"Bobby!" Shadow yells, kicking through the trash on the floor.

"Bobby!" he yells again.

"I don't think he's here," I say, trying to make a path to the kitchen.

I hear Shadow growl and curse as he makes his way to our bedroom, earning a chuckle from me.

I reach under the counter, pull out a garbage bag and start picking up trash.

"What the fuck are you doing?" Shadow demands.

"Someone has to clean this up." I answer as I pick up an empty pizza box.

"No, he's cleaning this shit up." Shadow walks over and rips the trash bag from my hands. "He must be at the club, let's head over there. I'm sure Babs will need your help and the whole gang should be there. Tonight is the bike show," he says, eyeing the apartment.

He looks over at me, "You think you can ride with your ribs all messed up?"

I look down at what I'm wearing; a shiny, gold sequined top that falls mid-thigh with black leggings and gold sandals. Not exactly something I would pick to wear for bike riding, but I've missed that feeling of freedom and I don't care to change.

"Yes, my ribs are fine!" I say excitedly.

"Good, I miss my bike," he says, grabbing two helmets off the couch.

We head downstairs and get on his bike. Within minutes we are hitting the highway. The sun's shining and the wind is warm. I should have grabbed my leather jacket for after the sun goes down, but I haven't been able to find it since before our trip. I hope I left it at the clubhouse.

Shadow curves his arm behind him to rest his hand on my thigh. My body screams alive at his claim.

When we pull up, the courtyard is nothing but a sea of bikes, more than usual. Shadow backs his bike into its usual spot and helps me off. There's loud music blaring from the clubhouse, kids running around with a basketball, and the smell of BBQ in the air.

"What is all this?" I ask. Did we miss the bike show?

"Looks like a pre-party before the after party," Shadow says, smiling. "This party is more family oriented, the after won't be."

He takes my helmet, looks me over and frowns.

"What?" I ask.

"Nothing, it's just you need a property patch. You look available, like a sweetbutt, and I don't want to have to beat another brother's ass for looking at you." He runs his hands through his hair.

"A sweetbutt?" I'm totally confused.

"Yeah, like a club whore," he says, seriously.

"Did you just call me a whore?" Now I'm offended. My mouth is gaping open like an idiot.

"No, I said you look like one."

"That's much better!" I say, sarcastically. I can't believe he just said I look like a whore.

"Shadow! Welcome back, brother," Bobby says, walking toward us from the house. He has a blond girl laced to his side who is wearing a tiny black skirt and a too small black tank top. You can see her hot pink bra covering more of her tits than the tank. She tops it off with fake jewelry and slutty pink heels.

"You look pissed," Bobby says to me.

"Sorry, that tends to happen when I'm called a whore," I say, looking off in the distance.

Bobby looks at Shadow with a raised eyebrow.

"It's not like that; I said she looks like a sweetbutt." Shadow sounds irritated.

Bobby laughs. "You look stunning as usual, Dani," he says and gets a glare from his arm candy.

"I think what Shadow's trying to say is, you're not wearing a cut. You're not patched in. Meaning you don't appear to be claimed, so you look like free reign. Girls who wear cuts that say they are property are not fucked with. You don't have one, so you look like a sweetbutt."

He points toward a woman standing a little ways off. "See her? Her cut says Property of Tank. Nobody will try to sleep or fuck with her unless they want the entire club up their ass. She's an Ol' Lady."

Then he points to the girl on his arm. "She doesn't have a cut, so men will be all over her looking for a good time. Most likely she will give it to them. She's a sweetbutt."

The girl slaps Bobby's shoulder in disgust. "You're a dick," she says and angrily walks off.

Bobby shrugs. "Sad thing is, she'll be sucking my dick before the night's over." He smiles smugly.

Bobby smacks Shadow's back. "Good luck, man." He starts to walk off before turning back, "I almost forgot, now that you're back, Bull's wanting to hold church."

"I would have explained it, but you got all offended and freaked the fuck out before I could," Shadow says, grabbing my hand and walking me toward the club.

As we get closer, I see more of the Ol' Ladies and their cuts claiming who they belong to. Why don't I have one; I'm Shadow's Ol' Lady, right? Do I even want one?

Shadow telling me I'm his behind closed doors is one thing, but to tell the whole world I'm property to be claimed seems a little fucked up.

When we walk into the clubhouse, I smell less BBQ and more cigarettes, cheap perfume, and booze. I can barely hear myself think over the loud music blaring and I'm squeezing Shadow's hand so tight I can feel my heartbeat pulsing through my fingertips.

Shadow leans down close to my ear and still has to yell, "I got church. Go into the kitchen and help Babs. Don't leave without her to go anywhere." I nod my head and start toward the kitchen. Then he pulls me back by my elbow, halting me. "I mean it, don't leave without her."

I nod again and head off to the kitchen. When I enter, there are a handful of women wearing cuts with property patches. They're laughing about something, but stop abruptly when they see me.

One woman narrows her eyes at me and says, "Bitches get younger and younger, I swear." Then she rolls her eyes.

"You can leave the way you came in," she says, turning her back as if I'm garbage needing to be taken out.

Babs scoffs and looks toward whom the woman is referring; me. Her eyes light up. "This is Dani, Bull's daughter. She ain't fucking your man, calm down." Babs eyes the lady.

Her eyes go wide and her face suddenly pales. "Oh, shit," she says, smirking. "My bad."

"Dumb ass," Babs says, snickering at her.

Maybe I need one of those damn patches after all. I have been here all of five minutes and have been mistaken for club ass more than I care for.

"Dani, this is Cherry, Molly, Pepper, and Vera," Babs says, pointing to each girl with a carving knife. They all have on cuts with property patches and look friendly; all but Vera.

Cherry is a strawberry blond, maybe a little older than myself, with blue eyes. She smiles and looks like she has a bubbly attitude.

Molly is a brunette with brown eyes who has to be in her fifties. She is a little more on the chunky side than the others.

Pepper has black hair with little specks of gray all over. She is obviously the oldest, but her green eyes make her look fierce and wise.

Then there is Vera. She looks to be in her thirties with reddish brown hair and the brightest red lipstick you can imagine. She looks like a total bitch.

"Hi, nice to meet you all," I say politely to the girls.

"Do you need any help, Babs? " I ask, ignoring the girls now as they're sizing me up.

"Nah, I think we about have it covered. Think we are all about to head out to the bike show as soon as the boys are done with church," she says, throwing the knife in the sink.

"You should be careful, not being patched in and all," Vera says, leaning against the counter. Her voice sounds condescending, sending red flags off in my mind. Top that with the look she is giving me and I want to stab her with Babs' knife.

"She's Bull's daughter, nobody would be stupid enough to fuck with her," Pepper says, lighting a cigarette.

"Yeah, but she's not from around here. She might as well be a civilian; anyone would think she's a whore," Vera says, eyeing me. "I did."

They are talking as if I'm not even in the room. What the hell?

I look right back at her, my pulse racing. My dad wouldn't appreciate me starting a fight after being back five minutes, but if I don't stand up for myself she will never respect me. Respect seems to be a high priority around here and I've gotta earn it.

"With that whorish lipstick you're wearing, someone could think the same about you," I say, pursing my lips.

Babs starts laughing along with the other ladies.

Vera smirks at my remark, cocking her head to the side. "Feisty. I like you already." Her smirk turns into a grin.

The kitchen doors are thrown open and a guy walks in; he looks familiar. He's wearing a black bandanna and has a black beard that's braided. I look at his cut in search of his name and see it says 'Old Man'. Then it hits me like lightening; he's the guy that hit on me the night I helped bartend.

"Hey, ladies, we're heading out. Pack up your shit and let's ride," he says, pulling Vera into his side. She must be his Ol' Lady, the way they start kissing. The way he talked to me that night didn't give me the impression that he had an Ol' Lady. I pray he doesn't recognize me; that could worsen things between Vera and I.

Vera starts kissing his neck. He turns his face to let her into the crook of his neck and notices me. He grins wolfishly and winks at me. Shit, he recognizes me.

With that, I turn to find Shadow. As soon as I open the kitchen doors, there he is.

"Ready?" he asks, pulling me into his arms.

I nod and grab his hand, heading for the door. He leads me into the chapel instead. "What are you doing?" I ask, confused.

He goes over to a chair at the end of the table and pulls up my leather jacket.

"I've been looking for that!" I yell, trying to grab it, but he pulls it from my reach.

"Wait, look," he says, holding it back up.

I look at it, but I don't notice anything different. Then he turns it so I'm looking at the back. I'm stunned at what I see.

It has patches; one that says 'PROPERTY OF SHADOW', and another of the Devil's Dust symbol.
I don't know what to say. At first, I thought wearing something so branding in public was ridiculous; like a dog with a dog tag. But after seeing the patches, and feeling the disrespect in the club of not having them, I want it more than anything.
Shadow slides it onto my arms and pulls me into him.
"Now you're mine and everybody will know it," he says, making me gasp with excitement.
I bite his bottom lip and whimper at the love and lust vibrating through my body, making Shadow chuckle.
"Let's go or we'll never make it to the show." He turns me toward the door.
When we reach Shadow's bike, Bobby starts clapping and everyone jumps in. I turn cherry red as I hear cat calls, and everyone congratulating Shadow. You would think I'd gotten married with all the excitement in the air. I feel respected as I get nods and smiles from other Ol' Ladies.
"'Bout time, brother," Bobby says with a face-splitting grin. I look over at my dad. He is not clapping and doesn't look happy.
"Yeah, fuck you," Shadow says to Bobby, with a matching face-splitting grin.
Everyone's bikes start up after Bull first starts his. The loud, thunderous sound of motors fills my ears. My whole body vibrates with the freedom.
Bull pulls off and everyone follows.

The bike show is held along the beach and zigzags up through the adjoining streets. There are street bikes everywhere and trucks hauling custom bikes pulling into parking spots. I can smell leather and exhaust before we even come to a stop.
I climb off the bike and wait for Shadow's next move. I look around at my surroundings and see a lot of rugged

men wearing leather cuts from Devil's, Silver Bullets, Ghosts and more. Off to the side of the road, I see an ambulance and about a dozen cop cars and black SUV's; ready at a moment's notice.

Shadow grabs my hand. "Ready?" he asks. I nod and we follow the others.

As we get closer to the action, I can hear Nickleback playing and can slightly smell chicken, but the leather and exhaust smells are stronger. We pass a lot of different bikes; most custom with half-naked chicks posing beside them. There are some people who aren't wearing cuts, but not a lot; they seem to dart out of our way when they see us. It makes me feel powerful. I love it.

"Want a drink?" Shadow points at a trailer with kegs on it.

"Yeah," I reply.

We walk over with Bobby to get our beers. They start talking about air intakes, fat tires, and more bike talk I don't understand.

After about an hour of walking around looking at bikes, and the beer Shadow got me, I'm about to piss myself. I look out for a bathroom but only spot port-a-potties a few blocks over. Shit.

The guys stop and start looking at more bikes. I look over and start eyeing a metallic green one that looks like a dragon. It's amazing what people can do with these things; the engine has a plate over it that looks like wings coming off the dragon and the wheel in the back is huge.

"Looks like Shadow patched you in," a voice rings off behind me. I stand and see Chelsea and Candy, both standing with their arms crossed, looking as slutty as ever.

I look around, but Shadow isn't near.

"Yep, sorry, ladies," I say, trying to walk off, but Chelsea grabs my elbow.

"Unless you want to look like her," I nod toward Candy's broken nose, "you better let me the fuck go." My voice is threatening and dripping venom. My brutal anger still surprises me. I am definitely not the same girl I was in New York.

Chelsea laughs. "You better enjoy it, hunny. It won't last long," she says, nodding toward my cut. They both smirk and walk off, leaving me angry as hell.

I stand on my tiptoes and see Shadow two bikes over. I make my way through the crowd and spot him talking with some biker bimbo. She has blond pigtails and is dressed in purple to match the bike she's posing with. A purple bra, purple thong, and purple fishnets are topped off by knee-high purple boots. She runs her hand down Shadow's chest cooing something at him, but he just leans his head to the side, and smiles.

I walk over to him and clear my throat. The girl eyes me with disgust.

Already angry from Chelsea and Candy, I want nothing more than to break her nose with my fist, but I really am about to piss myself.

"I gotta pee." I yell at him over the music and idle chit chat around us.

I walk off toward the bathrooms, not being able to hold it much longer.

"Dani, you can't get jealous every time a girl looks at me," he says, walking quickly behind me.

"Fuck you," I spit back, walking in-between box trailers.

Shadow grabs my arm and yanks me to him. "You can't just run off; it's not safe." He throws my back up against a box trailer.

"What the fuck's going on?" Bull asks, rounding the trailer.

"It's all your fault," a shaky voice rings out. We look over at the opposite end of the box trailer to see a disgruntled Cassie pointing a gun at us.

Shadow bolts upright and pushes me behind him when he sees his mother.

Then Bobby rounds the corner as well. "Hey, I saw you guys run off, everything alri-" Bobby cuts himself off when he sees Cassie.

"It's all your fault he's dead," she yells, trembling. She's so unstable her hands shake the gun uncontrollably; her finger is pressed tightly against the trigger, making me uncomfortable.

"I never should have taken the deal, I knew it. But I thought I could get that bitch to talk... and then Ricky... and blood…" she starts rambling and not making any sense.

Suddenly bodies surround the other side of the box trailer; men wearing cuts with crazy eyes.

"Well, well, well," one of them says, his head shaved.

"El Locos," Bobby breathes.

I remember them; they were the ones that were responsible for the drive-by shooting at the safe house. How could I forget them?

Cassie turns at the sound, pointing the gun at the El Locos, but only briefly before turning back to us.

She points the gun at me crying, "sorry." She drops her head and cocks the trigger.

A loud boom goes off, making me scream. I close my eyes and wait for the pain, but nothing comes. When I open my eyes, Cassie is in a state of pure shock. Her mouth gapes open and blood begins to pool at her chest. She drops the gun and falls to her knees, gasping for air.

"FBI, GET ON THE GROUND NOW!"

I look around and see a swarm of people in black gear surround the box trailers with guns pointing at us.

Shadow pushes me down hard and my head smacks against the ground. My heart is thumping so hard I can feel it pulsing in my fingertips. I look out under the box trailer and see black boots running away on the other side.

When the person is off a distance, I can see it's Bobby with a gun in his hand. Did he shoot Cassie?

"Look at me," Shadow whispers. Emerald green meets stormy blue as our eyes lock.

"Shit, they shot the Criminal Informant," I hear a familiar voice say. I look up and my blood drains from my body; my heart stops beating and I can feel my face pale.

It's Stevin, wearing a blue wind breaker that says FBI.

One of the El Locos gets off the ground and walks toward Stevin. "Man, if I knew she was going to do that, I would have tackled her," he says.

'You fucking traitor," another of the El Locos shouts out.

"You see who shot her?" Stevin asks.

"No, one of them though," he says, pointing toward us.

"They did what?" I hear a familiar voice say, coming around a box trailer beside us.

My mother steps next to Stevin; she's also wearing a blue windbreaker that says FBI.

My world starts spinning; I feel myself hyperventilating.

Stevin and my mother hear me gasping for air and start walking toward me.

"Shit," Stevin mutters.

My mother bends down and smiles like the devil.

"Someone get over here; we've got a witness," my mother yells. Suddenly, I'm lifted off the ground; everything moves in slow motion.

"Get her in witness protection now," she says.

"Say goodbye to Lover Boy," she whispers in my ear as I'm being pushed away.

I look over at Shadow, who's as shocked as I am. Then his shock leaves, replaced with a look of confusion and finally pure betrayal.

One of the El Locos is an undercover; my mother is an FBI agent; and I look like I am one of them. Shadow's eyes glass over with pure hatred; every little ounce of love replaced with distrust.

My mother signed my death certificate, making me a possible threat to the club. Shadow kills people like me. Before I can say anything, he turns his head away in disgust and I'm hauled out of sight behind a box trailer.

TO BE CONTINUED

Epilogue
Dani

    I'm brought to a stereotypical interrogation room. There's a metal table with a chair opposite of me and a two-sided mirror behind that. There's also a camera in the upper corner; guess they don't want to miss anything. It smells of bleach and coffee in here.
    I look down at the cup holding the brown java. My nails dig into the side making grooves as I try and make sense of everything. Looking back, I wonder how I was so blind. Things make sense now, like my mother resenting me more since she's been with Stevin. She used me; she knew the club wouldn't turn her down if she used me as leverage. Making me out to be a rat seals my fate in the eyes of the Club. Shadow's trust now nothing but a grain of sand in the desert wind.
    I sigh in defeat.
    The door clicks open and in steps a fat-bellied man with a folder. He sits down across from me, splaying out paperwork across the table. His black mustache curves and grooves across his pale skin as he scrunches his lips side to side.
    "Miss Lexington, do you recognize this man," he asks, pushing a picture across the table. Apparently he's not one for idle chit chat.
    "No," I say without looking.
    The man sighs. Laying his arms across the paperwork, he folds his hands together. "Miss, this will go a lot easier if you just cooperate." He wiggles his mustache as if it is tickling his lips.
    "Again, do you recognize this man?" He pushes the picture in my direction.
    I look down and my heart seizes. I take a calming breath at the mugshot of Ricky sitting before me.

"No," I say, crossing my arms and looking the other way. "We done?"

"Really?" he asks, lifting his shoulders. He digs in his folder and pulls out another picture. "Because in this photo, Adrian Kingsmen, also known as Shadow and the Sargent-of-Arms of the Devil's Dust Motorcycle Club, is carrying you out of that man's house."

My eyes widen at the picture shoved in my direction, displaying my lies in black and white.

"You want to try ag-"

Knocks sound from the other side of the tinted glass, cutting off Mr. Mustache.

The door is flung open and my mother steps in.

"Why didn't I know about this?" she asks, pointing at the picture.

"Sadie, you weren't given clearance on this. You were too close to the case and taken off. You need to go back into the other room now." The guy calmly points at the door.

My mother huffs, eyeballs me and steps out of the room.

"Now, where were we?" the man asks as he shuffles his fat belly into the metal chair.

"This man?" he asks, pointing at Ricky's photo.

I sigh. I know I have to give them something, but maybe I can give them something without giving them anything.

"He called himself Ricky. I woke up in that house kidnapped by him and Cassie. Shadow and the rest of them rescued me and took me back to the club. Other than that, I don't remember. I was pretty banged up; I had a slight concussion." I push the photo back in his direction.

"Is this Cassie?" he asks, pulling another picture out of the folder and laying it on the table. It reveals a strung-out Cassie mugshot.

"Yeah."

He nods his head.

He pulls out mugshots of Bull, Bobby, Locks, Shadow, Babs, and more.

"What can you tell me about the club," he asks, still throwing photos on the table.

"Nothing," I say, looking through the photos; Shadow's in particular.

"Based on your property patch, I would say you're close to Shadow." He leans back in his chair with a smug look.

I look up at him and then back at the photo of Shadow. His blue eyes pierce mine, even through a photograph.

"Look, I know you want to protect him, but you need to protect yourself. In your situation you're considered a threat to the club. I want to protect you, but you have to give me something." He starts picking up the mug shots.

I shrug at his threat.

I know he's right, but I would rather take my chances in the law of the club than any law this fat-ass and my mother have to offer.

Mr. Mustache growls in frustration.

He pulls out more photos and throws them on the table.

"You want to protect people that do things like this, Miss Lexington?" he asks, pushing the photos toward me.

I gasp at the gruesome pictures. There's a man with ghostly eyes, his tongue cut out and a bullet hole in his head. Another one shows a woman with her tongue cut out and a bullet wound to the head. I swallow hard.

"Nothing?" he scoffs. "Well, you can sit here and think on it for a while; see if anything comes to mind." He starts picking up his pictures and folder.

"I don't know anything," I shout, smacking the table with my hands. "They don't tell women anything!" I scream as the door closes behind Mr. Mustache.

What feels like forever later, the door opens and my mother steps in.

I roll my eyes.

"Here's a sandwich," she says, plopping it down on the table.

"Thanks," I say, sounding bitchier than I intend to.

"What are you doing, Danielle?" She sits in the chair across from me.

"If you're going to preach your 'I'm looking out for you' speech, save it," I spit back.

"When I met Stevin at the club, we realized we had something in common; Devil's Dust MC. I was suffering because of it and his case was at a dead-end because of it. We hit it off, he realized I was more of an asset than he thought, got me in training and I became an FBI agent. Together, we would bring down the club, but the only way in was through you, sadly." She leans in, tearing at the empty cup.

"I tried everything to get the information I needed while I was there, but they wouldn't give me anything." She starts tapping the table. "When they tried to take us to the safe house, I had to get back to the club, but they were smarter than I thought." She eyes me, as an awkward silence fills the room.

"Did you know about the drive-by?" I ask.

"No, my men weren't a part of that." She smiles, "but hey, it got the job done."

I bite my lip as my body involuntarily growls at her; I want to kill her. What mother isn't upset about a gang shooting at her child?

"You realize they will kill you now? Lover Boy will want nothing to do with you," she says, leaning back tongue-in-cheek.

"Yes, because of you. I'm sure you're happy, but you're crazy if you think I'm going anywhere with you." I sit up and glare at her. "I would rather live on the streets or take my chances with the club; hell, I would rather do time in jail, than to ever have anything more to do with you." I stand up and lean over the table, my face inches from my mother's.

"Leaving you there was the best thing for the case; if only you would cooperate." She turns her head and sneers at me.

"Let me put this so you can understand it. I hate you. You're dead to me. Take your case and shove it up your ass." I smile the fakest smile I can muster and sit back down.

She stands up and walks to the door. "You're wrong, I'm not happy. We didn't take down the club, but we'll get them. You continue to refuse to help and you'll go down with them." She slams the door, sealing the severed ties.

Acknowledgements

There have been many friends and supporters along this journey and I want to thank every single one of you; if I leave you out, it is not intentional. Every one of you has been special to me in some way.

I want to thank my husband most of all. He has had to endure temper tantrums, insecurities, loss of meals, and many more hells that come with me being locked away in my writing cave. He has been a huge shoulder to lean on and has constantly encouraged me to go forward with all of this. Plus, he's been my tech savvy IT guy in all of this. Lots of hugs to my children who hear, "Give mommy five more minutes" a lot. A big thanks to my parents who believed I had it in me to become a writer. A wonderful step-mother that listened to me in the wee hours of the morning on story lines and plots; and, of course, I cannot forget family and friends who have offered their feedback as well. Thank you all!

I want to thank the wonderful authors who have given me tips, and still do so, along the way: K. Bromberg, Pepper Winters, Chantal Fernando, Lili Saint Germain, G.L. Ross, Ker Dukey, Madeline Sheehan, Jodi, Ellen Malpas, Stephanie Logsdon. I want to thank my awesome beta readers for putting up with my disorganization: Tina Williams, Courtney Chebat, Tracy Gumke, Silvia Curry, and more. I want to give a special thanks to the blogs who gave me a chance even knowing this was my first book: Love Between the Sheets, Sizzling pages romance, Feisty Girls Book Blog, The Book Bellas, Kitty Kats Crazy, Sunfully Sexy Book Reviews, Mommy's A Book Whore, Sassy Divas Book Blog, Books and Beyond Fifty Shades, Kawehi Blogs, and so many more. I want to thank Cover it Designs for my awesome book cover, and a special thanks to Travis Welch for my internal artwork; it rocks! A big thank you to my editor, Belinda Forgy at forgyediting@gmail.com; you really made this book come together!

Thanks again to all of you, this book wouldn't be where it is today without you all!

About the author

M.N. Forgy was raised in Missouri where she still lives with her family. She's a soccer mom by day and a saucy writer by night. M.N. Forgy started writing at a young age but never took it seriously until years later, as a stay-at-home mom, she opened her laptop and started writing again. As a role model for her children, she felt she couldn't live with the "what if" anymore and finally took a chance on her character's story. So, with her glass of wine in hand and a stray Barbie sharing her seat, she continues to create and please her fans.

Stalk me

Goodreads:

https://www.goodreads.com/author/show/8110729.M_N_Forgy

Facebook:

https://www.facebook.com/pages/M-N-Forgy/625362330873655

Twitter:

@M_N_Forgy

Made in the USA
San Bernardino, CA
10 October 2014